Like a Lily Among the Thorns

Karen S. Bell

KSB Press Publication Copyright © 2022 Karen S. Bell
Cover Design by Karen S. Bell

This book may not be reproduced in whole or in part by email forwarding, copying, fax, or any other mode of communication without author or publisher permission. This is a work of fiction. Names, characters, places, and incidents either are the product of the author's imagination or are used fictitiously. Any resemblance to actual persons, living or dead, events or locales is entirely coincidental.

To find out more about this author's work, please visit www.karensbell.com.

ISBN 13: 9798426339408

Printed March 2022.

Printed in the United State of America. All rights reserved.

Acknowledgements

The final version of this work is the result of many hours of review by Julia J. Bell. Her keen eye and instincts improved the narrative tenfold, as usual.

Thanks also are extended to my beta readers: Rachel Hailey, M.D., Carol Willingham, Jenafer Howard, and Felice Seltzer.

Special thanks to Beth Isaacs for her time, patience, and excellent copyediting skills.

For Tim, as always

"Like a Lily Among the Thorns"
—Song of Solomon 2:2 Old Testament

In this work I have chosen to have the lily represent a shift in thinking and a movement toward saving this planet from an accelerated climate crisis.
May lilies begin to multiply.
—Karen S. Bell

Like a Lily Among the Thorns

Karen S. Bell

"What day is it?"
"It's today," squeaked Piglet.
"My favorite day," said Pooh.
— A.A. Milne

There are only two ways to live your life.
One is as though nothing is a miracle.
The other is as though everything is a miracle.
— Albert Einstein

Prologue

Here is a tale of romance and magic. Of love and loss and harrowing times. Here is a tale of adventure and pathways of changes and rhythms and possible crimes. A tale to enjoin, a tale that's inviting, a tale that teases and finally resounds. Resounds in the hollows. Resounds in the meadows. Resounds in the streets and then in the alleys. It starts with a notice and then with a letter. It leads to new friendships and then to a journey. A journey of trials, a journey of heartbreak, a journey for refuge and hope at the finish. But this tale also ends with a warning and burden. Ends with foreboding of what is the future. Take not for granted what rests in your hands. For sometimes the plans you make are not really plans. They may end up as tossed and not needed but may end up as too little too late and should have been heeded. Whatever will happen creates quite a story. Whatever will happen creates quite a tale. Gather 'round at once and be informed without fail.

Chapter One

The Notice

Journal entry:
O glory be, awake, awake,
from slumber filled with bits and bursts.
Awake, awake the conscious mind,
to embrace the day a newborn babe.
#Gratitude

On this ordinary day, we find Gabby Bernstein going about her daily ordinary chores. A lass of modest means, she hummed as she tidied up her small studio apartment. Although bereft of material accoutrements typical of a twenty-something New Yorker, she didn't dwell on it. Rather, she chose to focus on being grateful for all the kindnesses bestowed upon her by the universe and the miracle of life with the richness and diversity of the flora and fauna that blessed this planet. She was so attuned to the preciousness and beauty of all living creatures that she never was inclined to harm even the smallest insect preferring to capture it and send it out her window to climb down the fire escape or fly away. But most especially, she was grateful for *her* life, which she never took for granted. In fact, at this very moment, she paused to acknowledge her joy of just being alive and to mark her calendar with the #gratitude entry, giving thanks for each and every day she had her wits and her health.

As she went about her light chores, an unexpected random play on her music app added a spark to her usual sense of wonder and bliss. A coincidental gift from the cosmos of a cherished performance of Luciano Pavarotti singing the *aria Addio, fiorito asil* from Madama Butterfly, a captivatingly wistful melody that was one of her personal favorites. She gleefully acknowledged this gift and said a silent "thank you." To her surprise and again serendipitously, immediately after the Puccini came the Adagio in G minor by Tomaso Albinoni, another favorite. Humming along with these glorious harmonics she dusted and tidied while luxuriating in the lush sounds filling her apartment. When first stumbling upon these works in her music app, she had an immediate connection to their beauty created by composers from so long ago.

Although these sorrowful melodies were contrary to her normal and purposeful joyful optimism, she was attracted to their wistfulness but only on a superficial level. She chose instead to think of them as a soundtrack of the human spirit, her particular spirit to shoulder on, no matter what. Because she greeted each day with wonder, Gabby reveled in all of the senses, normal and paranormal (intentionally sharpened through meditation) that made knowing the world around her possible. These senses are what she believed made her life experiences vibrant and full of awe. Through practiced mindfulness, the magical state of being alive became a palpable feeling of bliss. Happiness, to her, was a sentient choice. Her heightened awareness brought into focus her five senses that we all have but often go unnoticed, taken for granted, and ignored. Habitually and purposely, she would lasso these five senses into her consciousness and experience them intensely.

The starting point for being consciously aware would be random. Today, she started with touch, feeling with her fingers the softness of her cotton blouse, then she took notice of the taste of the sweet sucking candy in her mouth, taking a deep breath she enjoyed the scent of her potted begonia offset by the stale odor of her recently burnt toast. The gift of sight, along with the ability to hear sounds, she found to be the most miraculous and celebratory. Right now, she could feel joy at being able to see the world that beckoned outside her apartment window. A glorious azure sky was dotted with cotton-candy clouds floating gently with the light breeze. The tumultuous New York city street below her apartment building was filled with dog walkers, joggers, and baby carriages being pushed by young moms or nannies.

In addition to the normal activity on this street, she could see the exploding richness of spring bringing vibrant shades of green to the orderly pattern of planted trees. Here and there, the odd yellow flower peeked among the unstoppable weeds growing in the tree beds as if mirroring the rare shiny clean car parked among the dusty compacts and SUVs. The magic of seeing all this while being able to hear this rapturous music was nothing short of remarkable. Life, specifically her life, was a gift for which she never stopped being grateful and for which she paid poetic reverence in her daily journal.

To the uninformed masses, to her friends and acquaintances, this childlike joy and optimism seemed misplaced given Gabby's daily challenges. Despite that, this was how she embraced her existence, a conscious decision to be thankful above all else. But that is not to say, she was not tested. Sorely tested, of which, she was painfully aware. Today, was perhaps exceptional bringing an abundance of tests. Today, her landlord had pasted a Quit Notice on her door right after her new puppy, Eliza Doolittle, had taken a poo on her brand-new white area rug just as she had laid it on the floor. Today, first thing this morning, in fact, her phone had pinged with a terse break-up text from her recent, short-lived boyfriend. "Sorry, not feeling it anymore," was all he wrote.

But Gabby would not be cowered, would not be brought down. She beat back the always near-at-hand negative energy by whispering her mantra, "Things could be worse." The dark forces that carried incurable disease, mental illness, being a victim of a crime, and poverty had been kept at bay. The power of positive energy in which she cocooned herself was strong enough, she believed, to thwart the negative energies that surrounded us all. And with this thought, after her daily acknowledgment that she loved her life, was the realization that her stomach flu had abated, and she could eat more than the toast that always burned in her cheap toaster. *Things could be worse.* There was great comfort in that thought. Positive thoughts, positive results.

Gabby's silver-lining attitude was an art form cultivated by years of watching her mother disintegrate after her father fled the household for another woman. She had just turned the vulnerable age of twelve when her father, who had stayed away for long periods of time all through her childhood, made his final move to his native Quebec and disappeared from her life. The only remnant in the household of his French-Canadian heritage was her name. Shortening it from Gabrielle to Gabby was, at best, a weak protest to sever this cultural connection to him. She could not speak or understand French and to some degree was glad her father never bothered to teach her. The sound of French or French accents reminded her of her loss and sadness would overcome her whenever she heard it spoken in movies or on TV. So, she tried to avoid any exposure to hearing that language whenever she could.

After her father left, Gabby's mother spent her remaining years staring out the living room window hoping to see her husband's car turning into the driveway. In that armchair, becoming increasingly worn, shabby, and used up like the woman herself, Gabby's mother sat all day, each and every day, seeing the world through dazed and vacant eyes. Only getting up for bodily functions or minimal nourishment, Mildred Bernstein wasted away while wasting her life.

With the help of neighbors in the Midwood section of Brooklyn who were her friends' parents, Gabby wasn't placed in a foster home because they engineered a charade of her being looked after. Since no one had seen her mother, it was easy to enlist a bogus parent for conferences, have report cards signed, and the like. Gabby went on to finish middle and high school, a pitifully neglected child with minimal friends due to her need for secrecy. She spent these formative years living under the constant fear of being discovered and taken away. She escaped into books, spending hours in the library. Books transported her from her lonely world. She loved spending hours browsing through the shelves and just being there. She especially liked books that took her to foreign places and those that brought history to life with stories based on real people.

Despite her aversion to hearing anything French, and also a complete mystery that would someday be revealed, she contrarily was intrigued by the French Revolution being oddly attracted to studying that period in history. She read all she could on Robespierre, Marie Antoinette, Guillotines, and the Bastille prison. Maybe because of all the chaos and death that the French populace endured? A punishment *deserved*? Because of her keen interest to learn all she could about that era her nightly dreams were filled with scenes of herself in fancy dress and enduring the hardships of those times. Reliving the Reign of Terror became an obsession she could not explain but provided her an escape from an isolated and boring existence. Besides books on the French Revolution, she also read all the classics and became engrossed with the strong and powerful goddess figures of Ancient Egypt and Greek and Roman mythology. She explored Jung and far-Eastern gurus to learn about meditation and the seeds of her shift in interpreting her personal reality were sown.

On the day of her high school graduation, her mother's disintegration became more than just an emotional and physical decay but the culmination of a pitiful life. When Gabby arrived home with her diploma in hand, she did not receive the welcoming excitement for which she had hoped but did not expect. Instead, the customary disappointment of silence was what greeted her when she called out her accomplishment. Her mother's normal unresponsiveness did not alert Gabby that something was amiss and it had taken several hours before she realized what had actually happened. As she had been for these past six years, Mildred Bernstein was sitting upright in her living-room chair with her eyes wide open facing the window. But this time something was different. Gravely different.

When Gabby decided after her initial disappointment to finally show her the diploma, she discovered the awful truth. Her mother's unblinking eyes were flat and fixed. Her skin grey and icy to the touch. She was dead. Stone-cold dead. Finding her mother thus, shocked Gabby but did not surprise her. This fear of discovering that her mother had passed away had always been tucked away in the recesses of her mind and many times she had felt for her pulse while her mother slept. This miserable woman's retreat from life had reached its ultimate climax and conclusion. A life thrown away. The coroner's report said she had died from starvation. But Gabby knew it was from a broken heart.

The shock of seeing the skeletal form of her mother as she was being carried away by the paramedics became indelibly sealed in Gabby's psyche. Vowing to never be like her, Gabby decided that happiness is a choice. The mind can interpret reality in all sorts of ways. Why focus on the negative when there's always a positive alternative? Why succumb to feelings of depression and rejection that had consumed her mother when you can fill your heart with joy? Let others give those feelings the light of day. In her world, they would have no traction. Now, here she was in her tiny apartment many years forward from that life-changing discovery choosing to be optimistic by ignoring the pull of fear or robust anger. So, in her customarily buoyant mood, she took care of the necessities that waited to be crossed off the to-do list for that day.

First things first, Eliza Doolittle needed to be walked so her training was reinforced, a book was due at the library where she worked, and the milk carton was empty. She would resolve her living arrangements later. Much later if she could stall the eviction. Things could be worse. Today, rays of sunshine had just burst through the clouds and pierced through her windows after several days of torrential downpours on city streets that created hazardous, swiftly flowing streams in the gutters and crosswalks. The racing water carried the odd plastic bag, soaked newspaper bits, and cracked Styrofoam cups. But, also among the garbage were edible scraps of half-eaten knishes, soft pretzels pieces, and pizza crusts. These fragments of New York City fare were swept into the sewers by the rushing stream, creating a party atmosphere for the hordes of rats dwelling in the tunnels below. A veritable rat-infested soggy food festival. Their joy became part of the collective positive vibe electrifying the now sun-drenched urban landscape. Rainbows and glistening cleansed sidewalks greeted the happy pedestrian.

Into this firmament of exultation, Gabby emerged from her third-floor walk-up with Eliza Doolittle in tow, a fluffy white ball of energy and tail-wagging jubilation. The little pup immediately curried the favor of passersby, who would stop and make sweet baby sounds or ruffle her head. Walks with this adorable four-legged delight connected Gabby, in a real sense, to the rest of humanity and became her drug of choice to enhance her interaction with society. In good weather and bad, Gabby lived for these walks each of which brought their own stories of new acquaintances and adventures. Needless to say, the excitement of the unexpected was the catalyst for these outings and they usually lasted longer than planned.

As she embraced this most welcome sunshine while absorbing the positive sub-atomic particles colliding with her skin, she decided to walk to the corner coffee shop where Leonard, the barista, always had a stash of dog biscuits for little Doo. The ever curious and friendly little Lhasa Apso mix enhanced Gabby's life and personal growth in more ways than she could have imagined. No one had chatted her up at this coffee shop before little Doo came along. Now, she was always bombarded with waves of "hello" or casual conversation whenever she entered. She chose the name, Eliza Doolittle because it was the perfect name for the disheveled, scrawny, and matted-down rescue dog who had the potential for being more. The recognition of being kindred spirits between Gabby and this downtrodden creature was immediate and life-affirming.

Inspired by a TV commercial asking for donations and adoptions by showing needy animals begging for love and a home had broken Gabby's heart. Right on the spot, she decided that as soon as she as she could, she would adopt a rescue dog from the nearby shelter. The poor little sweethearts. As luck would have it, she got a nudge from the cosmos sooner than expected. Purposeful synchronous events frequently happened in Gabby's life and such a coincidence occurred within hours of her seeing the soulful eyes of those wretched love-seeking creatures on TV. Later that day, when she went to get her mail, a flier had been shoved into her mailbox announcing that adoptions were open that very afternoon at the shelter just across the street. Indeed, the happenstance of receiving that flier on that particular day was not taken lightly by Gabby. She had great respect for the influence of cosmic forces in her life and paid attention to coincidences believing them to be messages not to be ignored. Before she fully realized what she was doing, Gabby found herself wandering over to the shelter. *I'll just look around.*

As she entered, she immediately felt a psychic pull to a cage toward the rear of the room and excitedly went over to investigate. There she was, a little disheveled mutt, her tiny face turned upward, her eyes pleading, her tail wagging. The connection was immediate and sustaining. Done. It was her! The fulfillment of the day's purpose. Gabby carried the scraggly cutie in her large purse while the puppy excitedly scoped out the territory from her place of safety.

And little Doo, like her namesake, cleaned up good. This floor mop with feet was transformed by some soap and water from a mangy-looking mongrel into an adorable ball of fluff making happy barking sounds as she ran around the apartment to dry off proving to Gabby, she had chosen the perfect name. Gabby's oft-repeated explanation for choosing this name became an icebreaker to begin interactions in the corner coffee shop and today on her walk with Doo was no different. Except for today though, the shop was also abuzz with the impending condominium project.

Everyone was impacted, even this coffee shop would now have to close. Gabby at least was not alone in this situation but that gave her no solace. Her cherished 18th Street apartment in Chelsea was on the chopping block and the reason for the Quit Notice. A luxury condo complex would take up the entire city block replacing all the neighborhood businesses. Stores like the mom-and-pop grocery with apartments above like Gabby's would be demolished. The lobby level of the luxury condo building would be rented to upscale street access shops and services replacing a dry cleaner, a kosher deli, a pizza parlor, a convenience store as well as the grocery and this coffee shop. Local businesses could not afford the hike in rent.

A hot yoga studio and specialty boutiques selling designer salt, designer olive oil, and an oxygen bar were slated to be some of the new businesses appealing to a yuppie clientele. Because she didn't read the Quit Notice carefully, Gabby now found out she had 10 days to find a new place before the wrecking crew came. Everyone murmured in unison that another rent-controlled building bites the dust bringing all of NYC closer to being an enclave just for the wealthy elites. The camaraderie of the group hardened but for a fleeting moment given their shared eviction problem. A brochure had been put in everyone's mailbox fishing for prospective buyers for the 100 plus available units. A laughable exercise demonstrating just how out of touch the developers were with the economic situation of the tenants they were evicting.

Leaving this neighborhood saddened her but in her normalized optimism, she expected that finding another rent-controlled apartment or affordable studio would not be a problem. Continuing her upbeat approach to the challenges in her life, she looked forward to the possibility of making new friends with this move. Her blind faith in positive outcomes propelled her optimism. *Things could be worse.* Despite the fact the inner Gabby was a bouncing free spirit of jubilant thoughts and emotions, her outward appearance, contrarily, was quite somber. Although she had promised herself never to be like her mother, her dour face and serious demeanor were the mirror image of her mother's woeful countenance.

Poor Gabby would practice in front of the mirror to look more cheerful, but it could never be sustained or appear natural. Her attempts at walking about smiling only made her look deranged and her inner circle of friends and acquaintances would ask if something were wrong. So, she gave up the pretext and accepted the disconnect. But it took its toll. Her dates never felt she was enjoying her dinner, the movie selection, or their company. It was rough sustaining her inner optimism when everyone thought you a pessimist, or worse, just an angry and frustrated singleton. It was especially hard when dealing with the public where she worked. To compensate, she perfected a soft tone of voice that created a calming energy. Carrying around Little Doo definitely helped.

Given the devastating news about the development project and Gabby's habitually, frowning face, the crowd at the coffee shop attempted to cheer her up. "No, it's all right," she said. "I'm ok. I'm fine, really, I am. Of course, this situation is not welcome. I will miss this shop terribly and all of you and being able to walk to work, but I know things could be worse." A collective "awww" cycled through the crowd and they spontaneously threw their arms around her in a group hug to cheer her up while whispering to Doo how they all were heartbroken. "Let's keep in touch and find another meeting place," they each said as they made their way to the exit. Gabby gave a forced smile as she waved to everyone when it was her turn to leave but that seemed to make it worse and tears flowed freely among the remaining group.

"Howdy, Gabrielle," said Walter the head librarian as she walked into the Lower Westside branch of the New York Public Library where she worked as an archivist. "Why so glum?" he joked knowing her well enough to tease but not well enough to be sensitive to her discomfort and annoyance at the jab and at using her full name not being privy as to why she never did. "How's that sweet Eliza Doolittle today?" he asked as he reached out to scratch the tiny head peeking out from her hiding place in Gabby's large satchel. Doo loved being carried about in that bag ever since that first walk away from cages and into a world of love. It worked for Gabby as well not having to slow her pace for Doo's tiny feet when they were crossing busy thoroughfares.

Handing him her book, Gabby saw him involuntarily grimace as he stamped it revealing how much he hated manning the return desk when staff was shorthanded, as it was most Saturdays. Walter was a simple man in style and needs. Working at the library had met his requirements for a job with no pressure where he could sail along with minimal effort. A cuddly bear of a man, he was well-liked by all, especially in the Asian community where his wife's family had a few prosperous businesses. Her work ethic paid for the extras and frequent trips back to Hong Kong to see her relatives.

"I see in the paper your apartment building is being demolished for luxury condos. What a bummer…this city keeps losing its charm and affordability," he said when she just nodded. "Lucky for me my parents bought my apartment years ago and left it to me. Can't touch anything on Riverside Drive anymore." At that very moment, Gabby noticed Countess Ivanova sitting at her usual spot in the computer area, a woman of rare gifts and charm. Seeing her was a happy accident since Tuesday was her regular day and it was always a treat to spend time with her. Obviously, a spectacular beauty in her youth and still quite attractive, Anastasia Ivanova was now, as the story went, an impoverished former Russian heiress who had been victimized by her third husband, a con man whom she'd since divorced. Although no one was absolutely sure if she were a real countess, her refined and regal mannerisms inspired all who interacted with her to treat her thus and the library staff did not disappoint. Certainly, the title suited her.

In addition to her aristocratic demeanor, her impeccable couture vintage clothing, an obvious vestige from her glamorous former life in London, enhanced her regal aspect. The story that circulated in hushed tones was that her astute grandparents and extended family of aunts, uncles, and numerous cousins had fled to Knightsbridge from St. Petersburg, Russia. They had grabbed what they could of their vast fortune quickly stashed in clothes and suitcases just before the Bolshevik revolution. Valuable jewels, cash, and small pieces of fine porcelain figurines were snatched quickly as they raced away from their lives to safety thinking they would come back to reclaim their property and live out the remainder of their days when Russia came to its senses.

Their summer and winter mansions held priceless art and artifacts that were eventually confiscated by the government. They mourned the loss of their significant assets and their former lives of luxury and the beauty of their home country but remained thankful for not perishing in the uprising.

As is often the case, the subsequent generations frittered away their modest inheritance in a rather short time and most of the remaining family had become quite poor. All style but no substance, they nevertheless traveled among the wealthy establishment as mannered and titled gentry and eventually married into the upper classes. The Countess's beauty served her well and, she too, married men who could provide the luxuries of life. Her first foray ended in divorce with a sizable settlement that solidified her place in society. The end of her second marriage could have been ripped from the tabloid headlines when Lord Joffrey Smythe III fell to his death scaling Mt. Everest for a documentary film he was producing. Her third and last husband was a charmer she met on a cruise crossing the Atlantic. As the social director of the ship, he was able to give her special privileges and made the voyage quite enjoyable. Before they docked in

New York they were married by the ship's Captain, who pulled her aside and told her to watch her money. Alas, the euphoria of love had thrown caution to the wind and so here she was using the library computer apparently not being able to afford one herself.

"Hello, Countess, how are you on this lovely afternoon?" Gabby asked as she approached the charming woman as she was totally immersed in some paragraph on a website and unaware of her presence. Startled by the unexpected interruption, she jumped slightly and then immediately closed the web page and turned to greet her young friend. Clasping Gabby's wrist with her manicured and bejeweled hands, she said, "Hello, my dear. Isn't it just marvelous that the rain has finally stopped? And how is my little sweetheart, Doo?" she said as she reached into the satchel to rub the puppy's head. No one was fooled by this hiding place.

"I've just been reading about the construction project that will demolish an entire city block. Everything razed to the ground. Pizza parlors, delis, convenience stores, hairdressers, all will lose their locations for a glamorous high rise that nobody from this neighborhood can afford. Terrible, terrible blight on this city. The privileged classes are taking over all the charming neighborhoods, especially on the lower Westside. So sad. I love this part of town. Chelsea is vibrant. I hate to see it change. Progress they call it," she sighs. "So, does this affect you by any chance? Because if it does, perhaps, I can help."

"Well yes, it does, as a matter of fact. I, unfortunately, got my eviction notice today. But it'll be okay. We'll find something. Doo and I will be just fine, won't we, Doo?" Gabby picked up the pup and snuggled her face.

"If you need shelter, I would be happy to let you stay with me until you figure out what to do. I have lots of room."

"That's so kind of you, Countess," Gabby said, "I might have to take you up on that offer if I can't get situated in time. Most kind of you, really."

Gabby was touched by this offer but also her curiosity was piqued. She had often wondered where the Countess lived and more importantly how she lived. Was it a walk-up like Gabby's? That situation might get difficult as the Countess aged. Even for Gabby, carrying groceries up to her apartment could be challenging. She guessed the Countess was in her late sixties but seemed in good health. She was slender and had a crisp gait, so stairs were still probably manageable and perhaps even good exercise. Although everyone assumed she was hard up for cash, she never seemed to be in dire straits, so it would be interesting to see her apartment. Most New Yorkers could not boast of *having lots of room* in their apartments. Her offer was intriguing, but of course wouldn't be necessary. *Things would work out.*

Although she tried her best to count her blessings and be upbeat, Gabby's forlorn childhood deprived of a mother left a gaping hole that only being part of a family could fill. So, from time to time, she would fixate on an acquaintance and imagine them as an aunt, a grandparent, or even as her mother. This mind game, which gave her much enjoyment, eased her loneliness. Her latest infatuation, the Countess, transported Gabby to a posh world where people spoke pleasantries with a refined British accent and ate caviar.

Because the Countess conveyed a sanguine attitude that Gabby consciously worked on for herself, the attraction to this woman was immediate and consuming. The Countess seemed to glow as if she had a spotlight following her wherever she went. Gabby was not the only one in awe. Anyone who came near the Countess felt lifted from their troubles. A sense of ease prevailed that could not be explained. For Gabby, it felt good just to think of her and she did so quite often in the quiet moments at the library or even sometimes in her apartment. The mystique of the Countess was top-of-mind, present, and real.

At times, she imagined the Countess as the heroine of old black and white World War II movies, a movie star from when Hollywood was in its heyday, glamorous and mysterious. She could picture the Countess with smooth coifed blonde hair pinned up and tucked under a floppy Fedora wearing elbow-length gloves while putting a cigarette into a bejeweled holder. She could hear the click of the lighter and imagine the Countess take a big inhale and blow the smoke out slowly and sexily. Or sometimes Gabby would picture her as a fun-loving divorcee living on a big estate in the country and having Gatsby-like parties with famous people. Certainly, her sitting in this library did not match Gabby's romantic notions of the Countess's life, but they prevailed, nonetheless.

Because Gabby was so consumed with thoughts of the Countess, sometimes when she went to the corner coffee shop, she would mimic the elegant way the Countess walked or held her mug to sip her tea. She would delicately bite into a pastry, as she had seen the Countess do the few times they had gone for a snack break at the bakery next to the library. Gabby became obsessed with inhabiting her style and grace even though she knew it seemed an affectation, not natural. Nevertheless, she practiced the moves.

She also envied the Countess's easy smile and her soft engaging laugh so as not to disturb the quiet when interacting with the other regulars at the library. She would practice mimicking the smile and soft laugh in front of the mirror, but it always appeared contrived. Even so, she felt closer to the woman as she pretended to be her. Although the Countess did not seem to need a companion, Gabby was convinced that one of the regulars, Captain Jim Jeffries, a retired captain who had been in the Merchant Marine was in love with her. The Countess seemed to enjoy his company and flirted with him shamelessly.

The thought of their courtship blossoming here at this library and the remarkable effect the Countess had on Gabby herself, gave Gabby a sense of destiny. *We've all come together at this little library for a reason.* True to form, Gabby's own interpretation of the meaning and mysteries of existence and how cosmic forces shape our choices gave her the satisfaction that she was on some lofty path not totally revealed to her. Accompanying her on this journey were these friends she had met right here. *We've all come together at this little library for a reason* was the often silently repeated phrase in her mind. *What has the cosmos planned for us, I wonder?*

The Captain, as he was known, had become a regular visitor several times a week perusing the travel section documentaries and books on miniature model building. He had enchanted everyone at last year's Christmas gathering with stories of his own exotic travels. Quite an attractive character, his bright-blue eyes glinted merrily while he stroked his pure-white handlebar mustache that matched the thickness of his long white hair pulled back in a ponytail that bounced slightly as he glided into a room. His unique appearance enhanced his ability as an accomplished storyteller that he had honed from holding travel seminars for several cruise ship lines after he had retired from the Merchant Marine. When the Captain had finished sharing his numerous exotic experiences, Walter instantly asked him to lead the story time hour for preschoolers. Twirling his mustache and making faces as he acted out the books he was reading made him an immediate success with the children who howled with laughter and never wanted the session to end. The Countess and the Captain...a pleasant thought.

After their conversation had come to its natural conclusion and Gabby was about to leave with Doo, the Countess grabbed her arm, "Wait, I have a marvelous idea, darling," she said. "Why not come for dinner tonight? You can see the guest room and there's a giant pot of beef Stroganoff simmering on the stove and some cold borscht. Come. We can have a nice visit. If you come right now, we can leave together."

To be invited to dinner at the Countess's was not only a pulse-throbbing honor given her obsession but also because as far as Gabby knew none of her colleagues had ever been invited. Except perhaps for the Captain, she chuckled to herself. And so, she accepted gladly and they left as soon as the Countess logged off the computer. Slightly taller than Gabby in her high heels and with her graceful stride, probably borne of finishing school, made keeping up with the Countess challenging for Gabby even in her weekend jogging sneakers and she scurried after her.

Everyone at the library assumed the Countess's apartment was a short distance away in their downtrodden and gentrified mixed neighborhood but as soon as they hit the street, she hailed a cab. The noise on the street made it difficult for Gabby to hear the address as the Countess leaned in to tell the cabby. She immediately realized they were heading uptown toward the posh area around Bloomingdale's and then turned further west passing Lexington Avenue and then to Park Ave. Her curiosity was more than piqued. Eventually, they stopped in front of a lovely but smallish Italianate brownstone townhouse on 65th street near Park Avenue while Gabby remained in the car unsure whether to get out.

"Come, come," said the Countess to a perplexed Gabby who was rather unhinged by this turn of events.

She exited the cab slowly with her mouth open and was gobsmacked at what she saw. "You live here?" Gabby finally found her voice to ask.

"Why wouldn't I?" the Countess replied sounding slightly annoyed.

Chapter Two

The Countess

Journal entry:
The world keeps spinning.
Turning, turning on its axis.
Never the same and always the same.
Turning and spinning.
What a remarkable ride.

Sometimes a major change in one's life comes on the heels of ordinary events. A dinner invitation and cab ride can be more than transportation from here to there for food. The Countess would become a very important addition in Gabby's life but as of right now, none of them knew that, particularly, the Countess. Frozen in place while staring at the luxury townhouse, Gabby was caught up short. Reality had suddenly become fluid, become a changeling, a stranger in the night. The hours she had spent imagining the Countess's life as a Hollywood starlet or Gatsby character now converged with the truth of her circumstances. It was hard to digest this shift in perspective when everyone at the library remained unenlightened and still believed the Countess was a brave woman struggling to make ends meet just to get by. The bombardment of the truth was too much to absorb right now, especially when her own life was in such flux. She also did not want to think of how this information revealed the Countess's damning deception, her disingenuousness to everyone. It was a mind-numbing disappointment, a gut punch that made her feel off balance.

Everything was suddenly out of step and off-kilter. Too much random noise was being thrown at her by the cosmos, a shock to the senses. In just one day, today, to be exact, she had been notified that her apartment building was being demolished, her friends at the coffee shop, albeit not close, would be summarily swallowed up by the cavernous city as they dispersed, and now this...this unexpected truth of the Countess's financial situation. A widespread misconception to her supposed friends at the library. Of course, the Countess had no idea that Gabby had elevated her to such high esteem, held her in such high regard, so that now she was shocked to her core at the apparent duplicity. But maybe she just rented a room in this townhouse. Maybe...she...

"Oh my," was all Gabby could manage as she stood there admiring.

"Lovely, isn't it? My solicitors found this fabulous deal because it

needed a lot of renovation," said the Countess unaware of the impact on Gabby who immediately quashed the notion of the Countess being a boarder.

As soon as they entered the ground-floor apartment, they were greeted by the savory aroma of slow-cooking beef. The decor was shabby chic, overflowing with knick-knacks and worn comfy seating that exuded the understated class and elegance of old money spent wisely. The apartment's somewhat modest but tasteful furnishings at least fit into the narrative of the Countess's meager finances. But owning this building was a different story entirely. This pleasant roomy living space had a far wall with large sliding glass doors revealing a compact rear garden. The outdoor area was handsomely festooned with several trees, dark slate walkways, colorfully painted ceramic pots filled with greenery, and festive brightly patterned patio furniture.

As Gabby looked around at this lovely home, she suddenly realized it pleased her that the Countess lived in this splendor. Enjoying a safe neighborhood. The spoils of a life well-lived. And why not? This woman could enjoy and should enjoy a comfortable lifestyle. She had the grace, style, elegance and obviously the wherewithal to live such a life. *That was good.* In a way, it was an enormous relief to know the real circumstances of the Countess's situation as a single older woman alone in the city. Gabby smiled to herself. No one need worry about the Countess anymore. The only remaining caution was her deception. Pretending to be downtrodden when you were far from it, still didn't sit well with Gabby. But she was sure there was some explanation. Certainly, she never seemed to be such a foolish woman who would lose all her money to a con man. And didn't she reveal she had lawyers who looked after her finances?

Unexpectedly, a woman entered the room wearing an apron. Another mind game about the Countess living alone immediately quashed. "Oh, Irina, there you are. I've brought a dear friend from the library to join us for dinner and enjoy your fabulous cooking." The Countess made the introductions. *A housekeeper? She has a housekeeper?* "I must say, Irina, the house smells so wonderful, I could eat dinner right now. But let's have some tea first in the garden, shall we Gabby? The weather is so delightful and it's much earlier than when I normally have dinner if that's alright with you?" Gabby nodded becoming rather submissive to the remarkable turn of events presented to her. "Also, Irina," the Countess continued, "please bring us some of the pastila that you bought yesterday from that fabulous Russian bakery. You will love them, Gabby, they have a flaky crust filled with fruit that has a texture like jam, but oh so much better. Come, let's go outside and enjoy my little garden and get to know each other better."

The garden was not as tiny as it appeared from the living room being ample-sized and even prettier on closer inspection. Early spring flowers were in bloom both in pots and planted in beds around the leafy trees. Manicured bushes were accented by tiny whimsical sculptures depicting gods and goddesses of ancient Greece or Rome. Nero played the fiddle and Venus blew a kiss, among others. The walkway made of slate squares led to a seating arrangement placed optimally for maximum viewing of the surroundings. One could whimsically describe it as a Bonsai version of the New York Botanical Gardens in the Bronx, a perfectly designed miniature array of indigenous flora. They sat down on white wicker chairs with overstuffed cotton cushions exploding in springtime hues of pink and green.

How extravagant to be sitting in a lovely garden in the middle of Manhattan flashed through Gabby's mind. Of course, one only had to look up to see the towering buildings surrounding them, and not yet the time of day that these towers would throw the garden into total shade. Nevertheless, it was a luxury most New Yorkers never experienced. To sit in your own backyard on E. 65th Street and hear birds chirping and insects abuzz as the sun warmed your face and the soft breeze nurtured your soul was quite a unique experience. This was now the way she would picture how the Countess lived. No more made-up scenarios, the real life of the Countess was just as glamorous, and just as exceptional, perhaps even more so.

True to Gabby's commitment to be mindful, she then took a moment to acknowledge the sheer joy of being in this place, to be fully aware of her surroundings. Paused her thoughts to combine her inner consciousness with the lovely greenery showing just a hint of colorful flowers as she lazily took in the setting. The Countess remained quiet for a moment as well seeming to take in and relish the lovely garden's gifts. Doo squirmed and broke their reverie. The Countess nodded her approval for Doo to be released.

The excited pup wandered about sniffing everything. They both laughed at Doo's small liquid deposit left at one of the bushes before settling down on Gabby's foot while Irina poured tea into fine china cups on trays she had set on the small glass-top tables next to them. A scene flashed through Gabby's mind of perhaps having afternoon tea with British royalty like the Queen of England. To her, the Countess could be the Queen with all the royal trappings. *Yes, a house servant to do your bidding*. One could get used to that. At least there was a companion in case the Countess fell or got sick, but nevertheless, it all was such a departure from everyone's image of her at the library.

"I love my garden as you can tell," said the Countess. "We've always had one in my childhood growing up in London and of course at our summer house in the countryside. As soon as I saw the neglected one here, I knew this house was for me. Turning it into an oasis from the city streets has been a most delightful and enjoyable undertaking. I even enjoy it in winter when it is covered with snow, and I can sit by the fire and enjoy feeling the warmth and coziness even more." She took a sip of her tea and a small bite of her pastry.

"I should clear something up, I suspect," she continued after a moment's reflection. "You were surprised about my living arrangements when we arrived here. I'm aware of the stories about me at the library and frankly, I don't really know how they started," she said as if reading Gabby's mind. "It was rather pleasant and quite endearing to have everyone be so protective of me, a woman of a certain age, struggling to survive in this overcrowded, harsh, and expensive city. So, I said nothing to dispel the notions about me. Probably that was wrong of me, perhaps even deceptive. I enjoyed the attention initially but enough is enough. I'm sorry if you sensed my annoyance." Gabby nodded in agreement starting to relax at this direction toward honesty.

"It wasn't all a charade. What was said about my third husband was partly true, he was a conman, but he didn't con *me*. Actually, it was the other way around. I made him sign a prenup that my solicitors faxed to the ship that said he would get nothing if the marriage didn't last a year and after that there were terms as to how much he would get for the years we stayed married. Well, right after we arrived at port, I realized my mistake. So…poof it ended. He got nothing except a kiss goodbye. Obviously, he wasn't too thrilled. Anyway, I was left quite well-off after my first marriage ended and especially so after my second husband's death in a mountain climbing accident, as has been factually retold around the library.

"My solicitors back in London always protected my finances and I am grateful to them for doing such a good job. When Joffrey died so tragically, I wanted a fresh start. To get away from all the sad memories but, alas, it took quite a few years to finally do it. I chose New York. Vibrant and bustling like London but new and different. That was the reason for my trans-Atlantic crossing as well as to have the experience of sailing on the QE2. Getting married was never part of the plan. Foolish and stupid. But I have no regrets. I never regret any of my actions. It makes for a more blissful and peaceful life. No harm done anyway.

"My solicitors suggested I buy this townhouse and convert it into three roomy apartments, one for me and the other two for income. An excellent suggestion. The two rentals have been occupied since they became available and my tenants are wonderful company. We're like a cozy neighborhood of friends that look out for one another. Very comforting for a woman of my age. Sometimes the strong arms of a male are needed and the two husbands that rent here are quite willing. I also love this location. I can walk to two museums, the Museum of Modern Art and the Frick. It's also an easy walk to Central Park and the Zoo. I love the sea lions and penguins. And I love to ice skate." Seeing Gabby's surprised look, she adds, "Yes, even at my age. Must be my Russian blood. Anyway, I'm glad you now know the truth, Gabby. Your predicament allowed me to do so. It's a relief because I cherish our friendship. You've been so helpful to me at the library and I sense a sincere goodness in you. I like and admire you very much."

This surprised and pleased Gabby. Imagine having the Countess feel that way about her. It was as if she knew how much Gabby had admired her. She settled into her chair and smiled inwardly. Irina came back into the garden and poured more tea. As the Countess sipped her tea, she studied Gabby. This child was always so forlorn, she mused. It would be good to take this little sparrow under my wing. Good for us both!

The ritual sounds of clinking china and the gurgling sound of pouring hot liquid into a cup created a sense of calm throughout the garden and the sweet birds begin to chirp. As they sat enjoying their respite, a palpable shift in their relationship to one of more intimacy was felt by the Countess and Gabby. Bringing Gabby into the fold, into this household, would help them both as it turned out. When Irina finished the tea service, she went back into the house. At that moment, the Countess sat back in her chair and laughed at a beautiful robin who landed on the table trying to pick at the pastry. She took a crumb and reached out to the bird. Gabby was amazed as the bird ate the crumb right off her finger picking at it carefully and then ate one more. The Countess gently shooed the bird away and took another sip of her tea. "I have never seen a wild bird do that," said Gabby. "It seemed to flap its wings and sing a little song like a goodbye gesture."

"Well, he, in particular, is quite friendly, but they all come 'round for the sweets from time to time because they know I'll feed them. Not that unusual really, haven't you seen people feeding pigeons in the park? We have many regulars who do that in London."

"Yes, I guess you're right. But it was quite remarkable to see a robin land right on your table while seeming quite tame."

"Yes, well this is the second spring that Morris has come back." She noticed the bemused look on Gabby's face and she laughed. "He, I assume he because his breast feathers are a rust color, and I know it's the same bird because he has a little white spot right near his beak. So, I recognized him from last spring. I call him Morris because somehow his gait seems like a little old Jewish man. His bird feeder is on the tree in the way back, so he's here quite often. The feeder is full because there are not too many squirrels in this garden to eat the seed. It's too difficult to get in here and I had the
ones that were here removed when I first moved in. They live in Central Park now where there are many more trees and nuts. Hope they're a good deal happier there. Oh, you must have loved the pastry, I see it's all gone. It's quite delightful, please have some more, won't you? I'll fetch Irina."

"Oh no, I couldn't possibly, not if we are eating dinner soon. But I did think it was quite tasty. So, there's a Russian bakery nearby?

Too bad there's not one on my side of town...hmm... I guess not my side of town for much longer now, so it probably doesn't matter."

"Yes, who knows what your side of town will be?" The Countess says quite playfully. "Anyway," she continues, "Irina found it quite by accident recently just when she will be leaving soon." She sighs. "Oh well, nothing stays the same. I will certainly miss her. Such a comfort to me being steeped in our shared Russian heritage. She had gone alone to a Rachmaninoff concert at the Frick because I had a cold and declined to go with her. She met a group of Russian ex-pats there who she went with for coffee and dessert afterwards at that bakery. Quite a find and reminded me of old family recipes. Now, I'll have to go on my own. Yes," she muses in a quiet voice, "it will be sad for me when she leaves. Her family has been close to my family for all my life. Her mum worked for my mum when I was a child.

"When I decided to come to New York, she wanted to come with me. She's like a sister, I guess, although I pay her quite handsomely," she laughs. "But like they say, the only constant is change. Who knew this adventure to New York would dramatically change her life? She will marry in a fortnight to a man who will take her to live in South America. Brazil, I think. Her last chance at marriage because she's in her early fifties. He was working for the contractor who renovated this place. I'm thrilled for her, but...oh well. What could I do? I gave her my blessing, of course. But it is still distressing to have her be so far away."

A look of consternation came over the Countess that quickly relaxed into one of pleased acceptance. "Perhaps, I'll find a roommate," she said and winked. This casual conversation was manifesting itself into something much more important that was beginning to take shape. A path forward for the two of them that they were just starting to comprehend. For the Countess, this important interaction first presented itself as a heartfelt interest to help this forlorn young woman but maybe it was something greater, maybe it was also mutually life changing. It was an uplifting notion and in total harmony with how the Countess had lived her life. Helping others gave her so much satisfaction but perhaps this time it would be beneficial to both. Gabby also was inspired to look at this possible living arrangement as engineered by the cosmos, as a reward for the good vibes she sent out every day. *Yes, we've all come together at this little library for a reason,* flashed through Gabby's mind and it pleased her to think so

"I'm curious," said Gabby inspired by that thought. "What made you choose the library in Chelsea? You're not too far from the New York Public Library on Fifth Avenue and it's so much more beautiful and majestic."

"Something...something drew me there...maybe you," she laughs. "Can't be explained. I was shopping on 14th Street and thought I'd go to a linen store on 23rd Street. I passed the library and stopped in on a whim. I loved the intimacy of it, the small space, and that there are regular patrons. I didn't realize libraries had computers, so that was an added bonus since I don't have one here. It has both a PC and Mac, so I've been trying to learn both. I will make a purchase soon." She saw the look of worry on Gabby's face. "What? It's okay that you know the truth about me. I don't mind if people know my true situation. It was fun being mysterious, but it was just a lark. I have nothing to
hide. Of course, the *Captain* knows because he has been here. In fact, he was the one who filled me in on the notions about me."

Gabby took a sip of tea, swallowed, and asked very perplexed, "Why me? Why have you chosen to tell me all this? Me and the Captain, of course."

The Countess thought for a moment before speaking. She wanted to find the perfect words to explain herself, to engage Gabby but not to offend her.

She began, "Quite simply because I like you and I sensed a kindred spirit. A similar worldview to mine. You are not frivolous, maybe a slight bit too sullen (Gabby grimaced slightly at this tired refrain), and quite intelligent. A big heart that belies your rather somber exterior. A big heart is what I like in a person. Your caring nature and tenderness for people. How you tried to explain the computer to me with such patience. Getting me coffee when you got some for yourself. Suggesting a good book that you had just finished. Always, always acknowledging my existence.

"Because of the way you treated me with such honest concern, you touched me. Appealed to my better nature, so to speak. And so, I studied you. It took me a few weeks, but I think I came to understand you. You are alone but not lonely. Not desperate for a boyfriend. You're in a precarious situation with your housing situation but ask for nothing. You accept your plight and move forward with optimism." At that, Gabby raised her eyebrows in surprise. The Countess saw her true self. Another human being who understood her...*really* understood her. It felt good...really good.

"Yes," the Countess caught Gabby's look, "I recognized your optimism. Your driving force. But I also understood it's something to which you have committed yourself. A personal choice. In the face of adversity, you always choose to find something positive. A wonderful trait in a person, but sometimes at odds with reality. Perhaps you might enjoy some guidance from an old broad like me. Might be just the ticket. And the timing seems synchronous. Irina is leaving and you're losing your apartment, as I learned from browsing the Internet today. As is often the case, I am pragmatic so, I immediately thought of a solution for both of us. Moving in here could be temporary or permanent, whatever suits you. I'm quite flexible. And my tenants are pure joy. Always looking out for me as I said. So, I'll be fine on my own as well. The option of living here is for you to decide, no pressure."

The Countess stopped speaking and slowly sipped her tea. Gabby did the same. A few moments of silence ensued as they took in what had just been said. The magnitude of this offer was hard for Gabby to digest. *Is this for real?*

"Would you be so kind as to tell me more about yourself, Gabby dear, so I can get to know you better? Where you grew up, where you went to university, and so on. I'm interested because I care about you. Walter hinted to me you have been on your own most of your life. And perhaps that's the cause of your underlying sadness. Would you mind telling me? Maybe having a confident would be of some help. Ease your burdens."

Gabby hesitated. *Should she? Should she tell her sad secrets to this person she so admired? Would it put her off?* The Countess, using a soothing tone, encouraged Gabby to open up. "It's alright," she said. "Your feelings and secrets are safe with me." This fabulous woman who Gabby had worshiped from afar was now insinuating herself into her life as if she were the important one. But a natural outcome of her obsession with the woman was that the Countess had become an authority figure. And as such, Gabby didn't have the wherewithal to tell her she was not comfortable denying her request. She had never developed these skills as most teenagers do when disobeying and fighting with their mothers. Even thinking about her childhood was never anything Gabby cared to do much less speak of it out loud. Gabby became visibly agitated.

Then the Countess did something peculiar. She asked Gabby to hold hands with her, close her eyes, take deep breaths, and exhale slowly. The very first time the Countess had touched Gabby's hand at the library, she was given flashes of Gabby's troubled childhood. This intermittent gift (she wasn't shown her last husband Don's true self, unfortunately) was sometimes a curse. But today, she was grateful to have been alerted to Gabby's pain. She knew if Gabby was finally able to unburden herself of her past heartaches, her life would be better. She might even blossom. The Countess murmured a chant while they both breathed slowly together. A sense of calm began to overtake Gabby and she started to relax.

"Now," said the Countess, "Now, it will be okay."

"Now," Gabby whispered impulsively in response. And so, Gabby sat upright and slowly and uncomfortably revealed all the sadness and confusion of her childhood. The suffocating loneliness and constant fear. Being brought up with no parental nurturing as if an orphan but for the kindness of neighbors. She retold the painful discovery of her mother's dead body sitting in her chair as if still alive. Calling 911 with shaky hands while gagging from the sorrow and sheer terror that engulfed her, a mere child still in her teens. She remembered all the emotions and all the minutia of that afternoon.

She relived waiting for the ambulance while feeling the anxiety of not knowing what her future would be. The overwhelming fear of being completely on her own even though she had basically been that way most of her young life. That shriveled woman in her chair had been a slim measure of comfort, and protection from foster homes. Now, this vestige of a mother would be utterly gone. Fatally gone. She would be forever alone. Really alone. The horrifying acceptance of that reality weighed heavily on her psyche, but it became a watershed moment, a defining moment for Gabby's survival. For her future self. It was at that moment that Gabby decided she would not let her torturous childhood determine who she was.

The tragic death of this stranger known as "mother" would not damage her potential. She would make her life productive and happy despite the negativity that surrounded her and, in fact, surrounded us all. She had a breakthrough moment of strength, even at this terrible, awful change in her world. From somewhere in the recesses of her mind came these words, *it's what we do that defines us. Not what is done to us.* And this thought immediately sustained her and made her stronger. It carried her into the current manifestation of the woman, Gabby, who managed to bring optimism into her life each and every day, *or did she*?

As she spoke, Gabby found herself choking back tears. She felt her heart begin to pound in her chest, a sense of panic clenching her stomach muscles. This immediate and visceral response belied all those years of control. Suddenly, she realized she was a fraud. Her optimism hollow and fake, evaporating in an instant as she told her woeful tale and succumbed to her overwhelming feverish and explosive heartache. Giving in to her mounting emotions, she finally let herself feel it all. Feel all the pain that had been subconsciously and consciously held in check. At last, giving in to feelings held tight for so many years, her suppressed feelings of sorrow and pain were given purchase. Her geyser of tears flowing wantonly was unstoppable in its force.

Right there, right then in that apartment with this new intimate friend, Gabby cried her heart out, wailing in a manner she had never done before. Floating out of the moment as a spectator, Gabby acknowledged that this display for her was extremely odd, embarrassing, and raw. Completely unexpected, she was powerless once it started to stop the outpouring of her repressed inner torment. As she wailed, she suddenly became aware she was in the perfumed and soft embrace of Countess Anastasia Ivanova, a tender moment of which she submitted gratefully. It was a surreal moment heretofore that she had never experienced. A simple thing woefully absent her entire life...a mother's hug. A consoling hug from this Russian lady of high status who had been her imaginary mother substitute now embodied the role with that much-needed hug. A physical expression of love to bring comfort and succor to dispel Gabby's misery.

As for the Countess, she herself had been overcome with such strong emotion that tears also flowed freely down her face as she listened to Gabby's anguish. It was brutal. Brutal but necessary, she told herself. When they both finally stopped crying, Gabby was exhausted but felt free, lighter. It was astonishing to feel so unburdened. Even her normal frown face began to relax somewhat, although she had no idea of it. As for the Countess, her motherly instincts, her nurturing self, had kicked into high gear. In that loving tactile exchange, the Countess had indeed become Gabby's mother figure and it would change hers and Gabby's life's path from then on.

For Gabby, the shared tenderness of that moment brought with it the realization that this was the reason for her obsession. This was what had symbolized the Countess for her. For as the Countess had become Gabby's mother figure with that hug, so too, Gabby's longing for a mother or a least a mother figure was finally realized. A gift from the cosmos. She was no longer alone. For this, she was grateful and, being true to herself, was mindful of its significance to her.

They sat silently for some time recharging their spirits from the tearful ordeal while gazing at the tiny birds nesting in the few trees and the Countess lovingly stroking Gabby's arm. Finally, the Countess spoke softly and tenderly, "Hand me your teacup, Gabby. Please, darling. I think I should look at your tea leaves. I'm getting nudged to do so, an urge if you will."

"An...urge to do...*what*?" Gabby said finding her voice with some difficulty.

"Oh, it's just something I do. I have perfected the notion that if you concentrate your energy, the universe will give you guidance. Bad situations can be avoided with cosmic knowledge. The tea leaves tell a story of sorts. They have absorbed your energy as you sipped and garnered information about you. I often consult the tea leaves. The day I stumbled on this townhouse was foretold by them."

Gabby was a willing participant in anything that dovetailed with her strong beliefs about the cosmic forces that shaped our lives. Yes, we are *kindred spirits*, she thought. This unusual request roused her from her numbed state while piquing her curiosity as she handed her the cup. The Countess looked inside the cup and studied the contents for several minutes. "Hmm, this is very interesting. Something is going to change for you. Quite a big change, actually. Yes...but it's different than moving from your apartment to this one. Something quite good. Something very unexpected...but perfect. Turns out to be just the ticket.

"You won't see it that way at first, but you will quickly see the wisdom of it. Oh, and, yes, yes, (she chuckles) I see *myself* in this future. How intriguing. Lovely, how lovely. Seems, there's room for me on this new path. That's a pleasant thought. Our friendship is sealed. Wonderful! Now, let's shake ourselves from what we've just been through and have dinner and a nice glass of wine. Let's also toast your mysterious good fortune. Maybe my good fortune as well," she adds merrily. Then they walked arm in arm into the apartment relishing in their new mother-daughter closeness.

The intimate dining table was set just for the two of them with fine floral patterned bone china. The pleasant dining room had library bookshelves on one wall and the other walls were painted a deep red with dark mahogany dentil crown molding and adorned with oil on canvas portraits of people, possibly relatives, in eighteenth-century attire. Cozy. They toasted with a glass of fine Malbec. "To my current favorite wine and my favorite people. To us, Irina, and to my dear departed cousins," said the Countess as she nodded toward the paintings.

They ate cold borscht soup followed by the Countess telling Gabby that she couldn't wait for her to taste "Irina's magnificent beef Stroganoff," said loud enough for Irina to hear in the kitchen. And then Irina served the mouthwatering traditional dish whose aroma made one feel transported to the palaces of Russian Czars and their infinite luxury. The regal cousins observing this meal ensconced forever in elaborate gold-leaf frames appeared proud while seeming to nod their approval of a meal fit for royalty. Gabby bowed her head slightly to acknowledge their presence and high status. *Did one of the painted cousins just smile at her?* Nonsense, but she threw her eye there intermittently.

The Countess could not refrain from making the sounds one does when eating a delicious repast. Perhaps, thought Gabby, this behavior was another Russian tradition. The cousins didn't seem to mind. She joined in with "It is quite tasty," to make the Countess feel comfortable with her sounds of pleasure accorded to this gastronomic delight. An exceptional homemade meal rarely enjoyed by this single librarian whose cheap microwavable entrees were placed on paper plates most nights and weekends. Being invited to dinner was not a usual experience for Gabby and her lifestyle. The odd exception was Walter, who invited her the last few years to a Chinese New Year's feast prepared by his wife.

For the Countess, the enjoyment of food was not just eating a meal, especially when eating Russian cuisine. It was a connection to her life's experiences. Her journey. Her essence. Her worldview. Whenever she tasted these distinct flavors and was surrounded by these familiar aromas, it had the overpowering effect of hearkening her back to her childhood. Images of her life as a young girl came in bits and flashes when just the aroma of a favorite dish swirled around her. Memories of family meals brought her a sweet nostalgia for things past. The taste of Stroganoff brought visions of sunsets viewed from the family's mini estate near Windsor Great Park in Surrey. How she loved their weekend getaways and summers spent there. The peaceful quiet, lush greenery, manicured gardens, and her lone walks in the woods and fields on beautiful sunny days. Strudel took her back to Surry's solitude on rainy weekends in front of the fireplace. Stuffed cabbage brought forth memories of Skippy, her precious, lovable Yorkie who begged for scraps and made happy barking sounds as she lapped up the ground-beef stuffing.

In contrast, she also loved the hustle and bustle of London and their townhouse in Belgravia. She appreciated every aspect of her privileged childhood. Never took it for granted. Blinis and caviar made her reminisce about fancy dress parties and being young and single anxiously awaiting invitations to arrive in the mail. Every moment in her past was relished for the precious memories they evoked and even right *no*w each bite of this Stroganoff was savored for its delectable thrill to her taste buds and her beloved and cherished memories of her youth.

As for Gabby, never having been exposed to this type of fare, she at first tentatively took a few bites until she decided it was exceptionally delicious. When asked if she had ever eaten borscht or heard of it, Gabby shook her head, *no*.

"One can eat this soup hot or cold. I prefer to eat it hot only in winter. It's made from beets and is very authentic Russian cuisine. Borscht recipes are unique to a family and have become a tradition. And so, the recipe for this soup you have eaten was handed down by my family members for generations. We never give the recipe to anyone other than family or close to the family. After Irina leaves, I will have to make it myself," she laughed. "You might think it peculiar to put a dollop of sour cream atop this soup. But we Russians love our sour cream and it's used in a good many dishes. Even the beef Stroganoff you are eating. And yes, the dish was named after a Russian nobleman who had a French chef that created it."

As the Countess ate, visions of happy family gatherings continued to play at the edges of her memory. The cold borscht, like the one she had just finished used to be prepared by Anna, Irina's mother. It would be set out on the lawn picnic table in Surrey when

Springtime temperatures teased their way into the changing winter weather. When this image came to mind, she usually recalled playing hide and seek and laughing with her brother or cousins along with the sweet fragrance of honeysuckle mingling with the scent of their rose garden. Grand times. Simpler times. A wistful yearning for family members happily being together when they were still very much alive. Mama and Papa. Brother Andrew. All gone now. Thinking of them always brought sorrow and longing for dear ones so very missed. Nevertheless, she was grateful for her life even with all its harsh realities. Because living is a miracle. A gift counted in moments of time. A gift never taken for granted by her ever since she could remember.

Born with a unique understanding of how the cosmos worked, the Countess had an instinctual grasp, a gift of realizing early on, the meaning of life. A knowledge that the spirit outlives the body and this knowledge above all else gave her much comfort. This special wisdom settled her and was the source of her powerful intuitiveness. As an enlightened child, she was sought after by family and friends who sensed she was special. Just being around her brought joyfulness to one's spirit while also making one feel safe and protected. Love of all things and sharing her wisdom was her life's mission. She emitted this energy and attracted the right people into her life, people like Gabby. Satisfied with this pleasurable day, she ate dinner heartily while silently being thankful for her blessings and reveling in her steady and profound happiness as she enjoyed the food of her heritage. Being in the glow of the Countess, Gabby became interested in learning all she could about Russia. She would educate herself on this topic because now Russia and the Countess were one and the same to her. Russian recipes would top her list. In the meantime, she asked the Countess these three questions as they ate. "Are you really a Countess? Have you been to Russia? Do you have family still living in London?"

Firstly, the Countess ended the myth of being impoverished aristocracy, which was only touched upon but needed to be fully addressed. Even though the extended family had hurriedly fled Russia in the wake of the Bolshevik revolution as had been told at the library, they had been able to take a vast amount of their wealth in jewels and cash with them. Although it had shrunk by wastrel relatives over time, the newer generation had been able to rejuvenate the coffers to some extent with smart investments in real estate and marriage into Britain's upper social class.

Her own parents, although born in London, were part of the Russian ex-pats that socialized with the lesser royals. Her father's connections after he graduated from the London School of Economics helped get him a position with the Bank of England as an economist. His inheritance after his parents passed when he was still a young man afforded them the townhouse in Belgravia and the cottage in Surrey. Her mother had met her father at a dinner party given by someone who worked for the Lord Chancellor. The Countess watched Gabby's expression and realized that this story was a far cry from the whispered tales at the library.

As far as the remaining relatives in London, the Countess had extended family, second cousins and the like, who still lived in around London, closer relatives, first cousins, aunts and uncles had moved to Devonshire and Surrey. As far as her being nobility, the family mythology was that a distant relative, third cousin to her mother was related to the Romanovs through marriage and some members say they were also a very distant relative of Catherine, the Great. But she didn't know if these stories were true. Most of the Russian ex-pats created stories of being nobility which nobody could disprove. Their wealth, although modest by the British royals' standards, would have made it difficult to socialize with the haut monde but not for their possible Russian aristocratic bloodline, so being called Count, Prince, Duke, or Baron and their female counterparts whether true or not was quite prevalent.

She had done some research on her surname but found nothing conclusive, and, of course, her first name, Anastasia, nostalgically named so by her mother to honor the Romanovs, had become rather common after the horror of the cold-blooded execution had died down. Perhaps she was a real Countess given these stories, perhaps not, but her second husband called her that for a laugh. The title stuck and she liked it. Especially being called so by the library staff. "Here in New York City, it seems very romantic to be considered a Countess," she said. And yes, she's been to Russia.

Her second husband took her to St. Petersburg on their honeymoon. A cultural immersion and genealogical expedition. They visited heritage sites and some mansions that once possibly housed her expat relatives. It was quite remarkable to be there. To come back to your roots. To intellectually not feel an outsider as she felt in Britain. Like a child coming home from a summer at camp or spotting your mum at your piano recital among strangers. Identifying with a place, the people, and speaking the language. Of being present and feeling connected at a subconscious level, recognizing who she truly was fundamentally. She spoke a Russian dialect that was understood by the populace and it was fun to do so. She was one of them. Like Jews visiting Israel or being in a support group where everyone has had a similar fateful experience. Not being the other. Belonging. It felt good.

The political environment at that time was still pretty strict and most people quite destitute. The average person suffered from a lack of common staples. So, on that level it was depressing. Cigarettes became currency. Dunhill's were especially popular and could be traded for the few Soviet-made products. She still had the nesting dolls that were exchanged for a cashmere sweater. But today, it's quite different there so she would like to go back and see St. Petersburg as a more thriving economy. Perhaps she would visit next year.

"As to immediate family back in London, the short answer is no. My older brother moved to Cape Town about 30 years ago. He needed sunshine. Craved it, in fact. But he suffered from Alzheimer's and died about 10 years ago. He never married. Sadly, my parents passed many years ago, too. First, my father had a major heart attack and my mother nursed him until he died a year later. Soon after my mother was diagnosed with stage 4 cancer. As for me, I've never had children. Too many miscarriages, so I gave up trying. Too painful. Adoption didn't appeal to Smitty, my second husband.

"So, there you have it. No close relatives in London but there are some of Smitty's cousins and a few of my second and third cousins. We are still in touch, so there's that. People to visit whenever I get back there. Never really been very social much with relatives. Might keep in touch more now being totally on my own after Irina leaves. It will take some getting used to since she's been with me her entire life and most of mine. I'm not worried about it. As I said, my tenants are quite nice and friendly."

They finished the meal making small talk about the library and upcoming parades and such in the City. It was very pleasant for Gabby to partake in this friendly conversation. It felt quite natural, not forced. This woman who was her idol. It was a no-brainer for Gabby to entertain the idea of moving in temporarily if she couldn't find an apartment right away. She imagined many evenings spent like this chatting at dinner, sitting in the garden. It was quite appealing.

"Let me know soon if you need a place to stay," said the Countess calling out to Gabby as she got into a cab. "And also let me know if something unexpected happens in a few days. I'm quite curious."

"It's been a very lovely evening, thank you," Gabby called back. But as soon as the cab pulled away a worrying fear of impending doom took hold. What was this unexpected event? Unexpected events usually weren't something for which to happily anticipate, like the Quit Notice. But then quickly her trained optimism kicked in. The Countess said it was a good thing. A good thing and trusting that the Countess had this premonition, she brushed away her doubts.

After Gabby left, the Countess asked Irina to join her for a cup of coffee. Her dear friend would be leaving quite soon and she was coping with all the emotions encased in that wrenching loss. As Irina poured the coffee, the Countess took notice of the subtle and dramatic changes brought about by the natural aging process. The two had been like sisters since Irina was born when her mother worked as the head housekeeper for the Countess's family. Although the Countess was ten years old when Irina was born, she nevertheless took a strong interest in the child. It had been a difficult pregnancy and the only one brought to term for Klara, her mother, who was in her forties when the pregnancy surprised both she and her husband. Klara brought the child to work and when the Countess was at home she would spend many hours with Irina, a preschooler, teaching her the alphabet and to read.

When Irina's mother died suddenly from complications suffered from the pregnancy and her father had become a hopeless alcoholic, it was only natural that Irina would be taken in by the Ivanova family. She later became the Countess's friend and confident standing by her side through all the turmoil of her marriages. Having someone to count on when life threw heartbreak your way became a cherished relationship for both of them. Irina had remained in this role until now and this change in their status left the Countess woefully unprepared for her feeling of devastation. Not the sentiment she allowed herself to tell anyone. Best make it seem it was fine with her, to make sure Irina wouldn't get a whiff of it.

A stunner as a young girl, no one had expected Irina to remain single for most of her life. She had silky, light-blonde hair with thick curls that danced around her shoulders. Now the color faded into a drab brownish tone interspersed with gray strands that she wore tied in a messy bun. Her once creamy plump skin was now drawn and littered with lines and the occasional dark spot. Her large, round blue eyes that in youth gave the immediate impression of gleeful wonderment now appeared hollow and dull. But occasionally, when she would have a good laugh or when her bright smile was consciously beamed onto a small child, the Countess would catch a glimpse of the young Irina in the blush of womanhood. Or the glowing version of Irina would emerge unexpectantly when the sweet scent of a rose would relax her features and recapture the flawless visage of the maiden.

During her glorious adolescence, everyone thought Irina had her choice of respectable suitors for which to make a life. But, alas, she took up with a married man who for many years strung her along with promises of wedded bliss but died suddenly from cardiac arrest never to fulfill his promise. When she recovered from this heartache, she was no longer young and no longer interested in the pursuit. Accepting her spinsterhood and embracing her housekeeper role, she remained content until Carlos, the contractor's employee, whisked her off her feet with compliments and chocolate. In *his* eyes, Irina was that young bright-eyed girl she had left behind many years ago. As she basked in his vision and perception of who she was to him, it also became the way she thought of herself. Once this happened, she could never go back to being the lost and lonely soul she had become. Now she wanted more. It was her time now and the Countess gave thanks for the opportunity to have known Irina so intimately and she willingly and lovingly let go of her dependence on her.

The Countess also understood it was time for her to be self-sufficient and she was ready for some solitude unless, of course, Gabby moved in. But that would be quite a different kind of relationship and frankly would work better without Irina. As for Irina, she was exuberant right now, but the Countess knew that marriage always presented challenges. And for Irina, there would be the additional challenge of moving to a country where she didn't know the language or customs. Of course, right now she was full of optimism, the first blush of marriage was always full of hope and idealism for a bright future. Reality and personality quirks, however, would become apparent sooner than either would be ready for them. The Countess hoped these obstacles were not insurmountable and in time could be worked through satisfactorily. But she knew from her own experiences that marriages do end prematurely either from a divorce or premature death.

As it happens when two people are such close friends, Irina simultaneously mused about her relationship with the Countess while the Countess was doing likewise. As Irina poured the coffee and served the sweets, she thought of how to her the Countess was larger than life. A spectacular specimen with the charm, grace, and aristocratic manners of royalty. It would not have surprised her if the family were indeed Russian nobility. The years had been kind to the Countess who retained her slim-waisted youthful figure. For some women, like the Countess, the aging process brings a softness and smoothness to their facial features and only a few lines marred her beauty. Irina knew that the calm inner spirit of the Countess, her generosity, and loving manner was reflected in her outward appearance. She would miss her terribly and the comfort of being in her presence. But the Countess had taught her to grab opportunities when they come your way and live life with gusto. Now, she would no longer be an observer but a participant in life. It was exhilarating.

The Countess had conveyed to Irina that she certainly hoped her life and marriage would be wonderful but given the uncertainties of life, it was important to remember she always had a place to call home. Irina understood how the Countess viewed the world and took her advice and offer with grace and loving appreciation. Although Irina was giddy at the prospect of being married and having her own home, she was comforted to know that the Countess also considered her family. As they finished their coffee, they wept together for the hard loss of each other's company and for the hope of Irina's bright future. It was a lovely parting conversation and one that kept their hearts connected even when separated by continents.

Afterwards, the Countess performed her evening toilette and mused about her own future. The tea leaves revealing some sort of life-changing event was suddenly welcome. She was beginning to become tired of her routine and realized that change was a life pattern on which she thrived. Her reminisces about her happy childhood in Surry made her long for a country environment away from the concrete, streetlights, traffic noises and all the other daily challenges of city living. How lovely it would be to rest her eyes on green spaces, distant wide vistas, quiet evenings with only the sounds of birds chirping.

Imagining herself in a country setting had crowded her thoughts that evening. Perhaps this was a premonition and she fell asleep with the scent of newly mown grass permeating her bedroom, a scent that signified her home in Surry.

Chapter Three

The Letter

Journal entry:
Oh, fear and loathing kept at bay.
Oh, fear and loathing came back to stay.
Turmoil, turmoil, turmoil from outside.
Turmoil, turmoil, turmoil creeps inside.

Once home from her cab ride, Gabby took Doo for a walk and virtually hugged her neighborhood. *These streets have been good to me. My adult life started here.* Graduating from Hunter College clasping her degree in Library Science was a happy memory. It was natural that Gabby would pursue a degree in Library Science because the local library was where she sought solace and escape as a young girl. Winning a full scholarship covering tuition, room and board, and a small stipend for books was the only way a destitute Gabby could attend. Her mother had borrowed all the equity from the house so she could sit in that chair and never go to work. It was an immediate shock to find this out, but she was young, strong, motivated, and hopeful. The scholarship solved everything. She had a roof over her head and a meal plan. The parents who had helped her get through high school wished her well and were greatly relieved she would not need any of their money.

After graduation, she went to the Hunter placement office to check the job postings. Hosanna! There was an opening at the library on W. 23rd Street. It was a small community library and Gabby loved it on the spot. She advanced from assistant to full librarian within one year of hire. Walter, the head librarian was planning to take early retirement in two years to help run his wife's family's dry-cleaning business, a fate he had managed to avoid until now but his father-in-law's health was failing. He named Gabby his replacement. Her future was set. For Gabby, it was much more than a job. It was a calling. Every time she entered a library as a child, she had felt a sense of excited anticipation. That feeling still remained. The quiet coolness of the interior, the muffled and hushed tones of soft speech, and her church-like reverence for the books became an addiction of sorts. The

outreach to the community when the adorable Hispanic kids from the local neighborhood
came for story time was one of her favorite activities. But she especially enjoyed the comradeship of the larger part-time and smaller full-time staff. The familial connection with the staff created a sense of belonging that had been sorely missing in her childhood. Because her past was filled with so much anxiety and uncertainty, her ambitions
in life were modest. She was easily satisfied with knowing for certain about what would happen every day. So, for Gabby, this simple, small library was a perfect situation.

During her job interview, Walter handed her an ad for her apartment within a short walk from their location. Furnished, cheap, and ready to move in. Her life's path was set. She had resolved all her graduation worries in one afternoon. Glorious. The cosmos was looking out for her that was for sure. There was only one full librarian on staff. Her name was Mona and she had worked there for ages and was quite elderly. Day in and day out, snow, wind, rain, or shine, Mona walked more than 10 blocks to work every day shuffling on her weary feet to get there before opening.

NYC has a grid layout. Easiest walks go North or South to uptown or downtown streets along the avenues. Longer and harder walks are when you go across town, that is, East or West on the same street. Most mornings, Mona, living east of the library in the Stuyvesant Town apartment complex on 14th Street and First Ave, arrived early giving herself several hours for the long, hard walk from East to West. She was found one morning sitting on the curb of Park Ave S. and 23rd street, quite close to the library. A passerby leaned over to ask if she were all right and called an ambulance when Mona fell over dead on the sidewalk. Gabby was immediately promoted to full librarian and didn't mind the extra work. She loved every minute and every aspect of her job but because of her normal sour expression, most people didn't think so.

As she strolled through her local streets with Doo playfully sniffing everything, she realized it would be sad to leave this friendly and charming neighborhood where she had grown used to the people and felt safe. She was happy here. Doo was too. Just when things were going great, a monkey wrench. *But things could be worse.* She had options. Fabulous options. She couldn't walk to work staying with the

Countess but with no rent, she could cab it. Wait. *Would there really be no rent?* She'd best find out.

When she got back from walking little Doo, she was ready to kick off her shoes and relax. There was a lot to mull over. As she was about to enter the apartment, she tripped over something left in front of her door that she missed seeing because she was carrying Doo and fumbling with her key. It was a delivery by FedEx. An ominous official-looking piece of mail. She threw it on the table to deal with later. First, a cup of coffee while watching her favorite television shows. The letter probably had to do with her eviction. Reading about that was something to put off for later...much later. And she went to bed later that night ignorant of what waited for her upon its opening.

With a few days to consider the Countess's offer to stay at her brownstone garden apt, Gabby decided to enjoy the Memorial weekend. Originally, she had planned to go apartment hunting and she perused the Sunday paper and online rental sites. She needed a furnished flat with a small deposit and low rent in the same neighborhood. Just like this one. Exactly like this one, in fact, this one was perfect. *What a bummer*! A quick search turned up nothing, nada, zilch, zero. She expanded out to Brooklyn, dreading the idea of a subway commute. Two apartments popped up in Crown Heights. *Ugh!* She looked at the subway map. Oh...well there were not too many stops to get into the city, but she would have to change trains at 14th St. or walk. It could be worse.

She looked up photos of Crown Heights and the images were appealing. Lots of brownstones and engaging tree-lined streets. Not too bad. She checked the neighborhood demographics. *Eh*. Not balanced, whites in the minority. She didn't feel comfortable standing out. But she was used to that on her street and in her building. So, deal with it. The first apartment was in a brownstone on the basement level, the second in an apartment building on the fourth floor, no elevator. She was only on the third floor of this building. It wasn't great with groceries but doable, so the fourth floor would be in the negative column. *But it would be good exercise.* And the basement-level apartment would be dark. Also, a negative.

She called the brownstone. The apartment had just been rented. She called the apartment building landlord; he spoke no English and she looked again and saw the ad was in English and Spanish. She hung up very discouraged and starting to get nervous that she didn't have the money to move to an area with a more evenly mixed demographic. And more importantly, available and affordable. *What should she do?* She might have no choice but to move in with the Countess. *Temporarily.* Not a bad option. *That lovely garden.*

Since apartment hunting seemed too daunting, Gabby decided to go to the Metropolitan Museum of Art instead. It always had an interesting visiting exhibit and she never got tired of the permanent collection. The landmark museum also made one feel a reverence for the culture of humanity over the centuries, the importance of understanding the mind of man like the books in the library. Devoted crowds gave off a vibe of excitement for just being there, witnessing the majestic achievements of past societies. Uplifting art and artifacts that enhanced the spirit while connecting modern-day people with our glorious ancient brethren as well as more recent contemporaries. She loved important public places like museums, libraries, and theaters. Yes, visiting the museum was a perfect way to spend the afternoon. Deciding where to live could be put on hold for at least a day.

As she folded the newspaper, she saw the FedEx envelope on her table. Oh yeah. It must be the official terms of the Quit Notice. It was distasteful but necessary to open it because perhaps there was the final date by which she had to vacate the premises. And so, Gabby tore open the envelope not realizing the portent of this moment. Information for which she was entirely unprepared awaited her casual nonchalant ripping of the enclosure. Alas, opening it before she went to the museum was a big mistake and ruined her plans for the day. Because the letter changed everything in the ordinary life of Gabrielle "Gabby" Bernstein. What it said was startling, horrifying, and had nothing to do with her imminent eviction. Simply put, this letter contained stunning news. Wrenching and devastating news. Apparently, the Countess was right about what she saw in the tea leaves. And that in itself was unsettling.

The sender was the law offices of Whitehead and Barnaby in Vermont. Vermont? She opened the letter with trepidation and her hands started shaking as she read. *We are sorry to inform you...* She stopped and gasped. *We are sorry to inform you...* She stopped and gasped again afraid to go on. *We are sorry to inform you*...and then finally continuing...*on the passing of your father, Philippe Justin Bernstein.* She read the opening sentences over and over trying to grasp their import. She sat stunned for a moment in disbelief. Her father for whom she had no real memory...was now...dead. A total shock. She glanced at the other words in the letter and the words *Last Will and Testament* jumped out. *There's a Will? Involving me? Do I feel anything? Yes, I feel disgust and anger.* But she also felt dread and sorrow...yes...sorrow.

The reality that her dysfunctional family was now officially and completely erased was surprisingly disturbing. It was alarming to have to deal with the pain of her childhood once again so soon after the meltdown in front of the Countess when for so long those feelings had lain in check. As she sat at her table, holding the letter, her emotions ran the gamut of a roller-coaster ride of twists and turns and highs and lows. Because she had trained herself to be stoic and calm in order to go about her daily life, she had not developed the coping mechanisms to face the harsh realities of her pain-filled past when thrown at her unexpectedly.

Trying to absorb everything, she wrote a eulogy in her mind about her biological father, although a father-in-name-only. This disturbing exercise was strangely calming and easy to do. He was a heartless person who abandoned her when just a child. He left her to be brought up by a woman who eventually became deranged because of him. He didn't even give her dire circumstances a second thought, never bothered to find out if she were well-cared for and if they had enough money. A no-good, absent, bastard of a father. He had been dead to her for her entire life, so his actual death was no real loss.

But it was a loss that she, unexpectedly, felt quite deeply. She was shockingly devastated. Whether she chose to admit it or not, Gabby had always longed for contact knowing deep down that she would instantly forgive him for everything if he would just call. Each day was a tribute to his neglect. Her sense of rejection was acute. And now...he finally reaches out at the end of his life or rather after the end of his life. Perhaps, that was something, *wasn't it?* Well, that depended on what he bequeathed to her. Could be nothing much. Maybe an old photo album with pictures of him and her grandparents.

Pictures of him would be good because she couldn't even remember what he looked like as a young man and at least she would know what he looked like through his life. Photo albums had been thrown out by her mother in a rage when he first left and before she was in the throes of her mental disorder. What had remained for

Gabby were snippets of memories. A dirty and well-used pair of running shoes left in front of the sofa. A 15-year-old champagne-colored battered Oldsmobile smelling of cigarettes. The strong scent of after-shave lotion on the shirts left in his closet. *Old Spice?* Whenever a guy wore that cologne or something similar, she walked away. A deal breaker. Eventually, even those meager belongings were thrown out or sold until he was completely obliterated.

She sat there ruminating over this new turn of events until she felt Little Doo licking her feet and pushing her cuteness into Gabby's consciousness breaking her dark mood. She was glad for the normalcy of routine. It was time to feed her. Then the walk around the block so she could do her business. She nodded silently to a few neighbors but was guarded. She didn't trust herself to speak. *Was it just yesterday that she took Doo to the library?* So much had happened in a small space of time. Dealing with finding a new place to live was enough change in and of itself. When she got back to the apartment, she turned her attention to the business aspects of this letter. It was much easier to focus on the logistics of the matter. Tamp down her emotions. Firstly, according to the terms, she must be at the Whitehead and Barnaby law firm in Rutland, Vermont by 9:00 a.m. on Tuesday for the reading of the Will, a condition of her inheritance. Just three days from today. *Should she get her own lawyer?* They didn't give her much notice and she wondered why. Perusing the envelope, she realized it had gone to a few wrong addresses over the past month. It made sense that they wouldn't know how to find her being estranged from her father. It was amazing that they had found her at all. In fact, she had thought he lived in Quebec not Vermont.

Well, if she were going to appear, she needed to get to Vermont and quickly. The inheritance could be something monetary. A photo album would not demand her presence at a law firm. With her impending move, an unexpected infusion of cash was sorely needed. It could change everything for her in her present predicament. But why would he leave her money, especially a lot of money? Although she knew nothing about his circumstances, this Last Will and Testament suggested assets of some sort. And if she were true to herself, she also ached to hear the words he used to write this Will. Something from him recognizing her existence.

Once she decided she would appear at the reading of the Will, she had to figure out how to get there. Should she take the train or rent a car? Stupid question. She would be taking Doo, so the train was out. Driving, however, was not something she was comfortable doing. She had gotten her license years ago because she needed a photo ID. Might as well learn to drive, she had told herself. Her friend at school rented a car for her test and she passed. Occasionally, she would rent a car for the day to drive upstate to see the leaves change or flowers blooming in Spring. She was a skittish driver but managed not to kill anybody.

She would start out first thing in the morning and stay overnight somewhere on the road. Take it slowly. Perhaps, she would get lucky and traffic would be light because the holiday was drawing to an end and people would be headed back to the city not away from the city. She found a Budget Rent-A-Car a short Uber ride away. Next, she called the library and left Walter a message. "I have to take off the next few days for personal business. Sorry for the last-minute notice but a family member passed away," she hesitated "...my father, my father passed away. I'll be back at work at the end of the week and explain everything."

Next, should she call the Countess? *Oh my!* A knot formed in her stomach as she again remembered what the Countess told her about something unexpected happening. Was this the unexpected event? Shouldn't she have known her father had died as she bizarrely studied the tea leaves for information pertinent to Gabby? But something powerfully unexpected did just happen, just as she predicted. And she said it would be good. Good is... good. How is her father dying good? Must wait and see what this is all about. After minor contemplation, Gabby decided to do this alone. After all, she had relied on herself her entire life, except for the aid of her neighbors to get through high school, but that was her own ingenuity making that happen, she told herself.

And this reading of the Will was probably a big nothing. Her inheritance also a big nothing. *Why embarrass herself in front of the Countess?* She needed a place to stay in Rutland and went on the computer. Soulless, cheap, chain motels were abundant. Rutland was near the ski resort of Killington and the legendary Green Mountains, so accommodations were plentiful. But then something appealing popped up in her search, an ad for a charming Bed and Breakfast. She always wanted to stay at one. *Why not?* So, she went on to the website. A picturesque setting in an old orchard near a pond. It was a white clapboard two story with a wide front porch.

Photos revealed that inside it looked homey with antique furniture sporting lace doilies and patchwork quilts adorning the beds. Unassuming and friendly like someone's grandmother's house. This brought up her empty feelings of longing for grandparents that had imbued her childhood along with everything else that was rotten. Both sets had died before she was born and were just figments of her imagination. *So, off to grandmother's house I go just like Little Red Riding Hoo*d, she smirked to herself.

The website touted that the property was only 20 minutes from the Paramount Theater in Rutland. The Paramount was on Center Street and that was also where the law firm was located. She called the property and asked if she could bring Doo. "As long as the dog doesn't bark too much." Perfect again. Everything was set. She packed a small suitcase and brought toys for Doo. First thing in the morning, she put the address in her map app, got the rental car, and with high anxiety headed north out of the city.

The day began with fair weather and a cool morning ground fog. A bombardment of the softness of Spring. Every sound in stark relief as an amplified reverberation echoing a perfect timbre. Reality clung to a fierce awakening of consciousness. The immediacy and awareness of nature coming alive matched the pounding of her heart. She drove thus to Vermont, got there in the late afternoon on Monday and checked into her room at the B&B. She had bought a sandwich on the road and decided to embrace her fear and got under the lovely quilt on her bed in her lovely room and stayed there in a fetal position with Doo at her feet for the rest of the day and night.

Chapter Four

The Will

Journal entry:
A big dilemma to decide,
the cosmos charts an unexpected ride.

"Speak up, my dear," said Mr. Andrew Whitehead, a precise, stern man who was quite short of stature and meticulously dressed in a three-piece navy-blue pinstriped suit, a crisp white shirt, and a periwinkle-blue tie with matching pocket square. After a sleepless night, she arrived at the law offices pale, nervous, and anxious. His harsh attitude caused an adrenalin hit of the fight or flight instinct and Gabby's blood rushed through her veins making her palms sweat. Her voice caught in her throat. Nothing but a croak came out when she tried to introduce herself. She tried to clear it a few times but only could produce gurgling sounds and then just fell silent feeling foolish. Everything about this meeting was terrifying. She was out of her league and wished now she had brought a lawyer or at least asked the Countess to come with her.

Aside from the disturbing prospect of her listening to the Last Will and Testament written by her MIA father, the man who had caused her and her mother so much pain, she was at the mercy of this Mr. Whitehead and quite intimidated. Also, the office with its glass-enclosed conference room lined with law books made her feel like an ignorant hick and a sitting duck. It reminded her of legal dramas she watched on TV but as the "perp", not the victim. She pictured herself being put in handcuffs and ushered out to prison. All nonsense because this was not a police station but nevertheless the fear was palpable and lodged in her throat.

Whitehead studied her and was decidedly annoyed. This nickel and dime stuff was not to his liking. Big real estate deals with developers were his preference but that had dried up with all the environmental regulations that had already passed with more in the pipeline. Vermonters with their "green" mentality were almost militant about that subject. Thus, his practice had morphed into whatever it was that his clients seeking legal representation needed.

Gotta eat. Gradually, he became the go-to guy in Wills and Estates and civil suits. At least he wasn't handling divorces, Russ Barnaby dealt with that horror.

He was somewhat interested in this unusual estate because he had liked Phil Bernstein and knew his wife since grade school having grown up here in Rutland. Being the topic of gossip, Bernstein's desertion of his family back in Brooklyn was habitually mentioned in the town but it was not his place to judge. He, too, had left his first wife for the cute paralegal that he had hired five years ago. He also knew about the hard times that had put the B&B in peril a few years back and Abigail Barnstable's sudden death from a strange accident involving a walk-in freezer that might have caused a heart attack—a woman only in her late 50s, and in apparently otherwise good health. And then of course Phil getting lung cancer, a man who never smoked, and dying rather quickly and recently from sepsis in the hospital. It seemed a black cloud hung over that B&B.

The Bernstein daughter, however, was another kettle of fish and he became immediately disabused to having taken on this case. She was like a frightened bird and her timidity did not sit well with him. He had no patience for this type of behavior. Well, at least it was a simple reading and he would be done with her quite soon and could go about working for his more important clients like *Mr. Root suing his neighbor about his barking dog,* he scoffed to himself. Whitehead sighed and focused on the immediate business of reading the Bernstein Will wearing the heavy cloak of failure for his inability to secure a spot in a powerful New York City law firm when he graduated from NYU law school.

At least he was a named partner after convincing Barnaby that changing it from Barnaby & Barnaby would be good for business. It would bring the firm into the present after the passing of the founder, John Barnaby, Russ's father. No one bothered to check if business had indeed picked up. It was Rutland VT after all. But Whitehead had gotten what he wanted and top billing. Russ didn't seem to care since he was always the second Barnaby in the firm's name.

Seated at the extremely long and polished mahogany conference table, Mr. Whitehead told Gabby they were awaiting another person in order to start. A startling and mystifying piece of information and most unwelcome given all of Gabby's inhibitions concerning this meeting. *Another person?* She didn't want to meet a member of her father's family. Petrified, in fact, to meet this person. It tuned out she needn't have worried. But at this juncture, she conjured up all kinds of thoughts concerning an offspring or two with this woman who had destroyed her childhood. Of course, there would be children. Why didn't she think of that and ignore coming to this meeting? How many children did they have? How old were these children? She hated them. These kids. His kids. Splitting his estate up among his heirs. A pittance was probably all she would get. *Why hadn't she just stayed home and spared herself all this embarrassment and stress?*

The phone placed in front of Whitehead began to ring startling her. Whitehead kept the conversation to a minimum saying basically, "Yes" "No" and finally "As you wish." Then he told Gabby they could begin the reading because the other person's representatives would be on speakerphone. "Oh, okay," Gabby whispered finally finding her voice. That was better, but she still felt nauseated. *What other surprises were in store?* Well, more than she could have ever predicted. Whitehead began by saying in a strong voice for those others listening on the speaker, "If you can't hear me, please let me know." A mysterious voice with a British accent said he could hear Whitehead quite well, and so he began the reading. "I Philippe Bernstein, being of sound mind...*something, something, something*..."

Gabby listened as still as stone. She was suddenly in an altered state. Not quite present. She heard Whitehead speaking but his voice seemed muffled, as if from a faraway place. To her, the words were out of context, jumbled, foreign, and then suddenly becoming coherent. *What?* She felt her world spin out but she remained ramrod straight to affect a state of being in control. It was rough. The Will was a story. The story of her father's turmoil, a man conflicted. A remorseful man. His sorrow at turning his back on her. Hoping someday Gabby could find it in her heart to forgive him. How he hoped that his final gesture would be well-received. Then came the stunning bit of information that knocked her back in her chair. Here it was...what he left her. He hoped she and his son Beau would jointly run the B&B he had run with Beau's mother who was the original owner.

The property was nearby in Rutland and was a going concern and for the most part in good condition only needing some light refurbishing. There was some cash for sprucing up the linens but more could be borrowed using the business as collateral. A P&L statement and cash flow statement had been provided to Whitehead. Her father had wanted both she and Beau at the reading so they could meet. Seal the partnership in person. It was a wonderful life running the business with his wife, who had passed away three years prior, and leaving it to them filled him with peace.

Mr. Whitehead shuffled some papers and was about to read the section of the Will pertaining to the other person referred to as Beau. The lawyers on the speakerphone abruptly interrupted Whitehead before he could start, "Please do not continue. Our client has just relayed to us that has no interest in the inheritance. He doesn't want anything. He will sign his share over to Miss Gabrielle Bernstein as soon as the Title and Deed are drawn." They hung up abruptly.

"Well, that was unexpected. To have someone walk away from their childhood home," said Whitehead. "But Beau, the only other heir, has been living in England for almost five years since before his mother passed, and didn't even come home for the funeral is my understanding. A professor of some sort of future-oriented biology at Cambridge, I think. Never had been around very much, very busy, off getting a doctorate at Harvard and then to a post-doctorate somewhere, maybe England, where he lives now. Well, case closed on that. Anyway, let's get to the particulars. Here, have a look at your inheritance. There is no mortgage. It was owned free and clear by your father."

He handed her a piece of paper. It was an advertisement or rather a brochure for the Bernstein and Barnstable B&B. Gabby noticed the silliness at once. The B&B B&B. A laugh. A laugh that wasn't funny. There was a photo of a very large red masonry building with a wide covered porch and two turrets. She would later find out it was a Richardson Romanesque Revival designed by the famous architect Henry Hobson Richardson at the turn of the 19th century. There were eight bedrooms each ensuite. A delicious breakfast was served daily from 7:00 a.m. until 9:30 a.m. Minutes from town and a short drive to Pico Mountain, Killington as well as other ski areas. Ten acres of pristine forest and meadows surrounded the property providing spectacular fall foliage color. The property had Rutland Lake access for swimming, boating, and fishing. A private pool with a spa pool was on the grounds. Address: 19 Possum Trot Lane.

Gabby held the picture in her now shaky hands. She was glued to the image. Her father had lived there. He had a wonderful life there while her mother decayed bit by bit in that awful chair. Gabby carried the burden of that decay in her heart and soul. She had lived through holidays, birthdays, special occasions that never were celebrated. A childhood isolated and lonely while her father enjoyed his life as the proprietor of a B&B, this particular B&B. A huge, beautiful house. Finally, she looked up at Whitehead, who had been studying her physical reaction to this photo, heavily chewing on a piece of Nicorette gum he had just popped into his mouth.

"I don't want any part of this," she said as she got up to leave grabbing the satchel where Little Doo was napping.

"Wait! Please don't be so impulsive. I would advise that it would be foolish to walk away and give this valuable property to the state. *And all the mountains of paperwork and filings I'd have to do.* Softening his tone, he said, "You should first take ownership and then you can decide to keep it or to sell it. It's probably worth at least two million dollars right now.

"As the paper I gave you said, it's a large property having an abundance of natural beauty bordering a swimmable lake. Why not sleep on this decision and call me tomorrow? Go look at it. I'll give you the keys. You can keep them. I have an extra set. It's been closed for about six months when your father took ill. But I had cleaners come, so it should be in pretty good condition to inspect. Just wait before you decide. You've come all this way. Please don't be hasty. You owe yourself that at least."

He leaves the room and comes back with the keys. It was an awkward moment. At first, she didn't take the keys but Whitehead didn't back down dangling them in her face. She finally reached out and snatched them angrily thinking she would throw them in the trash after she left.

"I know the circumstances of your family situation and your justifiable anger. Perhaps this life-changing inheritance is owed to you for past neglect," he said. "Please let me know what you decide. Perhaps you could call me tomorrow and we can schedule a time for you to come in to sign the papers. The flyer doesn't list that there is a lovely three-room owner's suite on the first floor. Have a look. No harm done."

"Uhhh, thanks," Gabby mumbled as she left in a fugue state of confusion. She got in her car and then drove over to the B&B she had checked into the previous afternoon. Once back in her room, she stretched out on the bed and Doo jumped up and snuggled. She tried to calm her thoughts but all she could see was her mother sitting in that chair and looking longingly out the window. Over and over that scene flashed in her mind. Gnawing away at any thought of her new situation. The keys represented all of that. The keys. She should get rid of them and go home to her familiar world. Well, familiar until her apartment was demolished.

She got up and stood by the window visualizing tossing the keys into the row of bushes below. But that's all she did. *Two million dollars. A game changer. I would be stupid not to sell it.* As she stood musing, she heard a soft knock on the door and it turned her attention away from the window and throwing away the keys. It was the proprietor, Mrs. Jones, a delightfully agile slim-wasted woman who looked to be in her mid-to-late fifties and exuded an air of refinement. Her opulent pure white curly hair framed her aristocratic, chiseled features and was pulled into a loose tie at her neck that hung down her back and bounced healthily as she walked. Her chunky silver and stone jewelry accented her funky Bohemian attire and gave her an approachable and comforting presence.

"I hesitate to bother you," Mrs. Jones said, "but you left this morning and didn't partake in our breakfast goodies and I was wondering if now you would like some of my blueberry walnut muffins and coffee or tea?"

A former model who had graced the cover of many a ladies' magazine, the never married Mrs. Jones took on that affectation believing being single in her fifties presupposed a previous coupling. *Why get into it?* Always on the lookout to improve her financial situation, she had considered herself quite fortunate to have stumbled upon this property. It was quite opportune because she was considering making a drastic change from managing a small Manhattan design studio in women's fashion after she aged out of modeling. She loved Vermont and wanted to get out of the dirty and downtrodden city to have a more peaceful old age.

Scouring the real estate section of the paper and perusing properties on the internet was entertaining but also instructive for knowing when there was a good deal. This income-producing property had come on the market during a real estate downturn so that miraculously her savings were enough for a mortgage and modest monthly payment that she could cover herself in off-season dry spells.

Mrs. Jones loved her peaceful life when the isolated hotel was devoid of visitors but also enjoyed the periodic guests that interspersed this solitude.

It was the perfect balance of serenity and commotion and it shone in the glint of her eyes and bright smile. Always having a soft spot for the lonely-looking child, Gabby's somber expression brought forth her under achieved mothering instincts. Gabby had arrived after the last Memorial holiday guest checked out and was most welcome. Realizing she was quite hungry, Gabby accepted Mrs. Jones's offer and they went downstairs together. After letting the pup out to do her business they went into the dining room with Little Doo skipping behind. A place had been set with a large pot of coffee at the ready.

"I assumed you would want coffee as most of us do, but I can make tea if that's your preference."

"No, this is wonderful. I'm in dire need of a cup. Thank you so much."

"I have breakfast muffins but also a lovely cream of broccoli soup that has been simmering on the stove if you'd like."

"Oh yes, I would. I didn't realize how hungry I am."

"Would you mind if I joined you?"

"Not at all. Certainly, please do."

And so over hot sips of soup, coffee, and bites of delicious muffins, a new friendship was created. Mrs. Jones was the perfect outlet for Gabby's conflicted state of mind and she revealed snippets of her childhood abandonment not wanting to delve in too deeply to this total stranger. After so many years of not dealing with her past, suddenly it had become a topic of conversation for her. First with the Countess and now here. But some information was necessary to convey her current bitterness over this strange inheritance.

It was an amazing coincidence that she chose to stay at this B&B, of cosmic implications, quite frankly. Mrs. Jones knew a lot about the establishment on Possum Trot Lane and had information pertinent to Gabby's situation and woeful lack of knowledge. Gabby listened intently as Mrs. Jones told her about the unusual stories floating among the locals concerning the inn. Happy outcomes and magical events were commonplace after Abigail Barnstable took ownership. Ill people brought there to convalesce left completely well. Marriages on the verge of divorce were reconciled after a weekend getaway. Students performed better at school, writers regained their creativity after being blocked, and artists were energized to begin new projects in their chosen medium. The length of stay didn't matter. Just being there overnight made a difference.

This spate of miraculous events suddenly stopped several years ago around the time of Abigail Barnstable's death. Her business had been built using that name, so she never changed it after she married Gabby's father. At first, people who had been expecting a miracle would get angry when nothing happened and then give the inn bad reviews. That caused a downturn in visitors and the B&B went through hard times for a while. It never fully recovered its former popularity and Gabby should be aware that it might become an albatross if she chose to run it. However, as in most things, people over time tend to forget especially when the original myths of rejuvenation could never be proven. Business had been picking up lately right before poor Mr. Bernstein passed. He probably thought he was providing financial security to his heirs.

"Possum Trot Lane would most likely thrive as another lovely inn during the seasons and it is worth a lot of money, I suspect," said Mrs. Jones. "You say you have the keys?" She asked idly. "Why not have a look? I'd be happy to go with you. It's not too far and I've always been curious."

"I'm not sure it's necessary. You were right, though, the inn is worth a lot. The estate lawyer, Andrew Whitehead, thought the property might sell for about two million dollars in today's market. That's quite a hefty sum and I know nothing about running a B&B and don't really think I'd want to. The timing is quite auspicious, however, because I'm about to lose my place of residence. My apartment building is being torn down to make way for luxury condos.

"But I love my job as a librarian in NYC and Chelsea, my neighborhood, which is close to the library on 23rd St. Even though I need to find someplace else to live, I'm not interested in changing careers or leaving the city. The property does look appealing from the photo, but I would sell it. Heck, the money might even help me stay in the neighborhood and perhaps buy one of those luxury condos. That would really be something."

"Quite right, that does sound like a very viable option. Two million dollars would be life changing if that's what you could really get. I remember it was put on the market just after your father's wife passed away. I read in the paper that it seemed to have sold but then

the buyer backed out. Town gossip was that during inspection, everything went wrong. A small fire was started in the kitchen when the inspector turned on the stove. No water came out of the faucets when they were turned on. It was like the house did not want to be sold. At least that's what people said. Your father ran it all these years until he got
gravely ill and passed. So, I don't know what condition it really is in. Can you afford to keep it and pay the property taxes and insurance until it sells?"

"Wait, *what?* Oh...boy! I'm so dumb to not think of that. Like I said, I know nothing of these things. I have no money to pay for anything. But...I don't know...hmmm...wait I remember, there was some mention in the Will of cash available, but I didn't think to ask how much. Maybe I should just walk away and let Whitehead give it to the state. My father's son Beau didn't want it either."

"That's not surprising. From what people have said about him, he hated it there as a teenager. Couldn't wait to leave. He's supposed to be brilliant. Went to Harvard and got a doctorate and post-doctorate at Stanford in evolutionary biology. Can you imagine? He's living in England, teaches at Cambridge, I think. Supposed to be quite handsome."

"I wouldn't know, he wasn't at the reading. His lawyers were on speakerphone. Apparently, he wants no part of this inheritance. His lawyers said he'd sign over his share to me. But what does that matter? I can't afford to keep it from what you have just told me. This inheritance and all it implies is very distasteful and also quite hurtful to me. This Beau person is older than me. When I realized that it hit me like a ton of bricks because my father left when I was twelve, so how can Beau be older than me? The only explanation is that my father was carrying on with Beau's mother before and after he married my mom. A despicable lying cheat."

"Oh my. How awful for you. Yes, I can see how all this is so painful. But maybe this inheritance from your father was his way of trying to make it up to you for his past neglect. Create a nest egg for you, some security for your future."

"That's funny, that's exactly what Whitehead said. But I'm not convinced of his good will, no pun intended. I probably can't afford to keep the property while it's on the market and from what you said, it might not be an easy sale."

"Well, actually, with the high value of the property, you could probably borrow some cash from it. Also, if you keep it, perhaps after you re-opened there might be a surge of reservations from pent-up demand. Become a thriving business right front the start. Although I've never been there, I hear it's lovely. Your father and his wife were not very sociable with the other inn owners."

"You know, Mrs. Jones, I sincerely appreciate your concern and advice but I'm thinking this inheritance creates more problems than it solves. All this is way over my head. I'd best just go home and forget about it."

"Perhaps you should take a look at it first. What's the harm of checking it out? I've had a wonderful life living here in Vermont. I highly recommend it. I can help you and honestly, I'd love to be your mentor. I have a wonderful group of professionals helping me. An accountant, handyman, financial advisor, and the like. And importantly great recipes that I'd be happy to share."

"Wouldn't Possum Trot Lane be competition for you? Why would you help me?"

"Well, when one B&B does well it helps us all. We share the overflow. People who like to stay at B&B's look for nearby properties when one is booked up. And since we don't have that many rooms, we get booked up quickly during the high seasons of winter for skiing and fall when the turning leaves are glorious. Like I said, it's a short drive from here, there's no real downside. Why not have a look?"

Chapter Five

19 Possum Trot Lane

Journal entry:
It beckons as if in a dream,
and brings on feelings that create a scene
of happy bubbles dancing on moonbeams.

There it was in all its splendor. The house. Impressive in size. Awaiting visitors patiently but stoically. Welcoming but not so much. Gabby was not getting the magical happy vibe to which Mrs. Jones alluded. She could not imagine herself running such a large inn, let alone living in it. Off-putting. The idea was quite intimidating, in fact. As if the house could read her thoughts, she suddenly got a location ding on her phone with the address. The house seemed to be saying, *Too much above your station?* Yes, she thought, *yes, it was* and now more than ever she was certain that turning her back on it was the right decision...but. Part of her was in awe of its expanse and there was also a tiny inkling toward having ownership of such an estate. Mrs. Jones had driven there on an impressively long, private tree-shaded road from the highway that wound through ample grounds and ended in this circular driveway. Her animus rekindled, Gabby got out of the car trying to absorb the injustice of her father's grand lifestyle juxtaposed against her measly and meager childhood circumstances.

There was nothing in her life, heretofore, to compare to this moment surveying this property that was hers for the taking. She paused and looked about before she walked up the front stairs and across the beautiful, wide, painted wood front porch. The dark wooden door with two leaded-glass Victorian sidelights was a perfect accent for the architectural design of the house. Gabby tried the keys in both locks and the door would not budge. It was stuck. After several attempts, she took that as a signal, a warning. She had not passed the house's scrutiny and was rejected. She turned to Mrs. Jones.

"Well, I guess that's that," she said.

"Wait, let's not be hasty," said Mrs. Jones while grabbing Gabby's arm. "Here, give me the keys and let me try. These old houses can be tricky, what with all the settling and expansion from seasonal changes in humidity and soil temperature doors habitually get stuck. Mine do all the time." With some finesse, she pushed the key into the bottom lock and turned it and then the deadbolt. "There...now...okay." And the door opened. Actually, it flew open as if someone were on the other side pulling it from within.

Gabby paused on the porch for a moment before she entered. This gift from her deadbeat Dad made her cautious and apprehensive while this persistent thought gnawed at her. *This is where my father lived when my mother was losing her mind and wasting away. When I prayed every day that he would come home.* As she stood at the entrance lost in thought, a vision appeared in the shadows on the far side of the room and startled her. There was a woman with wild flaming-red hair beaming at her and dressed in a white flowing robe. Her arms were outstretched in a welcoming embrace. When Gabby blinked, she was gone. *Oh my!* Mrs. Jones making her way inside didn't seem to notice what Gabby had just seen.

As Gabby was about to say something to her, it was forgotten as soon as they crossed the threshold. Both of them stopped in their tracks just inside the room and gasped in wonder. The interior of the house was nothing short of magnificent. "So beautiful," Mrs. Jones said in a hushed and reverent tone. The immediate impression was of wood. Golden-colored wood was everywhere (heart pine she would later learn). The floors, walls, and coffered two-story ceiling conveyed the overall ambiance of a rustic but elegant weekend getaway or hunting lodge. A dazzling spectacle, bright, charming, warm, and beckoning. They stood transfixed gawking. The eye gravitated toward the wooden staircase with carved wooden balusters that also supported the railings of the second-floor balcony overlooking this large public room/lobby and front desk area.

After the two of them regained their composure, they proceeded slowly into the room feeling overwhelmed and spiritually moved as if entering a house of worship. A large fireplace with a stone hearth covered one wall and comfortable-looking seating was arranged to enjoy its benefit. Homey touches of colorful throws and area rugs accented the decor. The large first-floor windows and those along the stairs featured stained-glass artwork throwing a colorful warm glow into the room enhancing the church-like atmosphere. As they absorbed the loveliness of the room in silence, Doo broke the spell by jumping out of the satchel and disappearing into the far reaches of the house.

"Oh no! Doo! Come back! What are you doing?" Gabby ran in the puppy's direction and found herself in the kitchen. Another welcoming space lined with brick walls and all the normal modern stainless-steel appliances. A large butcher block prep island stood in the center. The kitchen opened up to an adjacent room where another fireplace and giant hearth took up an entire wall opposite the long sidebar and several four-top tables. One assumed this was where guests enjoyed their free breakfast. Searching for Doo and constantly calling her name, Gabby opened a door slightly ajar thinking it was a closet but to her surprise, it was a walk-in pantry. Next to it was a walk-in freezer with shelves like at a wholesale market to hold, she supposed, enough stores if the winding road that led here got snowbound for days in the winter ski season and the hotel guest list was full. A large refrigerator completed the huge amount of food storage.

Mrs. Jones was duly impressed with the kitchen as well. "My word," she said as soon as she entered following Gabby, "what I could do with a workspace like this. I would finally set up the jam business I've been thinking about. Eight burners on the stove! Two ovens! And that amazing amount of storage," she said, as she peeked in to see what Gabby was looking at. "Unbelievable!"

"Doo," Gabby called as she closed the freezer door. "Doo, come here my sweet girl. Come here, my sweet," she began to get frightened. "Doo, where are you, Doo?" She started to panic. "Wait, was that a barking sound?"

"Yes, upstairs," said, Mrs. Jones. And they both ran up the back set of stairs to the bedrooms. A main corridor led to several rooms and made a turn leading to another staircase. "Doo," Gabby started to yell louder as her fear took hold in full. "Doo...Doo." And then miraculously, the rush of little feet as Doo ran out of one of the rooms and down the front stairs. Both women ran after her and Gabby caught her at the bottom. Doo was agitated but unhurt wagging her tale and squirming when Gabby picked her up and hugged her.

"Don't ever run away again, Doo. You gave me such a fright," Gabby said as she put the pup back in the satchel she had never put down.

"Well, this is certainly quite a place. Shall we investigate the rest?" asked Mrs. Jones.

"I'm too distracted right now, what with Doo scaring me and the overwhelming idea that this place was left to me. I need to go home, back to New York, and think about all this. There's really a lot to think about. It's a beautiful place, quite large. I'm thinking I should come back and carefully check it out when I've calmed down and digested all of this. I hope I can count on you to come with me."

"Certainly, it would be my pleasure. But wait, before we leave, how about we drive down to see the lake bordering this property? It's very popular with the locals for swimming, boating, and fishing. I personally love to go to the public picnic area on the other side from here and walk the trails. Parts of this lake, shallow areas in the coves, freeze solid in winter for some lovely ice-skating gatherings with colorful lights, music, and sleigh rides."

Once Gabby had made up her mind that she had had enough and was anxious to get back to the city, she felt trapped by this suggestion. Not wanting to insult her new friend, she nodded her consent just to be polite and leaned down to pet Doo's head and give it a little kiss. After they locked up the house, Gabby walked around the porch before she got into the car. It was in good shape, nice and wide, with plenty of rocking chairs that looked out to the mountain range view and lake. For a split second, she envisaged herself sitting in a chair sipping coffee.

It was a quick drive to the lake on a dirt road that traversed the property and was no problem for Mrs. Jones's SUV, "One must have a four-wheel-drive living here in winter," she advised. Gabby couldn't resist the vista and got out of the car. Crystal clear water lapped at the sandy shoreline and in the distance, the sparkling blue expanse was surrounded by an arboretum of lush botanicals. The manicured neat, neon green lawns of the houses dotting the perimeter were visible between leafy oaks and glorious thick blue spruce. The lake was easy on the eyes.

As she gazed at this peaceful scene, the warm sun on her face, and a soft breeze bringing the scent of flowers, she was startled by something cold and wet touching her hand. She quickly recovered from her disquiet when she realized it was a deer gently making its acquaintance. Then another. Soon there was a small herd. Mrs. Jones made a sign to be silent and the herd hung there eating grass and playfully poking Gabby's hands with their cold noses. Even Doo did not bark but watched mesmerized while protected by the satchel. Gabby inhaled the moment feeling as one with these mood-lifting surroundings and innocent wildlife. A sense of peace, a sense of unity with nature washed over her. She remained in repose for several minutes drinking in the calming effects and other worldliness of feeling connected to this herd. As soon as she reached out to pet a deer, they all got spooked and ran away but the high from the experience remained.

"Well, that was amazing. I have never seen anything like that," said Mrs. Jones. "They were almost tame. Perhaps, it's because there's no hunting in these woods. People must feed them rather than having them eat all their flowers. I, too, have plenty of deer wander across my property but never have any come so close to me. Quite thrilling. They actually touched you. You must have some magical attraction."

Gabby smiled but remained silent not wanting to break the spell of this pleasant spot and sweet interaction with the deer, it felt hard to leave. "I know you're conflicted about this unexpected inheritance," said Mrs. Jones seemingly reading her mind, "but do give it some thought...moving up here and running this place would be an amazing life-changing opportunity. I would envy you if I weren't so pleased with my own slice of heaven." After a few more moments of quiet contemplation, they left.

Gabby rolled into the city before dark luckily avoiding rush-hour traffic. She returned the car and finally got to her cherished apartment. Taking Doo out from the satchel, she asked Alexa to play Spotify and Chopin's Minute Waltz came on. The rapid notes of the piece mirrored her own agitated mood and she stood listening for a moment hugging Doo before she went to sit on her bed feeling quite emotional. And then it came. The overwhelming sorrow. The sobs rising up from deep within her tearing out her heart. She cried and cried and cried rummaging through all the sad thoughts that filled her with grief. Each thought bringing new force. She cried harder than when she was with the Countess on Saturday that now felt like a million years ago but really only a few days had passed. She cried herself out and finally stopped exhausted and played out.

She sat staring into space numb and stupefied before she succumbed to a completely opposite emotion taking hold. From whence the crying had come, now there was pure joy. Fits of laughter bubbled up inside her. She laughed uncontrollably. Laughed until it hurt. Laughed and laughed until she fell off the bed hitting her head and passing out for a split second. And in that second, she saw the woman in white from the house with arms outstretched. Then her entire life flashed through her mind until she was roused by Doo licking her face. In that split second, everything was made clear. She now understood both her tears and laughter. Her path was sealed. Her destiny determined.

The library. This apartment. Her life. The sorrow had come from deep within her. She was inconsolably tormented that she had not known her father and now would never know him at all. Never to see how he looked at her when he spoke to her. Never to feel him hug her. The vacuum of not knowing him intimately would now never be filled. Fantasies of a relationship were forever lost. Hopes gone evermore. Never to have a sense memory of any tenderness or of feeling her hand in his. Never a kind word from his lips to be heard. Any odd mannerisms to remain a mystery. A gaping hole. Finished. A permanent void. And a most unwanted half-brother. The thought of his existence made her sick to her stomach. In some unrealistic way, she blamed this brother for his existence more than she blamed her father. It was the only way to go forward.

Because unexpectedly, she would come to know her father through the things in his life that he had physically touched. Because now...now she would touch those same things. Mundane things. Chairs, dishes, and so on. She would come to understand her father by the life he had led because she had suddenly and surprisingly decided she would lead that same life. Her father would be present in her life every waking minute and she could not carry around such hate for him. She had always pursued her life's path based on grit and instinct. An inner core of wisdom and strength that came from a belief she was somehow guided by an unseen hand that she referred to as the cosmos. And now this unexpected change in her circumstances had also changed her understanding of what her life would be. The cosmos had opened a door and she would walk through it. For one truth steadfastly remained, you don't mess with the cosmos.

The depth of this see-saw of emotions was brought on by this decision. She would be saying goodbye to everyone and everything. Saying goodbye to a life that she had relished. Routines she had taken for granted. Walks around the block with Doo. The illogical sadness brought on by the parting of the ways that would have happened imminently anyway with her forced eviction. The coffee shop never to enjoy again, even if it was moving to another location. The library and Walter. The Countess. She sighed. She was leaving it all. It was devastatingly sad. A chapter of her life finished, completed. Done. Like facing the unknown after graduation. Time to move on.

But then...the joy. Once that acknowledgment of embracing change was made, it filled her with joy. An adventure awaited her. Her life would be changed dramatically. Owning something of substance. A business of her own. Being a proprietor. A participant instead of an observer. She remembered the magical uplifting of her mood once she passed through the front door. Like an infusion of happiness. Even through the frightening search for Doo. Not responding outwardly to the sense of elation as the deer touched her and sniffed her with their cold noses, she appeared aloof. Remaining stoic even as she signaled to Mrs. Jones, she was ready to leave that glorious lake and come home. But she was actually filled with joy. Unabashed joy at the thought of owning an inn, living in that beautiful house, the thrill of it, and she couldn't wait to get back there.

The next day, she showed up at the library and informed Walter she would be quitting and filled him in on all the circumstances for doing so. He was happy for her change in prospects, for her windfall, but sad she was leaving. Could she give him two weeks to find a replacement? That depended on whether she could hold off being forced out of her apartment, she told him. "Ah, yes," he replied. By coincidence, at that very moment the main door opened and the Countess entered, again not on her usual day. *Perfect*, thought Gabby. *Let's get this over with.*

"What's this?" the Countess said, "What have I missed? You all look downtrodden."

"She's moving to Vermont," said Walter matter-of-factly.

"Oh, my goodness," said the Countess as she grew pale and lost her balance grabbing onto the front desk. "Hmm...I guess my tea leaves were right," she said as Gabby reached out to help her recover her footing. "I'm fine," she said shrugging off the incident.

Walter looked puzzled.

"The Countess read my tea leaves at dinner last Saturday and saw a life-changing event. And so now here we are."

"Perhaps you should sit down for a moment, Countess, and have a glass of water," said Walter.

"No, no, no, not necessary. But I think what I would like is a nice hot cup of tea and a chat with Gabby at the Starbucks around the corner. Would you let her come for an hour or so, Walter?"

"I think I can spare her. We don't have any programs starting for a couple of hours. Always good to see you, Countess."

And they left.

The coffee shop was quiet with just a few customers, the morning rush being over. They chose a quiet alcove and sat down after they ordered their drinks. Latte for Gabby and English Breakfast Tea for the Countess. Leon the barista gave the Countess his usual big "hello" in a terrible cockney British accent that always made her laugh out loud. A friendly atmosphere for their honest conversation. Gabby took a sip of coffee to give her a moment to ruminate how she would begin. It was totally unnecessary because the Countess immediately engaged her as Gabby swallowed.

"Did you receive some money? You left suddenly. Walter said your father had died."

"Well, what happened last week was really quite remarkable and you somehow were right about life-changing."

So, Gabby sat back and began her tale of this amazing inheritance, the size of the house, a business of her own. Her father had a son who was older than she, a half-brother she never knew existed, and this knowledge was very troubling. It revealed that the relationship her father had with this other woman had been going on for years before he left her mother. Disgusting to think about. But this newfound relative wanted nothing to do with his inheritance. It would all be hers. The emotions surrounding her feelings about her father were so disquieting that tears caught in her throat as she stiltedly told the Countess all she had gone through. Her father finally acknowledging her existence when he was six feet under. The Countess all the while tenderly stroking Gabby's hand. She still had the brochure in her purse and handed it to the Countess who only response was, "Oh my, it's palatial.

At first, Gabby told her, she wanted nothing to do with this inheritance, it made her physically sick to digest all of her father's deception. She was going to come home straight away but Mrs. Jones, the proprietor of the B&B where she was staying, convinced her to take a look at the place. Just the sight of the property elevated her spirit. When she entered, it felt like she was transformed. Uplifted. It was hard to explain her sense of elation. She kept those feelings to herself not knowing how to handle them. Mrs. Jones had no idea of Gabby's newly discovered exuberance. Once back in the car for the drive back to the city, Gabby ruminated about it all. She wondered at the meaning of her spontaneous change in mood and if she were up to taking on such responsibility. It weighed on her for the entire drive home. When her favorite Chopin prelude began to play on her iPhone app, she took it as a sign. Done. Her mind was made up. She was now ready to totally change her life but also quite frightened and sad to say goodbye.

"I will miss everyone," she said. "Especially you, now that we've gotten to be real friends this past week. But being in charge of my own destiny feels freeing. Finally, not being subject to the whims of others. Except perhaps for filling up the rooms with future guests," she laughs. "But you know what I mean. Having a place to live without the threat of a landlord selling it or it being demolished. My spirit lightened at the thought of having my own business. I haven't seen the owner's quarters because I rushed out of there so quickly but whatever it looks like it has to be better than my threadbare and modest studio. I love my studio, don't get me wrong, my first real apartment. But it would be nice to have something bigger, finer, and something that I owned. Of course, this change comes with abject fear, a permanent knot in my stomach. I need to learn so much about running a hotel. But I made a new friend in the woman that runs the B&B where I stayed. Another amazing turn of good luck. She offered to guide me through the process, be my mentor." Gabby saw the look on the Countess's face.

"What? Why are you looking at me like that? Is something wrong with my thinking?"

"I don't believe you realize what has happened to you, my darling."

Gabby looked puzzled.

The Countess took out her compact mirror. "Here, take a look at yourself. While you were talking to me just now about your new future endeavors, your normal, forgive me, sour expression began to change. Look." She handed her the mirror. Gabby just saw her old face but then Doo jumped up and licked her mouth and she laughed while still holding the mirror.

"Oh. My smile looks normal. Not forced... huh."

"Yes, my darling. The cosmos has presented you with a path of fulfillment and you are grabbing it. It shows on your face and in your eyes. This is so right for you. Please let me know if there's anything I can do to help you with this transition."

"Well, Walter wants two weeks to find my replacement and that's probably pushing it with my landlord. I'm supposed to be out in a week or so. I've put off moving as long as I could and they've put a Quit notice on my door. Now it turns out that it's ideal because I have no lease to break."

"Well then, it's settled, you must move in with me. As soon as you want. Today even. Let me know which day works for you and I'll ask the Captain to pick you up with his car to help bring over all your things."

"It will only be clothing. The furniture stays with the apartment. Is Sunday okay? I promised Walter I'd work today through Saturday to make up for the time I missed this week."

"Sunday is perfect."

Chapter Six

A Family of Friends

Journal entry:
The cosmos hands you a surprise
that makes you see how very wise is
the notion that events sometimes
happen when most needed.
I love surprises.

Gabby was exhilarated for days. Each day the reflection of her poor mother's scowl that had been imprinted on her face for years began to fade more and more and then finally disappeared. Although Gabby herself was unaware of this transformation, the Countess was not. It was a joy to behold. Even Walter noticed the change at the library. *I never noticed how attractive she is*, he thought. When the Captain pulled in front of her apartment on Sunday, she was already waiting downstairs, anxious to get on with it. Several garbage bags were full of clothes and the odd knick-knack—her framed diploma, a hand-painted bowl bought at the weekly Union Square Greenmarket, and other innocuous small items. Minimal stuff that represented her minimal lifestyle.

This was the first chore in the process of changing her life forever; moving out of her place and then moving into the Countess's townhouse. After that would come the business aspects. She had to call Whitehead on Monday and tell him of her decision, then Mrs. Jones. She decided it would be a little scary staying alone in the big house, so she needed a place to stay for a few days. Besides, Mrs. Jones was now her touchstone for all things B&B. She marveled at how fortuitous it was that she had a mentor in this formidable undertaking. She decided that before she moved to Vermont, she must visit all the NYC sites that were on her "to-do" list and revisit those she loved. She made a list of museums, Broadway shows, and neighborhoods and realized that it would not be possible to do it all in just two weeks. It was silly really because Vermont was just a few hours' drive and the Countess would still be in NYC for visits.

"Come, my darling, sit with me," the Countess called out from the garden as soon as Gabby walked through the front door on the Tuesday of her last week at the library. Tea was set on the table near the Countess's favorite chair to have a good view of her bird feeder that was visited often by colorful goldfinches and robins of which her buddy and a regular, Morris, gave her much pleasure. As soon as Gabby sat down and kicked off her shoes, the Countess in an agitated state began talking immediately. She seemed to start in mid-sentence as if Gabby could read her mind.

"The house is spectacular," she said to Gabby's surprised face. "Your B&B," she explained. "I've looked it up on the internet at the library. There are photos of all the rooms and the outdoor scenery. It reminded me somewhat of Surrey, except for the looming mountains in the distance. I so loved my childhood there. Loved the countryside. I realized then and there that maybe I should rekindle my love of nature. That my mini slice of nature with this garden isn't quite enough."

"Well, you can come and visit anytime you want to," said Gabby not really getting it.

"No, my darling. I've been thinking about this very carefully and it feels perfect." Gabby continued to be confused. "I want to make this change with you."

"You...what? Wait. What exactly are you saying?"

"I want to come with you to Vermont. Help you run this hotel. It would give me a purpose. Now that Irina has left, I can turn this apartment into an Airbnb solely for people my tenants know. I've asked my tenants and they loved the idea. It would allow their families and friends to come visit and stay for a reasonable price while being close to them with one favor on their part. That is, keeping the bird feeder full for Morris and his friends for as long as he comes around. Of course, they wouldn't mind they said because they've met Morris and think he's a hoot. Pun intended," she laughs giddily. "In fact, when no one is staying here they would also like to enjoy my garden for cookouts and the like. So, everything is set and I'm quite excited about the idea. Well then...what do *you* think?"

Gabby sat in silence for a moment digesting the import of this amazing suggestion. This woman whom she so admired now wanted to become her helpmate in this venture. A shoulder to lean on, an advisor, a companion. It was too astonishing to believe. Answered prayers that had never been asked but lay dormant in her psyche. Acknowledgment that her fears had been assuaged in an instant by this offer, which was much more than just a business partnership. It was a familial connection for which she had ached her entire life. *This was what a mother would do for a daughter.* She blinked away the tears that welled up and coughed so that she could breathe. She couldn't speak without slightly sobbing.

"I've upset you. Oh no. I didn't mean to do that. I'm so sorry. I didn't realize you wouldn't want...so presumptuous of me, so sorry, never mind. Please forgive me, I didn't mean to add to your stress," the Countess blurted out misinterpreting Gabby's reaction.

Gabby gently touched the Countess's arm. "No, no Countess. You've misinterpreted my reaction. Please understand. I'm just so...stunned by your generosity. Overwhelmed really." Gabby sat back in her chair and her tears flowed light and steady. The Countess wore an expression of concern. She certainly had no intention of causing this reaction. She held her breath and waited until Gabby spoke again. Recovering slightly, Gabby managed to speak haltingly, "No one has ever been...this...kind to me and I'm...so full of emotion, a joy I've never felt before. You have...no idea...what this means...to me. But are you...sure? Sure that you really want to do this? Move from this wonderful house and everything you love to help me run the inn?"

"Of course, darling. I never say what I don't mean. I've had several days to think carefully about this decision."

"You can't imagine how moved I am and at the same time...well...relieved," said Gabby. "I wanted to do this, felt a compulsion actually to do it, but I was also so frightened. And now...you...single-handedly...have removed that fear. I won't be alone in this new endeavor and new life. To say thank you doesn't come close to conveying my feelings of joy and happiness."

"Remember, when I told you that this drastic change in your life might have something for me as well? As I thought about it more and more, it came to me in a burst of understanding. Perhaps by helping you, I would also be helping myself. Something new to freshen up my life, give me purpose. I love being social and being a hotelier, something I had never imagined for myself, would be just the ticket." She gets up and walks over to Gabby. "Come, darling, let's have a hug to solidify our new lives together." And in that hug, a new world was born.

They spent the remaining days in NYC planning and taking care of business. Gabby called Mrs. Jones and asked if she had two more available rooms. The Countess agreed that it would be best to take possession of the inn after they assessed if renovations were needed and, if so, depending on how extensive to complete them before moving in. "Of course, how exciting," said Mrs. Jones. The Captain would drive them up and stay to see them settled.

"Don't you want to stay in the same room as the Captain?" asked Gabby.

"Of course not, my darling. We're just friends. I'm much too old for him," she said laughing. "Besides, I'm done with all that stuff." *Oookay. That bit of information was good to know,* Gabby chuckled to herself.

When Gabby called Whitehead to tell him of her decision to take over the B&B, he seemed very enthused, well, as enthused as his personality would allow. They made an appointment for her to sign papers and where to transfer the cash.

"Might I ask how much cash we're talking about?'

"Certainly, it's yours. Well, let's see..." She could hear him typing on a keyboard. "Three hundred...yes...three hundred and fifty thousand dollars."

"Oh..." Several minutes of silence on Gabby's end as she nearly dropped the phone.

"Ms. Bernstein? Are you okay?"

"Yes, yes...sorry, thank you. Just a little shocked, actually quite shocked really."

"You should set up an account with First Vermont Bank as soon as you get up here and I'll wire it to your account. By the way, I meant to tell you that the owner's quarters have a lot of personal family photos. Shall I box them up and send them to Beau?"

Gabby paused for a moment thinking she might want some pictures of her Dad. To know what he looked like recently, but not in pose with his *son* and *wife*. Not interested in seeing that. "Why yes, how very thoughtful of you, thanks so much," she told Whitehead.

After they hung up Gabby tried to process how much money came with this inheritance. It was a small fortune to her. Way more than she had imagined. *Whew!* Then she got nervous about his only living son. *What if he found how much cash there was? Would he change his mind about walking away?* She was tempted to call Whitehead right back but decided to first ask the Countess.

"Leave it alone. This Beau person has lawyers you said. It's his problem to solve, not yours, darling. I wouldn't worry about it. After next week it will be in your account. He had his chance. But it is a windfall, lucky girl. Although, let's not get too excited until we look at the books and monthly upkeep costs. It may not turn out to be as much as we think."

In honor of their leaving, the two of them painted the town. After Gabby finished work, they went to museums on the days they stayed open late and went to fabulous restaurants where Gabby, of course, had never been. La Grenouille for French cuisine, Trattoria Dell'Arte for Italian, and Gallagher's for steak. Gabby tried to pay her way but the Countess wouldn't hear of it. "You'll have time to treat me after you get your windfall," she said with a twinkle in her eye. They were having so much fun they decided to stay for one more week after Gabby finished her job.

The Countess was able to secure tickets to *Hamilton*, the hottest show on Broadway. No telling what she paid for third row center an impressed Gabby thought as she sat enthralled being so close to the stage. They rode the ferry to the Statue of Liberty and took a boat ride around Manhattan island on the weekend. They ate corned beef sandwiches at Katz's Deli, something the Countess had never tried. "So, yummy. Good thing we'll be far away from these sandwiches or I'd gain a hundred pounds eating here all the time."

On their last Sunday in NYC, they went to the Central Park Zoo. The Countess said goodbye to all her animal friends and the workers she had met over the years. She was a big donor and they would miss her. She told them not to worry, she would be back to visit from time to time, Vermont being just a few hours' drive. She promised she would always support the zoo. They hugged and cried. It was a great visit. Gabby watched all this tender emotion, so grateful to at last have this feeling of connection, of family, finally brought into her own life. *The cosmos has really been good to me—more than just playing my favorite Chopin unexpectedly, she smiled inside grateful for her blessings.*

Her final meeting with Walter was harder than she thought it would be. He was very grave. He told her that he could see that her decision to take over the B&B was the correct one because he could see how her facial expression had changed. She looked happy. Somber Gabby was gone and that was wonderful to see. He hoped she would come for a visit from time to time perhaps even visit him at the dry cleaners after he made the change. She told him she most certainly would and that he should bring his family for a weekend in Vermont during the fall foliage time. Then he surprised her with a bear hug and gave her a present. A bottle of Champagne to bless her new home. It was quite emotional and made Gabby realize that she had been building a family of friends all along.

It was time. She and the Countess were now ready to start their new lives. The Captain came and put their things in the car. The Countess had the majority of her clothing and whatnots boxed up and sent by post to the property. These things would have arrived by the time they got there. All was going to plan. Better even.

Chapter Seven

New Life Old Friends

Journal entry:
The cosmos took us for a spin
with windows shattered door broke-in.
We cleaned it up thorough but something's
pending maybe tomorrow...or later.

Everyone was gathered in the main reception room listening to the Captain while reclining on the comfy sofas. As he spoke, he would habitually twirl his stark-white handlebar mustache while his brightly lit blue eyes were fixed in a gaze on no one in particular. They were, however, reflected inward as he revisited the beautiful scenery, relived the vivid memories of his adventure, and could not contain his visible sorrow as he conveyed through words what he was revisiting in his mind. The group was spellbound listening as he dramatically alternated whispering sounds with louder tones to tell the haunting tale of meeting his first love, Teora, the daughter of a tribal chief on the exotic isle of Bora Bora. For this simple young man who had only known Brooklyn, the beauty of the natural landscape of this Polynesian paradise captivated him to his very core.

A lush garden landscape greeted eyes that had only known cement sidewalks, vast ocean expanses, and the metal trappings of his ship. The island was, for him, a vision of startling beauty. The turquoise water was as if jewels had kissed the gentle sea and the soft white sand seemed to be made from crushed pearls. His first night at dusk when the salt air was bathed in the powerfully aromatic scent of the ubiquitous frangipani flowers and on leave of his duties as a merchant marine ensign on the cargo ship, Victory, a breathtakingly beautiful young woman seemed to just materialize out of nowhere at the edge of the beach. As she stood there in the soft light, the gentle breeze rustling her colorfully patterned skirt ever so slightly, it seemed as if she had just touched down to earth on her angel wings. For many years hence, he would often think about her brilliant white smile against her honey-colored skin as she beckoned him into the shadows of a secluded hideaway protected by dense greenery and tall, thick palm trees. She showed him how to get the meat out of a coconut using a big rock to break the husk and then crack it open. After they feasted on its sweet milk and tender flesh, they slipped into the gentle warm sea and watched the moon rise while a pod of dolphins played in the distance. Finally, he leaned over and kissed her delicately...then hungrily and they lustily hurried back to their hiding place. Reaching levels of ecstasy each had never known they remained entwined until the sun came filtering through the branches.

When he awoke the next morning, she was gone. For four days and nights, he searched for her to no avail. A nagging thought prevailed as he tried to find her. Perhaps she was just a dream, an imagined experience, and the entire encounter had never really happened. He drew a likeness of her on a scrap of newspaper and asked the natives if they knew her. Most shrugged their shoulders or just said "no." Nevertheless, he continued his search to find her or at least prove she was real. He came upon a weathered old man who looked at the drawing and told him she was the daughter of a neighboring island chief, her name finally made known to him was Teora. But, alas, his time on the island had run out and his search had come to an abrupt end. The fully loaded cargo ship was ready to get underway. Lost in the agony of not having the chance to see her once more, to tell her of his intense feelings and of his frantic searching, his sorrow knew no depths at the frustration of being so close to finding her.

As his ship set sail, he was on deck looking wistfully at the bend in the beach where she had first come to him. And right there he saw her. Was this just an illusion? No, it was her. Her golden eyes flashed in the sun and she slowly began to wave goodbye and continued thus until the beach receded from his view. Mesmerized and lovesick, he stood there for many hours reliving the magic of that one night and at finally getting a glimpse of her again. Eventually, he reconciled himself to her loss and went below decks.

Although he had numerous relationships over the years, none could come close to the rapture he felt when thinking about Teora. He chose to remain single until someday he could go back and find her or maybe meet someone who so fulfilled his life that he could stop thinking about her. He never did either one. Then he stopped speaking and let the story wash over everyone for a few moments. He stood up and bowed indicating the storytelling was over and all the women applauded, respectfully.

"That was a wonderfully romantic tale, Captain, but I think it's from a short story you might have read or a movie you might have seen," said the Countess, laughing breaking the somber mood.

"Nonsense, Countess," said the Captain. "Sometimes reality can be cinematic, don't you think...Mrs. Jones?" And he looked directly into her eyes as he said this and her eyes remained focused on him as he did so. Mrs. Jones nodded her agreement while a slight blush formed on her cheeks as she smiled broadly murmuring, "Yes, yes, I believe it can." And there it was ...something...something between them.

The storytelling activity was actually suggested by the Countess who knew the Captain's gift for creating enchanting tales for the children visiting the library for story time. It was a most enjoyable way to end a busy day and they all were now ready to turn in. The first stop that morning before checking into Mrs. Jones's B&B had been to Whitehead's office to get the paperwork giving Gabby ownership of 19 Possum Trot Lane. Then, on to the bank to set up an account and receive that humongous, as Gabby described it, influx of cash. Afterwards, they went to the property so that the Countess could get her first glimpse of the place and to collect the box she had sent. Gabby was anxious to see it as well. It didn't disappoint in the second viewing and, in fact, it was even more amazing. They went upstairs to the second level and investigated the four ensuite bedrooms and then the four on the next floor. A few steps up at the end of that hall led to a mysteriously locked door. Creepy, like in horror movies, but they didn't have the key. It could wait. Gabby next investigated the owner's quarters down a small hallway near the kitchen. Totally charming, it had two bedrooms with two ensuite baths and a sitting room with a fireplace overlooking the neatly mowed lawn in the backyard with a view of the pool, the lake, and the mountains in the distance.

Furnished in a traditional style matching the rest of the home's decor, the sitting room had a cozy plush sofa covered in a soft floral print and cushy leather club chairs. Gabby envisioned many an enjoyable evening spent there, reading by the fire or watching TV with the Countess. Wandering into the larger bedroom, she lay on the bed deciding it was quite comfortable. But just then a thought flashed in her mind of her father and *that woman* sleeping there, side by side doing who knows what and she immediately jumped out. It made her skin crawl. This bed had to go. She would buy a new mattress and bedding straight away. Then she opened all the dresser draws, nothing, empty. *Good.* She closed the last one. It felt heavy like something was in it. She opened it again and heard something rattling inside. Reaching into a far corner, she felt something. A book. She pulled it out. It had a lock on it. A diary. A locked diary. Curious, she examined it and placed it on top of the dresser to examine at a later time.

The Countess loved the place, especially the walk-ins for the storage freezer and pantry. She started to fantasize out loud about opening a full-time restaurant. A secret dream of hers. The huge sunroom where breakfast was served would be perfect. The others voiced their approval of the idea. Mrs. Jones had joined them on this excursion and she said that finding a chef might be a challenge but she knew of some possibilities. While they walked around, Gabby noticed the Captain and Mrs. Jones engaged in a private conversation interspersed with laughter reinforcing her notion that something was beginning to bloom. All in all, it had been a pleasant afternoon and festive feeling dinner back at Mrs. Jones's B&B capped off with the entertainment provided by the Captain. No hint for what was in store for them later.

The chaos started in the middle of the night. About 3 a.m. A rumbling of thunder in the distance. A sense of disquiet subconsciously in slumber. Dreams manifesting bombs and cars backfiring as the thunder moved closer. Then the torrential rain pounded down and the house shook with each thunderclap. At first, it felt cozy to be under the covers. And then the wind started pounding the windows and they shook violently, the night lights flickered. The house went dark. The overhead fans stopped. The refrigerator ceased its humming. Almost immediately, it got uncomfortably warm when the cooling system shut off. As the storm began to build, the lightning and thunder grew to a frightening intensity shaking the rafters at every thunderous discharge.

Gabby lay huddled in the dark with Doo who was shaking. She tried to adjust her eyes to the darkness but could only see when lightning flashed as if it were an intruder trying to break the window. Everyone began to call out to each other between the loud bursts of thunder as the storm raged on. Frightened, they all decided to go carefully downstairs to wait it out together. Each bedroom was equipped with flashlights and Mrs. Jones shouted to all of them to open the drawers in their nightstands. Slowly, they all made their way downstairs and gathered together in the living room. The noise of the storm was so loud they could not communicate easily and so all fell silent and just sat wide-eyed in fear hoping the house wouldn't blow apart.

Gabby knew tornadoes were rare in New England but this storm seemed unusually violent, angry, and downright scary. Could there possibly be a tornado somewhere out there? She strained her ears to hear the sound of a freight train, a sign there was a tornado embedded in the storm. There was so much noise, she really couldn't differentiate the sound of a freight train from all the rumblings. No one else could either, so they decided to huddle in the downstairs powder room just in case. It was a small windowless room in the middle of the hallway leading to the breakfast room. The kind of room recommended for seeking shelter during tornadoes. All five of them squeezed into the small space with Doo. It felt like a crowded subway train at rush hour to the New Yorkers, a familiar claustrophobia, except for the darkness lit only by flashlights. Ominous.

But the right decision.

Because they finally heard it. The freight train. The really loud sound of a train. It was unmistakable. Then an explosive, boom! Scary. Like a bomb went off. Next, something crashing to the floor right outside the bathroom door. The sound of an enormous weight falling and breaking everything in its path. It shook the walls when it landed. The whistling wind started blowing through the reception room tossing the furniture and what nots against the walls

Hearing the force of the wind had them shaking. Frightened out of their wits, the women started whimpering. They waited until everything got quiet and all they could hear was the steady heavy rain and intermittent gusts of wind. Opening the door from the bathroom cautiously, they peered out afraid of what they would see. It was an awful sight. Aiming their flashlights around at the once pleasant room revealed a war zone.

The lighter furniture, lamps, end tables, and the like, had been tossed around and smashed to bits. The front door had been blown off its hinges and hurled into the center of the room by the force of the wind and landed next to the fireplace. That was the crash they heard. One window had exploded and shattered glass was everywhere. No one had shoes except the Captain so they had him go upstairs to fetch theirs. They all worked together to shove the door against the doorway to stop the wind from whipping around the room and breaking more items in its wake. And then suddenly all the noise and rain stopped. Deathly quiet and still. The storm had moved on.

Gathering in the kitchen, Mrs. Jones turned on her gas stove and made tea and coffee by candlelight. Sipping the coffee in the semi-dark and reliving this nerve-racking experience, Mrs. Jones repeatedly worried if her insurance would cover all the damage. They chatted until the sun came up and went outside to investigate the destruction in daylight. It was worse than they had imagined. Trees were down everywhere. Beautiful old stately oaks, a few sugar maples, and a whispery birch were strewn across the yard. None had fallen on the roof, "Thank goodness," they all said in unison. And then they thought of Possum Trot Lane. So many large, beautiful trees close to the house. "We must go there, at once," said Gabby. "Hurry," said the Countess and they rushed out the back door. The Captain had parked in the driveway and the car was untouched. Funny, how the destruction seemed random. Apparently, the funnel was narrow in width as it whipped around willy-nilly destroying everything in its path.

The ride to the property was nail-biting. It was like a disaster movie to see all the destruction along the way. Some houses looked as if they had been lifted off their foundations, several had their roofs blown off but others were completely untouched. Small groups of people wandered about as if in a daze rummaging through personal items spread over several acres. Some could be seen sobbing. Gabby started to whimper, imagining the worst and regretting the decision to take on this responsibility. Her stomach was in a knot and just kept getting tighter the closer they came to the property. This storm had wreaked so much havoc that the radio only played static. No news about anything. Gabby and the Countess were sick with fear as to what to expect. The Captain drove slowly down the Possum Trot driveway dreading to get to the house and see the damage. And then they arrived. All sighed together while frozen in their seats. The house was...perfect. No damage. Front door in place, windows unbroken, no trees smashed into the roof. It was like a miracle.

Getting out of the car to assess the damage more closely, they were even more taken aback. It was as if the house had been encased in a protective bubble. It was beyond belief. The devastation of the surrounding countryside stopped at the property line of the house. Not even a leaf was blown onto the porch. They went into the house and everything was as it should be. No broken anything. In fact, there even was electricity. Kitchen intact. Upstairs, peaceful bedrooms. They drove down to the lake to see if there were felled trees. None. They could see that the nearby properties were not as fortunate. A lot of work needed to be done to clear the downed trees, pick up blown-off roof shingles as well as the odd road sign coming from who knows where.

They went back to the house and turned on the television set and got some explanation...maybe.

This storm and its impact on Rutland and its surrounding areas was remarkable and unprecedented. As residents might have surmised, there was a funnel cloud with a narrow circumference, so the damage hopscotched in a weird path where some homes were destroyed but others nearby had no damage. The fire department and cleanup crews are out to help clear the debris from public roads and to assist stranded residents. So far, thankfully, it seems there has been no loss of life. We will update you as more information is discovered.

Please stay indoors if you are one of the lucky ones with no damage so workers can clear the roads, especially since there are some downed power lines that have caused blackouts for a few areas. Fortunately, the weather forecast shows clear skies for the coming days. This storm, although, as I said, not large in diameter, caused millions of dollars' worth of damage. A storm with a bigger funnel with the same magnitude of force would have totally wiped-out Rutland. We can at least be grateful for that. Unfortunately, according to our local meteorologists, tornadic storms with a larger footprint might become more common in this area because of the changing climate and changing wind patterns.

Turning off the TV, they got up and made their way into the kitchen. "Well, I'm starving. Who wants something to eat?" asked Mrs. Jones to change the glum and pensive mood.

"Don't you want us to help clean up your establishment?" asked the Countess.

"Well, thank you, yes. But let's eat something first. I can check if there are any canned goods here and see if I can rustle something up. If not, we can head back to my place."

"Yes, let's eat something. We also should all stay here tonight. You too, Mrs. Jones, especially if the electricity is still off," said Gabby.

"I'll take you up on that, Gabby. Thanks."

They followed Mrs. Jones into the kitchen and she went through the giant pantry. There were a lot of canned goods and she found some meat and vegetables she could fry up together, canned peaches and apricots for dessert as well as coffee and soda. They ate heartily wishing it were pancakes or cereal but it was edible and they were quite hungry. Afterwards, they went back to Mrs. Jones's B&B and worked hard all day cleaning up inside and out until they were exhausted. As soon as they had gotten there, they put her refrigerated food in coolers and the Captain made a run back to Possum Trot Lane to put the food in the large refrigerator, freezer, and pantry. At the end of the day, they packed up and went to Possum Trot Lane to spend the night.

"Choose whatever bedroom you want," Gabby told the Captain and Mrs. Jones. "Countess, I'd love for you to share the owner's quarters with me since that's where we'll stay when we move in." Once in their rooms, Gabby gave the master bedroom to the Countess, the idea of sleeping in that bed was revolting. Exhausted, they went to bed early, but sleep was difficult for Gabby. An overarching anxiety made a slow progression throughout her entire body. Her feet got fidgety, then her legs became restless. She sat up and took a swallow of water and it caught in her throat. She started choking and then coughed continuously for several minutes. This caused her to have a runny nose and watery eyes that needed constant tissues. She went to the bathroom. Not ready to get back in bed, she walked around the bedroom in a state of agitation and contemplation.

She focused her mind on the good fortune that had presented itself. She was a far cry from the Gabby of just a month ago. Now she was a woman of means. An innkeeper. More importantly, she was a member of a group that once were strangers but now felt like family. She reveled in that sense of belonging. These were people who cared about her well-being and it was all brought about by a father who never seemed to care at all. Except, that in a way...he...*did*. He *had* thought about her even though he had never come to see her. The inheritance proved that. It was a real gift from the cosmos to have become close to these cherished people at just the right moment in her life. Serendipitous. For this she was most grateful…and ready for her life's new path.

After a few spins around the room, she went back to the bathroom and looked in the mirror. She was a mess and she began to inspect her eyes checking for streaked make-up when she saw it. There…whoa...in the mirror…a blurry face framed by with long hair. She gasped and turned around…no one. Little Doo who followed her everywhere began to bark. She ran out with the pup following her and jumped right into bed pulling up the covers.

Hugging Doo tightly she finally closed her eyes and suddenly started gasping having trouble breathing. *She was drowning!* Drowning in a sea of her own tears. She needed to find a branch, anything to grab on to. She saw it...a tree trunk and swam up to it. It wasn't a tree trunk. It was a floating barge with oil tanks dripping all over the deck. She held on anyway to the side and floated in a current that took many turns until she landed among a group of people hanging on to a rooftop screaming for help. They repeatedly cried out "It's gone. Everything is gone. All of it." The barge became a floating front door and she held on as the water surged propelling it forward until the door landed in the shallows and stopped. Then she crawled onto land.

Hot. It was so hot. She was in the midst of blazing heat that burned her chest when she breathed. She nearly collapsed but was rescued by someone putting a gas mask over her mouth. *What?* Everyone was wearing gas masks and marching. Marching to where? They all pointed to a mountain in the distance…there to high ground "The air is better and cooler over there," they said. Gabby looked at the mountain and then realized it was all detritus made mostly of plastic waste. Then she noticed the remains of people piled high atop the waste. She tried to tell the hordes marching what she saw but they wouldn't listen. Was that a circus clown? A man with orange hair, neon orange skin, and bright-white flashing fake teeth was shouting into a megaphone, "Don't believe what you see, just go. Just go. Move along."

She awoke with the Countess looking down at her and asking her gently, "Where dearest shouldn't we go?"

"Oh," Gabby said sitting up and rubbing her eyes. "I had an awful nightmare. Yeah. Huh. What? Did I say something? I don't remember any of it thank goodness." She breathed deeply. That was a lie. She did remember and it frightened her to her very being and she worried it might be some sort of a premonition. An omen. A horrible future. And not something to share because it was so frightening. Smoothing her hair and wanting to change the subject, she said, "Do I smell coffee?"

"Yes, dear. Mrs. Jones has baked her muffins and made coffee and tea. Come then. Oh, and this was sitting on top of the dresser."

She handed Gabby the diary which she immediately put in her nightstand drawer. Over mugs of coffee and cranberry muffins, they planned their day. Mrs. Jones had a call into her handyman to fix all the broken windows, blown-out front door, etc. Her insurance would cover it all and that put her in a fine mood given the circumstances. The Captain would take Gabby and the Countess to a car dealership to buy an SUV. Someone suggested a hybrid to cut down on pollution. All agreed that was a good idea. The Countess also suggested that the furniture in the main lobby room looked threadbare. After some inspection, it was decided that the wallpaper in the bedrooms also needed some freshening to cover the torn edges. A fresh coat of paint wouldn't hurt either. They made sure the stores were open and luckily the damage to the town was light.

So, after they went shopping for a car, they would go to a reupholster to pick out fabric. Wallpaper and paint colors would be next at a home-design store recommended by Mrs. Jones. She also suggested that an electrician and other inspectors should come out to check everything before a reopening was announced. A good going over was important because the storm might have damaged something they couldn't see. Problems arising when guests were staying there would cause bad PR and could hurt future business. Gabby was so grateful for her experienced input.

Since all of Mrs. Jones's food was still at Possum Trot Lane and she was not sure if her electricity had been turned back on, she offered to prepare dinner while they shopped. Everyone now had their plans for the day and would be back in time for cocktails. The three of them got ready to leave. Gabby was still under the influence of her scary dream and also had some unexplained nervousness as she peeked into her bathroom to take a shower. She remembered something frightened her in there but wasn't sure if it was part of her nightmare or if it had actually happened. Nevertheless, she proceeded with caution. The shower and other tasks like drying her hair were uneventful.

The Countess and Gabby were quite in sync. They bought a car in no time flat. Without much indecision, they ordered new fabrics to reupholster the sofas and armchairs. Wallpaper was also an easy choice and so was agreeing on the color of paint that would be delivered. A wallpaper hanger and house painter were hired. The Captain had left them when Gabby took ownership of the new car and headed back to continue to help Mrs. Jones clean up her place. Spying a cute coffee shop to grab a cup and recharge from all the tumult of the last few days, she and the Countess basked in their accomplishments.

"How about we go over to that shop across the street and I buy you a good suitcase set, Gabby."

"Whatever for?"

"An idea has come to me that I think you will like very much." Gabby perked up anticipating something good.

"What?" she said. "I'm filled with so much happiness as it is. This is all I need."

"Well, the reupholstering of the furniture will take at least six weeks. They have to order the fabrics and then do all the steps for completion. They're not picking up the old furniture until late next week. The wallpaper also takes time to arrive. So, we won't be able to open for business until late Summer, but at least we'll be ready for the Fall leaf-turning season."

"Yes, I'm aware," Gabby said really curious. "But what does that have to do with a suitcase?"

"Let's go on a trip. My treat. I haven't been back to London in ages and I would love to show it to you."

"But..."

"No buts. I've thought of everything, dear, while we were out and about. We can hire the Captain to be the caretaker while we're gone. He can handle overseeing the inspections. I know you've also noticed that he and Mrs. Jones have a spark between them, so I think he'll jump at the chance to stay up here. He loves yard work, well, I think he does. I think if given the chance he would. All men love riding tractors. I know he loves the outdoors. So, it's perfect. We can cruise over and fly back. What do you say?"

"Well...I say...YES!" Gabby enthusiastically cried out loudly and then shouted, "Oh my God!!!!" while getting up from the booth with tears in her eyes to embrace the Countess. A touching scene. You see, Gabby had never been on a cruise or for that matter—on a plane. The universe kept sending gifts and a more appreciative recipient could not be found. As for the Countess, having a traveling companion and seeing London through a first timer's eyes was just the ticket.

Chapter Eight

The Captain

Now we take a temporary step away from Gabby and her unexpected good fortune to get to know another major player in this drama, the Captain. The Captain's modest upbringing and natural skill at fixing things made him the cosmos's first choice to help our little group of women. A solitary individual but not lonely, he fit in perfectly with the psyche of the group. But who was he really? When we delve into the character of a man, we must consider the boy whose youthful experiences shaped him. Paramount is the father figure, the patriarch. For a lad such as Jimmy Ostrowski, his father was not worthy of his son. A laborer at a waste disposal plant, Alfred Ostrowski, Jr. was a first-generation American whose family had emigrated from Poland. Inherently nasty and short-tempered, he was mean and unpleasant in his interactions with his wife and every one of his children. He was most especially harsh toward his youngest son, Jimmy.

"Bring me a beer, Jimmy, and make it snappy, you good-for-nothing wastrel," said Alfred Ostrowski with a snarl as soon as he sat down for dinner. "Look at me, boy. Did you hear me?"

"Yes."

"Yes, what? Yes, what? You, disrespectful fool."

"Yes, Sir."

It was a typical conversation at the dinner table free of anything important. No tenderness from either the father or the mother who lived in fear of her husband. Mr. Ostrowski, an abusive man, did not need drink to make him violent although it exacerbated this tendency. Violence begets violence and Alfred, unfortunately, knew the back of the hand of his own father whose poor command of English was a roadblock to a decent job after he came to America. Thus, Alfred, Sr. spent his days toiling as a low-level runner at a construction site with no hope of advancement and the constant worry that he would grow too old to do that kind of work before very long. Irritable and miserable because his dreams of a good life in America were never realized, he took out his frustration on his only son, who, in turn, now took out his own sense of hopelessness and normal state of depression on *his* youngest son James, the only remaining child living at home.

The youngest by eight years of his three brothers and three sisters, Jimmy remained at home after his siblings escaped as soon as they could. The girls fled the autocratic rule imposed by their father by getting "knocked up" and then kicked out by forced marriages while still in their teens. The three boys joined the military and eventually were killed in Viet Nam. As the solitary child, Jimmy suffered the abuse of his father's wrath and his mother's indifference stoked by her fear of her husband. Then one day, he saw a flyer stapled to a pole about the Merchant Marine. Here was his chance. During peacetime, after the war was finally over, the Merchant Marine was strictly used for transport, shipping cargo, and providing passengers lower-priced travel to exotic ports in Asia, the Middle East, as well as Europe. It was like being in the Navy but not having to enlist.

Joining the Merchant Marine fit perfectly with Jimmy's hopes and dreams growing up in Brooklyn on Voorhies Ave. near Sheepshead Bay. Actually, other than his dysfunctional family, his childhood wasn't all that bad. Living by the sea was exhilarating for him. It woke up his spirit and filled his emptiness. Each season had its special gifts. Escaping the summer heat at Brighton Beach, although packed with people, still offered a cool breeze and an ice-cold ocean. He went to the Tuesday night summer fireworks on the boardwalk. Young people gathered by Bay Three of Brighton Beach, the terminus of Coney Island Ave. or grabbed some privacy in the alcoves below. In winter, the biting salt air, the empty stretch of sand, and the squawking sea birds all made his connection to nature tangible. The motion of the waves breaking on the shore, sometimes gently, sometimes violently, was forever changing and never boring. He loved those winter walks, the sound of the breaking waves, and the force of the bitter-cold wind.

When he went to the piers at Sheepshead Bay, which he did quite often, his pulse would quicken and his imagination would come alive. He got hooked on the feeling of being transported to a New England fishing village inexplicably tucked away and thriving in a New York City Borough. The scent of wild-caught fish in the salty air, the pitch-dark and ominous-looking water lapping at the bulkheads was a departure from his brick and cement charm-free neighborhood inhabited by sour and heavy-hearted blue-collar workers. The colorful dilapidated charter fishing boats laden with their catch brought seagulls and onlookers creating a festival atmosphere bustling with delightful shouts of conversation and laughter. Giant tunas were weighed amid the sound of awe welling up from the average Joe who had whisked one out of the sea with his tiny rod and clever maneuvering. This Brooklyn seaport anomaly was where Jimmy's soul was nourished and it precipitated his desire to become a sailor.

Unbeknownst to his mother, Jimmy had been filching cash from her wallet for years. The odd dollar bill, a handful of change. Small amounts she never realized were missing. Money for his eventual escape and now maybe this day was the time. He had used the stolen money to take the necessary Merchant Marine coursework and get the necessary certificates in case he got the guts to go. Although still unsure after he passed all the requirements whether he could handle leaving everything and everyone he knew, the last conversation with his father had given him no choice.

It started out as a normal evening with his father swearing at his mother and throwing his dinner on the floor.

"This tastes like shit," his father yelled out fiercely at his useless mother who began to whimper while being shoved out of the kitchen. "Stop that crybaby shit. I can't stand it. DO YOU HEAR? I CAN'T STAND IT!" his father screamed. Then he grabbed the arm he was using to push her out of the room and started to squeeze it. Tighter and tighter. At this, his mother desperately tried to pull away shouting in agony. "Stop! Stop! You're hurting me." And then as she started to wail in pain, she began smacking her husband in the face with her free arm, a most unusual reaction on her part, startling the out-of-control bully for a moment. When he realized she was attacking him, he let out a growl and with all his might punched her on the side of her head knocking her to the floor.

Jimmy rushed over to help her up as an ugly bruise began to form on her face. Making sure she remained conscious and able to sit upright at the kitchen table, he went angrily over to his father who was about to take a swig from a bottle of whiskey and knocked it out of his hand. The bewildered old man lunged at his son who then grabbed his father's neck and began choking him. As his hands clutched his father's throat, time slowed and then went full stop. Frozen in this pose, Jimmy could see every pore and scrub of grey hair on his father's face, his open mouth exposing teeth thick with tarter, and his complexion now a subtle shade of blue and with his eyes bulging from lack of oxygen. As soon as Jimmy absorbed this frightening scene, he willed himself to remove his hands from their tight grip around his father's neck. With that move, his father reeled backwards and then unsteadily made to swing at Jimmy. He missed completely and instead punched a giant hole in the wall as he lost his footing and then fell into the hole.

Seizing the opportunity of his father's distraction, Jimmy was roused into action as if from a numbed sleep. Shaking his head to clear his mind, he high tailed it into his bedroom snatching the bag he had already packed in anticipation of just such an unexpected departure. Quickly, before his father could regain his balance and stumble over to him, he grabbed his coat from the coat rack by the front door, threw the door open then slammed it shut as he hurriedly left. He never looked back. In fact, he never came back. Disappearing from the family forever, he never called his mother or sisters and certainly never again spoke to his dad.

This life-changing event happened with perfect timing as life path's sometimes do. A few days prior, always checking for job openings, he had come across an entry-level deckhand opening posted in the local paper for a ship that was about to sail from the New York/New Jersey port. So, without a second thought, Jimmy Ostrowski joined the Merchant Marine and turned his back on his rotten family. Chapter closed but the cruelty of his father and indifference of his mother were never forgotten. Important lessons learned, always be prepared for change and be a survivor not a victim.

He loved his new life and the excitement of travel. He was reborn into a self-assured man capable and personable. Over the course of his career, he was promoted to positions of increasing responsibility and reached the level of Chief Mate in record time that led eventually to his becoming Captain Jim. His unusual ability to stop time, as first happened with his father, spontaneously popped out on a few occasions when as a sailor he was set upon by locals in port and one time by more-seasoned crew members jealous of his quick rise in the ranks. Always unexpected and coming on during violent altercations that gave him an amazing edge, he managed to prevail with no one being the wiser of his strange ability. In Shanghai, he was attacked by street thugs who were frozen in place as they surrounded him with clenched fists and then he knocked them down one by one as he walked away. When the group of five finally roused they were lying on the ground quite confused as to how they got there forgetting about Jimmy who was nowhere to be found.

Aboard ship, the jealous and angry crew members became a mob when they were suddenly frozen in mid-step on a stairwell in hot pursuit of Jimmy who was running to get away below decks. When time resumed, they each lost their footing and tripped and fell over each other down the narrow circular stairs. With only minor injuries like sprained ankles and bruises, they soon forgot why they were there in the first place and nursed their wounds for several weeks. All Jimmy needed was a racing pulse fueled by fear for the strangeness to occur. The perps forgetting it happened was an added benefit in tight quarters. Over time, these attacks died down to nothing as he got older and moved up further in the ranks finally reaching the rank of Captain. No one would dare start anything with a Captain from whom they all took orders and whose title they respected.

By the time Jimmy retired in NYC he had traveled to all the continents except Antarctica and had seen all the Wonders of the World, both old and new. His curiosity was boundless and each new adventure filled him with extreme excitement. He would surf the internet or look up information in the ship's library before personal computers to find out whatever he could on where he had just visited or where they were going next. He became a wellspring of knowledge from antiquity to modern Europe and Asia about and area's socio-economic history, culture, architecture, and native species. In addition to his keen intellect and curiosity, he was a handsome lad with thick flaming red hair and hazel eyes. He had no trouble attracting women. When in port he usually found an obliging female who showed him the local attractions and gave him a free place to stay. Being a man who lived in the moment, he enjoyed the fierce casual relationships that lasted for just a few days until the next time in port. A bounty of good memories kept a gleam in his eyes and a bounce in his step.

As he aged, he realized that perhaps he had missed out on the normal attachments of a wife and family but he was by nature a loner and his wandering life suited him. He loved the scent of salt air in his nostrils, the undulating rhythm of the water, and the sense of isolation from civilization in ocean crossings. He never tired in his fascination with the sea. The glorious vistas of sky and clouds and the unexpected bounty of pods of breaching whales or dolphins tickled his imagination and brought forth awe and respect for life's diversity. He lived fully, always in the moment, and he had no idea of what became of his family and didn't care. He felt blessed and happy every day with no regrets.

Settling down in NYC when it was time to retire was difficult at first. After 40 years aboard ship, it was rough to stay put in one place and to fall asleep without the gentle swaying of the ocean. It was also weird to be back in NYC and witness the vast changes time had wrought. The peep shows were gone in Times Square replaced by tourist attractions showcasing popular children's candy and toys. An increase in theaters with legitimate productions replaced bachelor party raw nightclub nudie shows. Eventually, he went to Voorhies Avenue in Brooklyn. Although he had never visited while his parents were alive, he experienced a nostalgic pull to see the modest clapboard house once again. His parents were now long gone and his sisters scattered who knows where. Huzzah! His house was replaced by a high-rise apartment building. Good. Although he could not fathom why he was obsessively drawn to visit his childhood home, it had paradoxically made him uncomfortable to even think about seeing it.

Now the horror of the old place was totally erased from reality if not totally erased from his mind. He stood for a few moments where the house used to be and imagined himself coming and going. Imagined the sparse and threadbare furniture, the grimy kitchen, his father snarling at nothing, his mother a frightened sparrow hiding in the dark. Maybe the negative and evil vibes were demolished with the house as well. It felt good to walk away from his memories as it had been to walk away from that life. It seemed appropriate that nothing physical was left of his miserable existence while living in that house. He felt at peace.

Choosing to settle in Manhattan when he retired was a very strategic decision. A few miles away from his Brooklyn roots, it was light-years away in lifestyle but close enough to waterways being bordered by two rivers that meandered to the sea. Although he would be a two-legged human from now on

he would never lose his love for all things maritime. Finding affordable housing on his modest pension was quite challenging and his expectations were trimmed so far down that when he found a studio in Spanish Harlem that barely fit a twin bed, he took it gladly.

He bought a beat-up used car that he could park on the street for sojourns out of the city when fresh air and greenery were a necessary diversion. These excursions out of the cement jungle were how he gained a thorough appreciation for the gentle lush mountains north of the city. The mountains and the sea were a gift of nature's bounties. He also availed himself of pleasures denied him at sea by walking as much as he could when fine weather would oblige. Loving the sheer freedom of an invigorating stroll as if in a drugged reverie, he could walk for hours at a stretch. Such a luxury was an impossibility on the cramped space of a cargo ship. It was also a welcome escape from his tiny living space. Whenever he grew restless for the smell of salt air and marine wildlife, he would go to the Central Park Zoo and listen to the barking seals and sea lions and catch the scent that carried him back to fond memories of Fisherman's Wharf in San Francisco. He could sit for hours and watch them playfully dive off the rocks in their habitat while their noisy interactions would reach a crescendo that personified the sea and all its romance. It was on one of these visits that he met the Countess.

Sitting on a bench taking photos and videos of the sea lions with his phone, he noticed an elegant older woman walking past the outdoor habitat. As she walked with a brisk step, she was suddenly surrounded by a group of young teenage boys who started heckling her. Someone made for her purse but she held it tightly only to have it ripped from her grasp. His antenna up, the Captain immediately ran over and tried to pull it from the boy's grip. Two of this gaggle of ten boys got unexpectedly aggressive and shoved him savagely knocking him off-balance. Before he fell and hit his cheek on the pavement while yelling obscenities at the boys, time stopped for an imperceptible split second and the boys froze in mid-air giving the Captain a chance to snatch the purse before they ran away. He was lying on the ground when the Countess leaned over him.

"Oh dear, are you hurt, love?" she asked.

"No, just my pride," he laughed as he slowly got up and brushed the dirt off his jeans while handing her the purse.

"I can't thank you enough," she said. "My whole life is in that purse. Credit cards, money, photos of special people in my life, and my apartment keys. Oh, tsk, tsk," she exclaimed, "you have a break in your skin and a bad bruise is starting to form. It should be cleaned out right away to prevent infection. Please let me do it for you. Come back to my place, it's not far. It's the least I can do."

She cleaned out his wound and bandaged it after the short walk to her apartment. They sipped tea served by Irina in the garden and ate a variety of sweets and scones with clotted cream and delicious thick, homemade jam, the likes of which Jimmy had never tasted before. Relaxed and enjoying each other's company, they told their personal stories. He was taken with her glorious food, glamorous history, and celebrity lifestyle of several husbands, as well as being so down to earth with her obvious wealth living in and owning this substantial Brownstone. He was also intrigued with her Russian heritage and possible royal ancestry. It was a mutual fascination.

She was enchanted with the cinematic romance of a mariner's life and began calling him Captain as a joke. She could imagine him on deck peering out of binoculars or going ashore at intriguing ports of call. He didn't disappoint her with his adventures, and to her delight, was a great storyteller. He stayed for dinner, and their friendship grew into such a close bond that Gabby mistook it for a courtship. The Countess and the Captain, nicknames both given on a lark, would become how they were to be addressed for the rest of their lives, although Jimmy had been a real captain.

For the Captain, settling in NYC and meeting the Countess brought all that he had missed in life. A closeness to another person, a confidant, a sense of place and connection that he embraced wholeheartedly. Realizing at this time in his life the value and importance of having one good friend. Yes, there were friends he made while at sea, but he had never wanted to get too close. People tended to ask too many questions. He didn't like that. Didn't want to talk about his family and his love-starved childhood. Better to keep to yourself, focus on the work. He made good money that he socked away because he had no expenses except when in port.

Being frugal, the outcome of an impoverished childhood, he chose to live on his meager pension and leave his savings to continue to grow in case, just in case, he would become infirm when he was quite old. Both he and the Countess recognized their common desire for financial security and the unpretentiousness in each other, although the Countess was not averse to splurging every now and again and had the means to do so. But at this moment, they were both pleased with their common outlook and style. For the Countess, the Captain offered protection, someone to call to fix a broken light switch, and someone to dine with or go to a show as well as being delightful company. They quickly became great friends. Introducing him to her favorite library to become one of the regulars, *was just the ticket* for everyone.

"Sometimes, I get fidgety," he told her on a beautiful Sunday afternoon. "I feel like I should be shipping out somewhere. Hard to get used to being in one place."

"How about we do something then? Something on the water perhaps? Let's take a boat ride circling Manhattan island."

And so, Sundays with the Captain became a thing. Of course, they visited the seals as often as they could, enjoying the noisy playfulness of those robust and silky sea specimens while eating ice cream cones and laughing at their antics. It was a real treat for both of them when they visited the New York Aquarium in Coney Island, watching the shows and recapturing the joy they felt as children. Innocents before the harsh world became too real. It was a good warm friendship filling gaps they didn't realize were needed to be filled. The Countess enjoyed all the Russian influence in Brighton Beach and bought knishes on the Boardwalk for both of them. They also went on excursions further away, drives to the mountains stopping for lunch at the small, picturesque villages and towns dotting rural New York. One Sunday, he took her to the Sheepshead Bay Pier. It was a busy day for the fishing boats and fun to watch. Sitting on a bench eating pretzels, they watched the crowd. Suddenly, the Captain jumped up and ran over to a person about to throw a plastic cup into the bay.

"Stop! Don't you dare do that," he screamed." And all at once, everything stopped. The cup was poised in the air with the man's hand extended. People were caught in mid-step, the days' catch weighing scales stopped spinning their needles, pelicans with wings outstretched just hung in the sky. Everyone was in freeze-frame except the Captain who reached out and snatched the motionless cup out of the air. Then, suddenly, everything returned to normal. No one seemed to miss a beat, the play button was again pressed and everything resumed. The cup thrower pulled in his outstretched arm and was overtly confused until the Captain spoke.

He made a big display of throwing the cup into a recyclable garbage can. He turned to the still confused litterer and said loud enough for everyone to hear, "We are drowning in plastic detritus young man. Our seas are not waste dumps. Miles of garbage float around in the Pacific causing havoc to sea life. Beached whales are found with bellies full of plastic. It's heartbreaking what we humans are doing. Have some respect, man, for this planet that sustains us." A small crowd had formed and began to clap. The Captain nodded and went back to sit with the Countess.

"Well, that was something," she said.

"My speech? Yes, I get really upset about how, except for primitive indigenous people, most humans have so little understanding of how everything is connected. Microplastic has even been found on Mt. Everest and Antarctica. Just shameful."

"Well, that too of course, but the scene in front of us came to a complete standstill. Frozen in time. It was quite remarkable. Did you do that?"

The Captain just shrugged his shoulders, not wanting to commit to an answer, but then said. "I have no control. It just happens. It started with a very violent attack I perpetrated on my father who was abusive to me and my mother. The freezing of time allowed me to see that I was committing murder. Patricide. With that realization, I stopped my attack and left. I joined the Merchant Marine—a life-changing event and decision. Now when it happens, it's brought on by others acting violently towards me and has gotten me out of a lot of messes. But this time was different in a good way. Usually, everyone around doesn't realize what's going on. But you were aware while you witnessed it. The same thing happened when you were attacked in the park, although then you were recovering from your own altercation and didn't notice that was how I was able to grab your purse."

"Oh my. You are quite right. I didn't realize what was happening at the park that day. But today was different because you see, dear, I, too, am quite sensitive to the paranormal so to speak. But your powers are quite astonishing. If you can figure out why this trigger event was different and you could control these moments, it probably would be quite useful. Let's go back to my place and have some tea and discuss this further."

Chapter Nine

The Trip

Journal entry:
A stately ship, an unexpected rough crossing.
I am now called Gabrielle at the Countess's request and don't mind at all.
A handsome Captain, oh my!
Is this a fairy tale?

Life goes on. People plan. Weather changes. Sun-filled cloudless blue skies with balmy temperatures made for glorious days in the aftermath of the Storm of the Century as Vermonters referred to it. The beautiful weather seemed odd against the backdrop of fallen giant old-growth trees, wind-damaged roofs, swollen ponds, and downed power lines. The precarious storm had hit one or two shopping strips and caused crashed-in store-front glass from the hurricane-force winds. This resulted in rain-damaged inventory from the onslaught of downpours when the stores were left exposed, but contrarily, other retail areas were miraculously untouched. Clean-up crews were out in force. The pleasant weather created a sense of relief and with it a feeling of hope that circulated through the populace.

It felt good to be alive and to have survived the thundering, lightning-charged war-like assault of Mother Nature. There were no casualties, amazingly. Caught up in this blissful mood were Gabby's intimates, her new family of friends. All were in the throes of optimism for the re-opening of the B&B. Gabby awoke every day with eagerness and joy, heretofore, feelings she had to consciously and intentionally manifest in her tiny studio. Sheer giddiness. For the Countess, anticipating her upcoming sea voyage was especially exciting. She suddenly was quite homesick for London and couldn't wait to get going.

"Let's go shopping for our trip!" she blurted out one morning a week before the ship was to sail. "We'll bring empty suitcases to my apartment in the city and have fun filling them up. I have a great hairdresser near the apartment that can give you a makeover and make-up tips, Gabby. A new life and a new you, awaits!"

"That's totally unnecessary," Gabby protested outwardly but was secretly thrilled at the thought of the Countess taking charge as a mother would. So, they went to the city to begin the adventure of a lifetime for Gabby. The Countess was right about the Captain. He was most eager to stay in Vermont and oversee the rehabilitation of the lodge and take care of Doo. Mrs. Jones would find cooks, cleaners, and gardeners. The Captain would also help Mrs. Jones repair her place as well and stay with her while repairs were made at both places. There was much to oversee and plenty of supplies to buy to get ready for the opening slated for the Labor Day weekend. Before they departed, Gabby and the Countess hired a marketing company to create brochures and place ads in magazines, online venues like Facebook, Google, and Instagram. They also would paste fliers in local stores in Rutland and the neighboring towns to announce the reopening of the inn. Gabby had some second thoughts about it being frivolous to take a vacation at this important juncture in her life, but the Countess wouldn't hear of it.

"Nonsense," she said, "the timing is perfect. The inn is in excellent hands for its refurbishing and once we're up and running it will be impossible to get away."

So off they went in a hired car to the Countess's apartment in the city. It had not been made available yet as an Airbnb because the Countess had had a feeling that she might need the place for a least one more month. They happily dropped their empty suitcases in the middle of the living room having just a small overnight bag for toiletries. Gabby laid in the bed in the guest room that night too excited to sleep and marveling how her life had changed so much in so short a time and already missing Doo. The Countess also laid in bed thinking of what had seemed to be a rash decision to manage a bed and breakfast inn was not really so rash. The tea leaves had told her this change would be coming and her dreams had been filled with visions of a large house beside a lake with a wide front porch. As soon as the Countess saw Gabby's B&B, she knew the decision to live there was a path chosen for her. A very important path as it would turn out. But that came later.

Gabby's makeover was nothing short of astonishing. Now that her features had finally relaxed and the outward Gabby reflected her true inner feelings, she had developed an easy smile. Quite remarkable to her whenever she caught her reflection and for all who had only known her grumpy demeanor, like Walter. With her new hairdo and expertly applied make-up, Gabby was ravishing. Transformed from the drab, self-conscious librarian into a woman of independent spirit. It was as if by magic that she had morphed into this person. Like Cinderella going to the ball transformed by the fairy godmother. Only this was at the hands of the Countess, who also helped in choosing flattering clothes, both casual and upscale finery. It didn't hurt either that Gabby had the height and body type of a runway model. *Who knew?* Walter's mouth was agape when they came to tell him of all that was going on and to come to the B&B when it was open. His mouth was still agape when they left.

It was time. Supercharged butterflies of excitement rushed through Gabby's bloodstream and she could not keep her emotions in check as they set sail. In a high state of elation, she giggled and bounced from thing to thing to check everything out. The Countess had booked the most expensive and luxurious stateroom on Cunard's famous ocean liner, the Queen Mary 2. The Grand Duplex had a floating staircase to the bedroom level where they each had their own bedroom and marble full bath. Gabby could not stop saying, "Oh my," as her giggling turned into shrieks of joy as she looked around.

"My personal fortune is not just to provide salaries for others," said a delighted Countess. "It's for my own enjoyment as well. I've always loved the finer things in life and having a good time, and I've always wanted to stay in this suite. When I crossed before, it seemed too large for just me. Besides, my living expenses will be covered from now on. I've been rather conservative with my spending compared to my wealth for most of my life. So why not be extravagant now?"

On the first night after a long day, they decided to stay in for their evening meal and discovered the personal service was impeccable. Their butler, Harris, was assigned their room and saw to their every need. The spacious stateroom had its own dining area and they decided to alternate their meals between eating in and the fun of dressing fancy for dining at the Queen's Grill, which was dedicated to the first-class guests.

They enjoyed walking excursions around the deck, treatments at the spa, the raucous nightclub entertainment, and the casino. Gabby loved gambling and discovered she had quite the knack for winning at poker. On the third day of their seven-day Atlantic crossing, a formal invitation was delivered on a silver tray by Harris with their in-room breakfast.

"How lovely," said the Countess as she read the invite. "We've been invited to have dinner tonight with Mr. Mark Davis, the ship's captain, at his table. Let's get pampered and go to the spa and beauty shop. What fun."

The positive energy of the cosmos was greeted and acknowledged by an overwhelmed Gabby. With each sip of coffee and each bite of egg, she expanded her consciousness by being mindful and present. She took a moment to absorb her new reality and paid homage to the forces that led her to her new life. Here she sat in this well-appointed luxuriousness stateroom, surrounded by the calm ocean sparkling through large windows while enjoying a breakfast served by their staff. True to herself, she vowed she would never take her good fortune for granted and would share it by doing good works for others. It would be easy, she thought, to provide meals or temporary housing now that she was the proprietor of an inn. Always being cognizant of her previous rough existence, she would remain humble and grateful. She reminded herself that the material extravagances she was now enjoying were not at all equal to the emotional security she was receiving from her new family. Tears of joy welled in her eyes as she was once again overcome with the raw naked emotion brought on by her new reality.

"Are you alright, darling?" asked the Countess. "Have I done or said something to upset you?"

"Quite the contrary," said Gabby controlling her urge to break down sobbing. "I'm overcome with feelings that have been foreign to me for my entire life. Real joy soars through me. I used to talk myself into feeling grateful just to be alive but this is different. This sense that you really care about me makes me weep with gratitude. I'm sorry. I don't mean to embarrass you by constantly bearing my soul. Forgive me. I know my gratitude and tears have become repetitive but I'm just so utterly grateful. So much good fortune and love has come my way and now staying in this luxurious stateroom, something I never would have experienced before I met you. An abundance of riches."

The Countess took a moment in contemplation while she spread jam on her toast.

"It is very important that you hear this, Gabby, my dear. What we have together is also very special to *me*. Just as you have been missing something, so have I. The prospect of spending the rest of my life alone, no Irina, no husband, was devastatingly sad for me but I was making the best of it. Hoping my friends at the library and my tenants would be enough to not make me feel so all alone. To feel connected. My entire adult life, I coped with the reality of being childless. When I would observe families together, fighting and laughing with their children, I would feel a profound sense of loss. It would last but a moment because I wouldn't dwell on it. No sense to drown oneself in sadness, especially over a situation for which I had no control. I know I could have adopted a child, but my brief marriages weren't conducive. And I guess I was too selfish to strike out as a single mother. Or too frightened. It is what it is, as they say.

"But, Gabby, you and I have, by a coincidental and quite amazing happenstance, filled a void for each other. Relationships formed by choice and not biology can be just as real, just as valid. You are like a daughter to me or probably more like a granddaughter," she laughs, "and I feel blessed to have you in my life and all the change in my life that comes with it. I, too, now have a sense of being part of a family, of belonging." The Countess paused for a moment and sipped her coffee, "Please take what I'm about to say in the right way. But I have a suggestion for you, love. In honor of you being reborn into this glamorous personage, a woman of substance, and great beauty, I might add."

Gabby put down her coffee cup and looked puzzled having no idea what would come next and needless to say was quite surprised when it did. "I believe the name, Gabby, no longer suits you. Henceforth, I shall call you Gabrielle."

The Countess then took a long pause to study her sweet newfound "granddaughter" fondly. Finally, she said, "Would you mind, dear? If I called you Gabrielle from now on?"

Gabby thought for a moment and realized the Countess was correct. All the ill will for her father had evaporated with this new life he had handed her. Keeping the name he had given her would acknowledge her forgiveness and how grateful she was.

"Yes, I think you are correct. It seems like the right thing to do now is to honor my father's memory and use the name he gave me. In doing so, it will acknowledge that in some way leaving the B&B to me makes up for all his years of disinterest and apathy. His act of generosity started a monumental change in my circumstances, of which the inn was but one aspect. Without realizing it, he gave me a family for which I have always craved. Yes, I agree to be called Gabrielle from now on."

"Wonderful, my darling, Gabrielle. Now, let's get more lighthearted and have a fun day preparing for our dinner with the Captain of this ship."

They got up and gave each other a tight hug and then the Countess made their appointments for massages, facials, mani/pedis, and hair. While the Countess was on the phone, Gabrielle waited on their private balcony feeling the strong wind on her face and blowing through her hair. She connected to the forward movement of the ship as it sliced through the waters. Clouds were forming in the distance but the sun was glorious and warm in the cool breeze. She paid attention to all her five senses that were each responding to this moment and stayed in that mindset all through her day of delicious pampering.

Back in their room, they took bubble baths before they dressed. Gabrielle, who now realized just how much she enjoyed these spa treatments, was quite relaxed while she soaked in the scented bath. It was time to get dressed in her Dolce and Gabbana black tight sheathe with sweetheart neckline accented with a red patent-leather belt and matching red Louboutin spiked heels. She could hardly believe it was she. Her long, black hair was pulled away from her face and fell in soft waves. Her flawless makeup and green eyeshadow accented her almond-shaped black eyes and long lashes. Gabrielle had transformed into a stunning butterfly from the caterpillar she used to be. It took her a few moments to accept this version of herself. *I am the same inside as I've always been. Remain humble,* she reminded herself.

"Ravishing," said the Countess in her own finery when Gabrielle emerged. She was wearing black silk palazzo pants over which she wore a silk embroidered jacket she had had custom-made on a trip to Hong Kong. They both looked marvelous and headed over to the Queen's Grill private dining room. The Countess knew from past crossings there would be others attending because all the guests staying in the larger Grill suites would be invited to attend this dinner. But no matter. It was still special since the Captain would be sitting at their table. By the time they arrived, there was a small crowd milling around. Servers walked through the group offering glasses of Champagne and they happily accepted. Gabrielle still hadn't internalized her transformation into a sophisticated beauty and wasn't aware of the interest shown to her. Women paused to study her and men unabashedly stared. Captain Davies was alerted of their entrance and quickly walked over to them.

"Good evening, Countess Ivanova, so lovely to meet you and your granddaughter, Miss...?"

"Gabrielle Ivano..," she started to say with a wink to Gabrielle before the Captain interrupted.

"Ah, yes. Lovely to meet you, Gabrielle. Won't you both join me for a drink before dinner?" he said as he stared directly into Gabrielle's eyes. The Countess realized she should have given this glamorous version of Gabrielle that *talk* about the workings of the world, especially concerning men. She worried she had opened a Pandora's Box of minefields for the young girl, attracting men like a fly to honey. *Ah, yes*, she had a fleeting memory about her own youth and the fun of being sought after. She realized that frumpy Gabby must have had trouble attracting handsome men of substance who were marriage material. She had probably just dealt with inconsequential relationships with inconsequential boys who were not real prospects. It would be fun to observe Gabrielle's passage into visibility with important men, to help her make a good match. Sort of a "coming out" period like the old days, like her own Debutante Ball season. Yes, watching and advising, as if Gabrielle were really her granddaughter. She mused at future events, such as planning a wedding, raising great-grandchildren. But she was getting ahead of herself. Way ahead, she laughed quietly… but fun…and happy thoughts to mull over.

The Captain led them by the arm to a small cocktail table and motioned to the waiter. Although he made small talk with Gabrielle's newfound "grandmother," he kept darting his eyes back and forth to engage the stunning young woman who also studied him while observing the others attending this event. Everyone was very smartly dressed. It was an intimate group of 14 people. The richest among the wealthy elite of which she was now a wide-eyed member. She couldn't help noticing how handsome the Captain was. A tingle tickled inside her—an excitement blooming. He looked to be in his mid-to-late thirties. No ring. But that didn't mean anything. He cut quite the figure in his dress uniform of a waist-length white dinner jacket with gold buttons and gold and black epaulets on each shoulder. The formal outfit was complemented with a white bow tie, white formal shirt, and gold cummerbund over black dress slacks. His dashingly handsome soft features were perfectly accompanied by thick wavy blonde hair that fell softly on his forehead enhancing his emerald, green eyes framed by thick black eyelashes. Dramatic, elegant, and extremely sexy. Gabrielle was besotted.

Intermittently, as they both studied each other furtively, whenever their eyes would suddenly meet...WHAM—a spark of electricity arched between them. Sitting there, on this elegant ship, flirting with this stunning male, Gabrielle felt reborn. A far cry from that frowny-faced girl that just a few weeks ago would have been shy and intimidated in this setting. That girl was light-years away from who she was now. Never having been someone who fawned and fussed over her looks, she had been quite astonished to realize how attractive she had suddenly become with just a few beauty tips. Her once limp hair was now cut and treated so it looked thick and wavy as it tumbled down her shoulders. Her elegant high-cheekbones and fine features were enhanced with just the right amount of make-up to make her large dark eyes sparkle. A touch of color on her full lips enhanced her dazzling smile that no longer looked forced.

When they finished the Champagne and light hors d'oeuvres, they moved on to a larger table where more people joined them. A spectacular dinner of epicurean delights was paired with a delicate Chablis, a sparkling rose, and a full-bodied Cabernet. The Captain was a delightful host making all the dinner guests feel welcome and special. He had a knack for making small talk and put everyone at ease. An accomplished man of style and grace and very well-educated in the arts and sciences, he spoke of the wonderful London museums with curated collections that ran the gamut from ancient Egypt at the British Museum to the Tate Modern art collection.

He made sure he sat Gabrielle next to him, so he could lean over to whisper compliments from time to time. She reveled in the attention and noticed the approving but also worried look of the Countess as if saying "enjoy the attention but be careful." What fun. She had read stories about shipboard romances and felt she was about to write one of her own. They planned to meet for a nightcap in the Observation Bar after everyone had left the dinner party. Dessert and coffee were served and afterwards, the Captain mingled with the crowd as Gabrielle went with the Countess to the casino to play a bit before meeting him at the bar.

After the Countess went back to their room with a smile and a friendly warning to "be careful" Gabrielle went to the Observation Bar with great anticipation. She reminded herself that she was now the owner of an establishment, an eight-room inn on ten acres of land in Vermont. Filled with confidence, she ordered a glass of Malbec and caught the attention of an older gentleman at the other end of the bar who said something to the bartender. As the glass was placed in front of her, she went to hand over the ship's charge card but was told that the man had already paid for it. She looked over and he waved, she nodded a "thank you" as he got up and was making his way over when the Captain entered. *What a relief.* Then and there, Gabrielle realized this new world of hers would be fraught with uncomfortable situations in which she must take charge or be subjected to the unwanted attention of others. Lesson learned.

"Thank you so much for meeting me tonight," said Captain Davis as he pulled over a stool and sat down next to her. Gabrielle noticed the other gentleman stopped moving and walked back to his seat at the bar. The Captain made a sign to the bartender who brought him a double Johnny Walker poured from the blue label, his usual order apparently. He raised his glass and clinked it with Gabrielle's, "Here's to a fabulous voyage and the beginning of a special friendship, I hope." Gabrielle just smiled not knowing what to say. "Tell me a little about yourself. Your grandmother has quite the credentials being a member of Russian aristocracy. I was just a Chief Engineer on one of her previous crossings. She always caused quite a stir whenever she showed up for dinner and such. Very regal, but approachable. I remember on her most recent trip she married the social director or something. But I guess that fling didn't last long," he laughed. "How is it you are American but she's from London?"

"Well perhaps I should just tell you the story of my life and you can put all these pieces together. Quite sad really. I was basically an abandoned child emotionally, left alone to figure out how to take care of myself. Luckily, I had the parents of a school friend step in when an adult was needed. When my mother passed after many years of mental illness, I went to college in New York City on a full scholarship and earned a degree in Library Science. In no time at all, I managed to get hired at a small local library on the lower West Side of town and met the Countess who was one of the regulars. Very recently, we became close friends, more like family really, and she has agreed to help me run a bed and breakfast inn in Vermont that my absentee father bequeathed to me, rather unexpectedly."

"A frightened child all alone. A very sad tale indeed. Tragic," he said softly. "But one in which I can relate, unfortunately. Life's pathways can take interesting turns. For you it certainly has...and... for me as well, I daresay. It's hard to imagine you as that lonely forlorn child because what sits before me is a rather sophisticated, lovely, and self-assured woman."

Gabrielle was startled to hear him refer to her as self-assured but it pleased her. A thought flashed in her mind of the frightened little "namby-pamby" when she first met that lawyer, Whitehead. What would Mark Davies say if he had seen her in that office just a few weeks ago? Deep down she knew she hadn't changed all that much. She was growing into her pretense of sophistication that would perhaps become real with the help of the Countess. Because of her help, she at least looked the part. Right now, she was still playing at it. She knew she was a fraud but he didn't. And who knows how sincere *he* was? In any event, what did it matter? Just a fling. His ease in complimenting her kept her charmed and his attention was very pleasant. *Leave it at that.*

As for the Captain, he was truly captivated. Not only was she beautiful but obviously well-connected and financially independent. Most of the women he wined and dined on these cruises were quite comfortable, obviously, because it was a small fortune to travel first class, and he only socialized with those privileged guests. All aspects of this job were perfect for him. He loved the ladies and they, in turn, loved him. A fantastic life. On each voyage, he met a special someone who kept him intrigued. It was perfect for a man like himself, who needed no permanent attachments in life.

"Let's finish our drinks," he said, "and take a stroll on the outside deck and I'll tell you of my similarly sad childhood, unfortunately."

Although they had been enjoying each other's company, acknowledging their not-so-happy memories of their childhoods put them both in a pensive mood as they walked to the outside deck. It was a glorious evening with a full moon that lit up the calm ocean and the starry, cloudless sky. The light sea breeze brought on by the forward movement of the ship fluttered around them belying the surrounding water that was as still as a lake. The peaceful and gentle rocking of the ship was relaxing. The mild temperature cocooned them and made being outside extremely pleasant. They leaned on the railing and looked out enjoying the scene, then he put his arm around her waist and they stood like that...close.

Gabrielle leaned in enjoying his masculine physical presence and put her head on his shoulder. His strong arm wrapped around her made her feel safe and protected. Nice. It also aroused her. She felt liberated by accepting her sexuality and its power. All worthy pursuits on this cruise and in her life. She was broadening herself and becoming...becoming just being in the state of becoming. That was enough. At this moment she did not need to remind herself to be grateful as she had trained her former self, the old Gabby. Now, as Gabrielle, it just flowed through her organically. She felt sheer joy and was humbly thankful for life's gifts. So many welcome changes. The Countess, the inn, this handsome accomplished man pursuing her.

As she stood there taking in all her positive feelings before their first kiss, Gabrielle reveled in the anticipation of it. She knew there would be a complete erotic physical connection if she so chose. Should she wait or devour it? Had it not been for the Countess waiting back in their stateroom, she knew what her choice would be. She lusted for him and it excited and thrilled her. This man would be quite different from her previous sexual encounters with young boys who had no finesse. Yes, Mark Davies would be an experience for which she was ready.

He pulled her closer and leaned down and kissed her lightly and tenderly on her forehead. "Just like you," he began speaking softly, "my young life was a rather miserable and lonely existence. My parents died in a tragic accident after many alcoholic years accompanied by horrific fights with yelling and screaming obscenities, throwing objects, and slamming doors. Luckily, I was sent to boarding school so I was just exposed to it when home on holidays. I was an only child having lost my younger sister at age twelve in a car accident when my inebriated mother was driving. I'm sure the terrible fights were an outcome of that tragedy, but nevertheless, I kept away whenever I could. Some holidays, I chose to spend at a schoolmate's home in Devonshire. A kind invitation from Alec, my friend, who knew of my home situation. On one of those holidays at Alec's, my parents drove their car off a bridge into a lake and drowned. Was it a murder/suicide or an accident? No answers on that. Either way, the outcome was the same.

"My paternal grandmother, a stern and heartless creature, became my legal guardian. When I finished my studies in geography at Oxford, I wanted to travel, I desperately wanted, rather needed, to get out of the country and experience the world. Most especially, I guess I wanted to get away from my past. I had a small inheritance that I didn't want to blow on a year abroad. At Oxford, one meets the right people. And that's where I found the ideal solution. A classmate's father was a big shot at Cunard. I could travel *and* earn a living. A perfect setup. I thought that perhaps I would just try it for a few years, but I soon discovered I loved being aboard ship. The lifestyle suited me providing the adventure of seeing the world and meeting new people on every cruise. I quickly and easily moved up the ranks and made captain in record time, so they tell me." He paused for a moment lost in his memories of good times and wonderful women. For him, Gabrielle would be another special memory and he was looking forward to making love to her. He then went on, "Quite happy with this turn of events for me. And I suspect the same goes for you."

Gabrielle turned to look at him touched by this story. His eyes revealed his honesty and she immediately felt a kinship towards this man. They were traveling on a similar life's journey. He also reminded her of dear Captain Jimmy back at home who was now a most welcome part of her entourage. *Seafarers must all be romantics and have similar angst-filled childhoods,* she thought. They made small talk to lighten the mood. She discovered that he was only 32 years old, just a few years older than she and younger than she had originally thought. Never married, he currently was unattached, no girl waiting in London. No serious one anyway. Well, no matter his eligibility, she was focused on the now, being mindful and present. And it was very pleasurable to be in this high state of excitement. The scent of his cologne standing this close to him was alluring and captivating. She could feel his breath on her neck.

As she turned to look up at him again, he grabbed her and kissed her deeply and long. It further aroused her. Lost in his embrace, the world receded and there was only him kissing her sweetly and longingly. He touched her softly down her shoulder and her arm. Pressing her against him, she could feel his desire for her. They kissed like that for several minutes and then he whispered in her ear in a thick and husky voice, "Come back with me to my room." Her thoughts about slowing this down and not wanting to worry the Countess blew away with the breeze. She wanted this as much as he did and she was ready and willing. She'd made up her mind to give in to her lusty turned-on feelings and was helpless to stop it. They kissed a little longer sealing the deal, "Ok," she said softly.

Just then she lost her balance. The ship rocked hard. A small deck chair slid a few feet and then turned over. And then another. Everything not tied down started sliding. The calm seas became choppy and then angry with giant waves forming. The waves began to crash against the ship and flooded the deck. This weather event was deteriorating very quickly. From calm to a raging storm in just a few minutes.

"Uh oh," Mark said and pulled away quickly, "this is not good. This storm was not on our radar. Very strange. I'm sorry but we have to get inside. I must get back to the bridge. I'll call someone to escort you to your room," he said. Just then a young man ran out from the bar in an excited manner telling the Captain about what a huge storm this weather had become. They all hurriedly went back into the bar and Mark rushed back to the bridge with not so much as a goodbye. *Well, that's understandable,* she thought. *But still.* She felt foolish but then came another strong rocking motion and the young man grabbed her arm to steady her. *Okay, gotta pay attention.* He escorted her back to her room while trying to help her keep her balance as well as his own as the ship's pitching back and forth increased its angle dangerously. Scary. Very scary.

"Oh, my dear, thank goodness you're here. What is going on?" asked the Countess holding onto a chair arm for dear life in the first floor living room.

"I think this might be a hurricane-type storm. Mark was very worried that it just showed up with no warning on the radar. I don't think we should try to climb the staircase with this rocking. Let's take the private elevator outside."

"Will you both be, okay?" asked the young man who helped her back to the suite.

Just then the butler came to escort them both upstairs, so he wished them well and left. The elevator was slightly nerve-racking but better than trying to walk up the stairs as the ship swayed and dipped. The butler offered to bring them some tea. Gabrielle went into the Countess's room to calm her as well as herself having never traveled on a ship before. The tea was served with covers on the cups to help keep them from spilling. A small plate of petit fours was brought also. They sat down at the cozy seating arrangement in the bedroom and sipped their teas. The swaying calmed down a bit. The butler told them the ship's stabilizers were state-of-the-art and not to worry. "This strong rocking motion would soon quiet down," he said. "No cause for alarm." Just as he said that the ship took a really hard bounce and sway and everything fell that wasn't tied down. He, himself, fell on the floor, the teacups flew out of their hands, and then the butler tripped into one of the tied-down chairs as he tried to get up. He jumped up to pick up the fallen dishes and food.

"So sorry for this rare weather disturbance. Most unusual. I believe we shall sail out of it soon, perhaps in a day or so...maybe sooner. I'll check with the Captain. Shall I get more tea?"

Gabrielle and the Countess told him they were fine and just wanted to retire for the evening. "Certainly, shall I turn down the beds?" They shook their heads 'no" and after a few moments picking up the tea remains, he unsteadily left.

"I'm so frightened, can I sleep with you?" said Gabrielle? They spent a sleepless night hanging on to the bed frame and exploding frequently with "Oh my god" as the ship pitched at sharp angles and the fear of it capsizing keeping them terrified.

Luckily neither one got seasick but that changed slightly when in the morning the storm had not abated. As they moaned in bed, the butler came by and handed them some pills. "Fast working stuff," he said. And he was right. It worked like magic and they slept for several hours and woke up hungry. That was good but the storm was still raging. That was bad. The butler came in. *How does he know when we are awake?* Was a thought that quickly passed through Gabrielle's mind and she looked to see if there were any security cameras. She point-blank asked him and he told them there were sensors that alerted him when they were moving about. And he always knocked. Well, that was true. So here was the deal. They had to change course to get away from the hurricane. *So, it was a hurricane!* This will add two days to the trip but very pleasant ones after they sail into calm waters in the wee hours of the morning. By tomorrow night's dinner, we all would have enjoyed a day of fine weather and a fabulous meal will be provided in the Princess Grill dining room to celebrate. Shortly a full English Breakfast will be brought up or if they would rather, he could help them downstairs. They both preferred going downstairs and cautiously traversed the staircase.

Still woozy from the pills and the motion of the ship, they ate in slow motion but steadily. They were famished. After they finished, they decided to relax in the living room and catch up on a conversation that was waiting to happen.

"So how did you enjoy your drink with Captain Davis?"

"I think he's quite nice and very good looking, but the evening was cut way too short. Whatever you have done to make my appearance more attractive has opened a whole new world for me. It takes getting used to. A man like Mark would never have been interested in meeting me just a few weeks ago. I can't believe all I've missed in the dating world because I didn't know how to apply makeup or wear my hair. Seems superficial though. I'm still me."

"Well actually, not really. There has been a pretty drastic transformation that is reflected itself as a most pleasant aspect of your face and smile. Your new life's path has caused a miraculous change. Yes, your true inner self remains but now your outer self is more of a reflection of the inner. A melding of the old Gabby and the new Gabrielle. It's been quite remarkable and a joy to witness such a rapid change. It began right after you came back from your first trip to Vermont. You may not have realized it then or see it now. But others certainly see how beautiful you are. It's like there's a spotlight that shines on you, and when you enter a room, you give off a vibe of charming enthusiasm, youthful hope, and optimism. It's no wonder the Captain was entranced."

"Thank you, dear Countess. I don't see myself as you do, in fact, I've thought the same about you, but it's nice to hear. Indeed, Captain Davis's invitation was a surprise but he also attracted me. Maybe my interest in him was the impetus for his attention. He is after all a red-blooded male."

"Yes, I wondered if you would come to our room last night," she laughs, "before the dangerous seas changed everything."

"Well, needless to say, I think I rather like this changed world of mine. As I said, I owe it to your expert guidance and I hate to admit to my father's generosity. Gabrielle Bernstein is suddenly a force to be reckoned with and I've become more independent and self-assured by the minute."

That arrogance took the Countess by surprise but then Gabrielle noticed her look and said, "Just kidding. What I really feel like is that I'm playing dress-up, swept up by life in a dizzying ride that I'm not quite sure is real. What I will admit is that I toyed with spending the night with Mark and was disappointed *and* a little relieved when it didn't happen. But we'll see if I even have drinks with him again. You know, I just realized that the ship is not rolling as much. How about we get dressed and check if the casino is open."

They managed to get upstairs using the elevator and enjoyed bathing and getting dressed. The seasickness pills the butler gave them were still working or their inner gyroscope had gotten used to the ship's heavy rocking motion. The casino was dead. A few machines were turned on but the rocking motion made it hard to stand or sit in front of them. No one was at the tables. Getting to the casino from their room was a challenge as well and somewhat unpleasant. There were only a few people out and about but some would stop and hurry over to the side of the ship and throw up. It reeked. They gave up their outing and went back and called for the butler who this time didn't just show up. They needed more pills. The excursion to the casino had not been a good idea and they were starting to feel sick. Knocked out they slept the day away, got up for a light dinner, and slept again until morning. Just as predicted when they woke up the water was smooth and calm. *Now we're talking. Wonderful!*

It was a marvelous couple of days of fine weather. A most welcome relief of tranquil seas and smooth sailing. The festive dinner the first night of calm brought out everybody in their finest attire. An electricity of happiness was in the air. A gaiety of mood permeated the room. The joy of survival was palpable and radiated off everyone. "We lived through it, huzzah," was on the tip of everyone's tongue. It even emanated from the servers. We are alive and we are grateful. Nothing will be taken for granted anymore. Lesson learned…for now. And the food was delightful. Crisp, cold, plump jumbo shrimp cocktails. Melt in-your-mouth filet mignons with grilled salmon and a salad bar brought to each table. Tiramisu to die for and cappuccinos all around for dessert.

Gabrielle was anxious and her eyes fluttered about the room. She hadn't heard from Mark and she kept checking the dining room entrance to see if he would show. She and the Countess agreed to share a table with a delightful couple from the South of France. The Countess loved conversing in French and Gabrielle had lost her aversion to all things French when she forgave her father but was glad she was off the hook to socialize and could concentrate on watching the entrance. A vision of her insane mother sitting in that old worn-out chair at the living room window searching for the return of her father flashed through her mind. *Not good.* Immediately she ordered a stiff drink of Vodka rocks and focused on the food.

And then there he was.

She was all aflutter. He glanced around the room but was summoned to a table before he noticed her. She watched him while he made witty conversation as the two older women laughed sexily and their husbands laughed heartily. Obviously regulars, people who knew him, she told herself. Old friends that found him charming. Made him feel like a rock star. *Who can compete with that?* When dinner was over for her and the Countess, they said their goodbyes in English and in French and she glanced over at his table and caught his eye. *Finally!* He smiled and nodded his head and then turned back to his dinner companions. *That was it?*

Once back in the room, the Countess turned in immediately, exhausted. Gabrielle stayed in the living room and turned on the TV. She poured herself a cognac. And then another. After three or four or more she was numb. She admonished herself for thinking the way men treated her had changed. The Countess had given her those ideas. It's true, she was probably more attractive in her style and facial features with her new hairdo and makeup application. But men still treated her like garbage. Lesson learned. *Don't kid yourself.* After one or two more cognacs, well maybe she finished the bottle (it wasn't that large), she stumbled up to bed and collapsed until morning.

This was the last day of the cruise. They decided to luxuriate in an in-room breakfast on their private deck. The weather was sunny, clear, gorgeous, and a well-earned serenity, just a gentle breeze. The temperature was chilly but not cold and the warm sun kept them toasty. After the heavenly stack of blueberry pancakes, breakfast pastries, and honey-cured bacon were devoured lustily and the final cups of coffee were poured, Harris brought a silver tray that had a note for Gabrielle. It was from Mark. *Well, well, finally!* It was an invitation to join him for afternoon tea at the Howard hotel in London the day after next, four PM. The final leg of the journey before arriving at port would keep him too busy to get away. Please respond on the accompanying notepad.

"What is this?" asked the Countess.

"Mark has invited me to afternoon tea at the Howard hotel for Tuesday."

"Well, that sounds lovely and in fact is perfect. I have an appointment with my solicitors that very afternoon. Tea at the Howard is quite lovely as it is at the Savoy, where we're staying. You can judge which is better. We probably could have had a real English tea experience on this ship, if not for the weather and all the other mountains of food," she chuckles. "Oh well, it will be far superior in London, I suspect."

"I, of course, have never had this sort of thing. What is it really?"

So, the Countess explained the tradition of steeping teas, partaking of delightfully prepared scones (like a biscuit but better) and clotted cream (like whipped cream but a liquid and much richer and served with all cakes in England), thick, delightful jams, finger sandwiches, and little cakes and pastries. "We eat supper here much later than in America. Eight pm or later is pretty common, we call lunch dinner and have tea to stave off the hunger before our late supper. Nowadays, we also include a split of Champagne to start," she said. "I've really missed a delicious afternoon tea whilst in America. There's a pretty good one served at the Palm Court at the Plaza hotel in New York City with nice relaxing chamber music. But it's not as widespread an experience as it is in England. Yum, now, I can't wait! We'll go to the one at the Savoy before you meet your Captain so you'll be a pro at it. Oh, my darling, we will have such fun. So much to see and do. I've actually made a list that you can look up and check out before we go. I totally forgot about giving it to you what with all the commotion and the awfulness of trying to stay alive these last few days," she laughs, "I'll text it to you. The Howard is a lovely boutique hotel. This Captain Davis is quite civilized. The Savoy where we are staying is not too far. Why is Harris hovering 'round?"

"Oh, I'm supposed to respond."

"Well of course you should go, darling. Harris, please take her response."

And so, it was settled, she would meet Mark in London, how exciting.

Chapter Ten

London

Journal entry:
A stranger who was not a stranger,
a forbidden dalliance. Flee, I must flee
...and so, I did.

It's time to take a moment to pause and reflect before Gabrielle disembarks and steps into her future. The Gabby that started this adventure was now the Gabrielle who would live it out. A manifestation by the dear grandmotherly woman of elegance and wealth who turned Gabrielle into the image of the daughter/granddaughter she never had but always wanted. As for Gabrielle, pleasing the Countess would be paramount to how she ran her life going forward making the Countess into the mother of whom she had always felt bereft. It was a beginning, a birth if you will, of a family not biological but born of mutual desire. It would serve them both well and their lives would be the better for having each other.

Once Gabrielle alights from the ship onto the shore, her preordained future, of which she is most unaware begins. The import of her connection to all her new friends at the inn is not as life changing as what awaits her in London. All the pieces must be put into place for the important duties and responsibilities of this cosmically formed clan. One wishes that it would not be needed. And maybe there's a slim chance it won't be. But nevertheless, it doesn't hurt to be ready.

As we turn now to the moment of disembarkation, Gabrielle was aware that just stepping onto a foreign shore was the most adventurous moment in her young life and was once again, or maybe by now obnoxiously so, grateful for the experience. She whispered her gratitude to the cosmos for all the love that had come her way. The love that was expressing itself in this shared adventure. The calm assurances of the Countess whose knowledge of this strange place, made Gabrielle feel quite safe being thrust into the unknown. The Countess knew the important sights to see, the best restaurants, the perfect day trips. It was exciting and quite reassuring to have a tour guide such as her.

They had arrived in Southampton port during the wee hours of the morning and watched the commotion sipping coffees from their private deck. The staff was packing their clothes because they had also unpacked. Luxury living was quite easy to enjoy and Gabrielle decided that she would not feel guilty by partaking in the pleasures of a wealthy lifestyle. Soon enough she would be working hard at the inn and experiencing a completely different daily routine. *Grab it all while you can, and there's no crime in doing so*, she told herself.

When they disembarked there was another surprise, a Rolls Royce waiting to take them for the long drive to their hotel. It was an included amenity when staying in the Savoy of London's Royal Suite, the most expensive room at the hotel. "I will spare no expense," the normally frugal Countess had said of this trip. "Who knows when we will get another chance to get away like this and I'm not getting any younger." This first-class trip would be her treat and she was going to enjoy spoiling Gabrielle as well as herself before she became an innkeeper working seven days a week. When planning this trip, she had decided to bathe the two of them in the luxury she could well-afford and consciously paid no attention to her penny-pinching alter ego welcoming instead the extravagant and frivolous Anastasia of her youth. It was an easy transition. Glasses of mimosas were poured by the driver as they sat in the back of the Rolls and they toasted each other giggling like schoolgirls. *What fun!*

After nearly two hours' drive, they were whisked up to their penthouse suite for a private registration and given their room keys. On the way, Gabrielle noticed the lovely lobby of black and white marble checked floors and deep polished wood. Elegant. The suite had two bedrooms and two baths and an enormous walk-in closet area outfitted in dark wood with storage shelves built into the closets. Their private butler would get them sorted and unpacked and handed them a list of amenities. Hair and makeup daily, in-room breakfast with a menu but anything they wanted not on the menu would be provided, the Rolls and driver were available for daily trips around town and for dinner excursions, a bartender would arrive every day to serve them drinks from their private bar located just off the living room.

When the staff had unpacked and left, they explored the suite. It had a fantastic view of the Thames from every window. "Is that like the Ferris wheel in Coney Island?" asked Gabrielle having gone there once with a group of friends.

"It's called the London Eye and rotates very slowly compared to the Ferris wheel and the enclosed pods hold more than two people. It gives a great view of the city. I've only been on it once. I'd love to do it with you tomorrow morning. We both have the entire day to tour around. Let's make the most of it. I'll show you all my favorite haunts." Just then the doorbell rang and the butler came with a note on a tray and quietly left. The Countess tore it open. "Well, I'll be. My distant cousin Sofia is having a dinner party and we're invited for tomorrow evening. How fun! She throws the best soirées. How about for today, we have a light lunch brought up and relax for a bit. I'll have the concierge make reservations at Rules restaurant for some traditional British fare. My mouth is watering just thinking about it. Let's say for 8:30. Is that good?" Gabrielle nods. "Good."

The Rolls dropped them off at the restaurant in Covent Garden. The oldest restaurant in London, Rules was like an elegant pub. Cozy and posh. They were seated at a tucked-away table with two beautiful red-velvet banquettes, one of many that lined the walls. Just like the Countess had said, the menu was very British as well as the service being quite formal. The Countess was disappointed that grouse wasn't in season so she settled on the lamb. "You Americans don't eat much lamb and I've missed it." Gabrielle found something "normal" and had Dover Sole. All in all, it was an exceptional meal, the ambiance and service were first-rate. Gabrielle took it all in. The new world, this new life. The following day was a whirlwind of adventures.

After the vista seen from the London Eye had excited Gabrielle to take numerous photos, they headed to Westminster Abby where Kings have been crowned in coronation ceremonies since the 13th Century. It is the iconic Gothic structure that one pictures when thinking of England. Then on to Parliament passing by the clock known as Big Ben and finally to Buckingham Palace for the changing of the guard. A spectacle not to be missed. Gabrielle snapped away with her iPhone and had fun getting close to one of the guards, like all tourists, to try and make him smile, which they never do. Afterwards, it was time for tea at the Savoy, her practice run before she was to meet Captain Davis, the following day. It was just as the Countess had said. The clotted cream was to die for and the scones heavenly. "We must find out how to make these to serve them for breakfast at the inn," Gabrielle said.

They were done for the day and filled with anticipation for the Belgravia dinner party. Important events sometimes seem to come out of nowhere in an unassuming manner but that's only how it *seems*. The cosmos likes to play tricks. Kismet can start way back, many moons back. Perhaps it was the very first meeting between Gabrielle and the Countess that put the wheels in motion. Of course, Gabrielle could not know that this dinner, just as her friendship with the Countess, would eventually be life changing. It had started quite innocently with a surprise invitation and its import would not be understood immediately. One wonders why Gabrielle was singled out for all this. Gabrielle herself felt perplexed at all her good fortune. She contemplated how to give back, to show her gratitude. How she could help the world gnawed at her. How could she help people less fortunate? What was expected of her? It was an odd state for her because heretofore her life was something to be pitied, a person to be thrown away. An ordinary nothing. But now a sense of destiny was taking hold. A life's path was materializing. These were grand thoughts, large thoughts, and quite overwhelming so once they emerged into her conscious space, she would force them to stop. Stow them away to contemplate at a later time. But whispering in her ear were words of strength and resolve. Feelings of empowerment. She rejoiced in those feelings.

The two ladies had a rest before getting ready for dinner. Then hair and make-up rang the doorbell and they were off to a fun start of the evening's merriment. Gabrielle was thrilled because the Countess's cousin Sofia lived in Belgravia, just a few houses down from where the Countess grew up. It was the reason why even though they were distant cousins they still kept in touch. It was a beautiful neighborhood near Buckingham Palace and located in London's fashionable West End. Gabrielle had searched the internet during their downtime and realized just how upper class were the classical terraced white stucco-fronted townhouses.

The Rolls dropped them off at Sofia's six-story residence. An elevator or "lift" that fit seven people per the capacity sign provided access to each floor. They entered the lift to reach the first-floor reception room where an intimate crowd gathered for drinks. Hot and cold hors d'oeuvres were served by formally dressed butlers. The hostess, Sofia, spotted them as soon as they exited the lift and ran over toward them screaming for hugs and kisses.

"I can't believe you didn't tell me were coming, naughty girl," she said.

"Yes, well how did you know? I would've called everyone in a day or two."

"Brightsmith. I use him as well and just went there the other day to sign some papers. You were on your crossing so I thought I'd wait and just send an invite. He gave me all the info about where you were staying." She turns to Gabrielle. "Hello, I'm Sofia, Tasa is my second cousin, whom I adore." She notices my confusion, "Oh, the family calls her Tasa, much less work," she laughs.

"I'm Gabrielle her...friend and...business partner." The Countess reaches out and puts her arm around Gabrielle's waist and says, "She's more like an adopted granddaughter, really. We have quite a tight bond, actually. She's given me a whole new lease on life now that Irina's left me to get married and live in Brazil."

"This late in the game? Good for her. Life brings so many surprises. You moving to America for one. Let's have a lazy lunch some other day whilst you're here so we can catch up. I've so missed our talks." She looks at Gabrielle and says, "Tasa was my life coach, knowing just the right words to inspire me to recognize the cosmic cues in life. Helped me to figure things out. Now without her, I'm a total mess. Well, dearest ones, I must see to getting the dinner served that I planned just for you, my darling Tasa. All traditional British fare that I'm sure you can't get in the states. Oh, I see my dearest Professor friend over there. So handsome ...should introduce you two," she says pointedly to Gabrielle. "But now, I must speak to him about a business matter." She saunters away slightly tipsy in her spiked heels and skin-tight gold lamé dress. Right out of a British vintage Noel Coward comedy. All she needed was a cigarette holder and Betty Boop hairdo. The two ladies grinned at each other as they watched her disappear into the adjacent high-ceilinged drawing-room.

"This house is quite stunning."

Gabrielle agreed.

"I've actually stayed here when I was much younger and her parents were still alive. Some of their parties got quite raucous and one had to sleep over, especially my brother even though we lived down the street," she laughs. "You must go on and have a look after dinner. Belgravia is quite renowned for these lovely terraced Georgian mansions. Some of the most expensive homes in the world can be found here. This one, in particular, is probably up there with the best of them. Sofia's father, my cousin Lev inherited it from *his* parents and passed it down to her. No telling how long it's been in the family. Our house was much less grand. Lev had some financial difficulties before he passed, but lucky for Sofia, he was able to hold on to this place to hand it to her.

"And Sofia made a good match for herself. Ronnie, her husband over there," she looks over to where he is standing in the reception area and he nods, "comes from a long line of squires and is quite well off so I suppose it's his money that keeps it afloat. Today, this home is probably worth three times what it would have sold for when her father died ten or more years ago. These homes have such a history. Glorious furnishings and appointments. You *must* have a look around," she says again pointedly.

People were starting to be ushered into dinner by the staff. Gabrielle hung close to the Countess not wanting to be separated at the dinner table. She felt entirely out of her element and an unusual shyness overcame her. She kept her head down so that no one could direct her to the dining room to sit among strangers. As they all moved into the dining room, she felt eyes on her and turned to see a startlingly beautiful woman staring at her. Wild flaming red hair. White flowing dress. She was ethereal and seemed out of place smiling brightly at her. Was she real? She looked familiar. *Where had she seen her?* Her attention became diverted by the forward-moving crowd. When she looked back, the woman had vanished. *Weird.*

Comfortably seated next to the Countess, she began to relax and read the printed menu. It was very British just as Sofia had said it would be. The Countess was delighted just as she was at Rules. She couldn't get enough of these local delicacies, but not so for Gabrielle. In the end, though, it was quite enjoyable. The meal started with an Indian mulligatawny soup, which the Countess explained was shredded chicken in a veggie chicken broth. The fish course was fried sole. The main course was a choice of fowl or a saddle of mutton. They decided to order one of each and share. For dessert, there was a yummy Conservative pudding which was a steamed pudding made with sponge cake, ratafias (a liquor flavored with almonds), macaroons, rum, cream, and preserved cherries.

As she ate, Gabrielle couldn't help but notice an exquisite-looking gentleman in an elegantly designed tuxedo sitting between Sofia and her husband. Sofia was quite the flirt giving him her complete attention and laughing boisterously at all the comments he made. Her husband watched in silence and annoyance. The man must have sensed Gabrielle's gazing at him because he paused and looked directly at her. She flushed from embarrassment but also felt a sudden quickening of her pulse accompanied by a flash of sensuous excitement. She immediately diverted her eyes but covertly stole glances at him all through dinner. A few times when they accidentally engaged, she would look away quickly. Cat and mouse through every course. By the time the pudding was served, she was in a high fever of arousal.

Like most flirtatious women, Sofia was aware of not having complete control over her quarry. She followed his gaze and saw that it was Tasa's ward or whoever she was, that had grabbed his eye repeatedly. She made up her mind at once. *Why not?* If she made the introduction and it worked out, he would be most grateful and who knew where that could lead...for *her*. Everything that motivated Sofia had an angle for her benefit. She startled Gabrielle who was taking a sip of coffee by suddenly standing behind her chair and announcing quite loudly for the entire room to stop and take notice.

"Hello, darling, I'd like to introduce you, Gabrielle, to my close friend who we fondly call, Professor, because...well, he actually is one at Cambridge in some sort of advanced science area. Handsome and brilliant, a perfect package, don't you think?"

The Professor laughed heartily, "Sofia is quite the exaggerator," he said in a deep melodic voice with not even a hint of a British accent keeping his eyes fixed on Gabrielle whose heart fluttered and pulse quickened at his closeness and intense eye contact. She also closely scrutinized *him*. His amazing dark brown eyes were framed by thick long lashes and he had dimples that peeked out when he smiled accentuating the sexy cleft in his chin. She longed to run her hands through his full head of long, thick, messy, curly hair as one would expect for a professor. *A real stunner and surely not interested in me,* thought Gabrielle.

"Perhaps you might take Miss Gabrielle for a tour of this place?" Sofia said breaking in on Gabrielle's mind game and jerking her back to the moment. "I don't believe there are any properties quite like this in America. It's quite old compared to properties there. It's been here since the 1800s and in my family for that long as well. I'm quite proud of it and I believe it deserves all the notoriety it garners. It has been the choice for many locations in movies and TV shows. You might even have seen some. So be a dear, my dear Professor, and show it to her. I suggest you start in the media room downstairs."

With that Sofia sashayed away and the Countess gave a slight nod of approval. She had zeroed in on the give and take between Gabrielle and this handsome professor and was tickled to be part of the intrigue. The Professor helped Gabrielle pull her chair back and they made their way in silence to the elevator where they both began speaking at once, causing them to laugh. Before they could begin a conversation, the elevator arrived and they went inside and it got awkward again. The elevator took them down to the media room and gym where there were also staff accommodations, laundry, and direct access from the house to the underground car park. They looked around still in silence and then as they approached the media room, he grabbed her arm and spun her around, and kissed her passionately.

"I can't believe it's you," he said. "My darling."

Gabrielle started to speak slightly confused but he was kissing her again and they tripped their way onto a sofa and got lost in their fervent passion that could not be contained. Gabrielle felt with that first kiss that she somehow knew this person, had known him, would like to know him better. Both of them were surprised at how caught up they were in this tidal wave of sexual arousal. They couldn't stop. Did not want to stop and so...they did not stop.

Afterwards they got up and put back the clothes they had thrown off and then fell into each other's arms again kissing passionately. They heard the elevator and broke away. Gabrielle combed through her hair with her fingers and tried to look nonchalant. It was a young couple being taken around by one of the staff. They were invited to tag along grateful for the distraction or they would have stayed down there for the rest of the evening and aroused the interest of the partygoers upstairs. They touched hands through the tour of six bedrooms, with the master suite having its own floor, they gazed at each when the group looked at the garden and city views from the balconies, and they snuck a kiss as they hung back when the numerous bathrooms attached to each bedroom were looked at.

The tour ended and they waited for the elevator standing so close they could feel each other's heart beating. Then the elevator door opened and an elegant couple emerged, apparently houseguests on their way to their bedroom.

"Well, hello, Professor Barnstable," said the woman. "How nice to see you this evening. Darling, this is doctor, or shall I say, Doctor Professor Beauregard Barnstable, he was Jenny's first-year Biology professor when she was at Cambridge. So nice to see you. Jennifer Wimple was her name."

"Ah yes, I remember her. Quite a good student, excellent in fact. I hope she is well."

"Quite well, thank you. Dropped out, married the son of a Duke, and is the mother of a two-year-old. And we just got the news she's expecting another 'round the new year."

"How nice. Tell her, I said hello, and that I wish her much continued happiness."

"Yes, certainly. Oh, my, I've just realized, we've gotten off at the wrong floor, darling. Our bedroom is one flight down. Shall we?" she said indicating getting back into the elevator.

The professor turned to Gabrielle...but she was gone, vanished, leaving him quite perplexed. Feeling as though she had just gotten hit over the head with a sledgehammer, all the color drained from Gabrielle's face and her veins began to throb in her temples when she heard his name. Beauregard Barnstable! He's Beau Barnstable! Beau Barnstable, oh...my...god...my brother! Incest! One of the biggest taboos! Luckily, she spotted the door to the staircase next to the elevator shaft and slipped silently away and made for it, while everyone was busy chatting away. As soon as the door closed gently behind her, she ran all the way down from the top floor to the dining room floor, ran over to the Countess, and told her in her frenzied manner they must leave at once. The Countess was shocked but seeing how distressed Gabrielle was grabbed her purse. The Rolls was parked outside waiting for them and they dashed away without so much as a "thank you for dinner" to Cousin Sofia.

As far as Gabrielle was concerned the trip was over. Unfortunately for her, there were several days before their scheduled flight. The Countess had her appointment with her solicitors and then a day trip planned for the two of them to visit Windsor with a private guide. Gabrielle refused to talk about what happened and, of course, the Countess imagined the worst.

"Did he assault you? Are you hurt? Shall I call the police? Was there someone else upstairs that frightened you? Please, dearest, tell me. I can help with this whatever it is."

The barrage of questions was relentless but still, Gabrielle would not speak. The Countess went to her meeting the next day and Gabrielle sent a note to Captain Davis at the Howard Hotel canceling their date for tea. She ran to the pharmacy and bought the morning-after pill and that calmed her down...somewhat. How could she have gotten herself into this predicament? Being intimate...say it! *Having sex with my own brother!* It was revolting. Just the thought of it was revolting. Nauseating! But how was she supposed to know? How could she even imagine they would meet? Was she so attracted to him because she saw something that reminded her of her father? Ugh!!! YUCK!!! She didn't even know what her father looked like in person so how could she see her father in him? But that would have been even *more* creepy.

Her behavior was debased. There were many more words to describe her loathsomeness. She ticked through them. Vile, putrid, sinful. And on and on. She remained isolated in her torment and horrified all day. Oh, how she wished she could go home immediately. She could never think about this trip without wanting to throw up. Could she ever tell the Countess about this? Never! It was beyond awful.

She went back on the London Eye to distract herself from the endless images of them together. She rode alone in the pod, a happy accident. She paced the pod in turmoil and grabbed the view from different aspects while she tried to quiet her mind. At one level, as the wheel slowly spun around, it would stop and she could watch people get on and off at the bottom. As she watched, she couldn't believe her eyes. There was that woman with the red hair exiting a pod. She looked up right at her, smiling, knowing exactly where Gabrielle's pod was, and nodded her head as if to say, "Everything's ok, not to worry." Gabrielle turned her back on her until the pod began to move again.

She couldn't resist another look so she turned around and just like yesterday, the woman vanished nowhere to be seen not even walking away.

After the ride, she went back to the hotel in a somber mood. Disturbed by the woman magically appearing, disturbed by her abhorrent behavior with that stranger who wasn't a stranger. Just basically continuing to be in a disturbed frame of mind. She withdrew into herself, withdrew from the world to try shoving down her feelings of shame. The remainder of the trip would have to be endured, so she became wooden in order to cope. To stop her mind from thinking. Dropping out emotionally and putting herself on autopilot for the immediate sightseeing plans. She would somehow get through this.

It was a pleasant enough drive to Windsor, although without conversation it was rather somber. They had tickets to tour the world's oldest and quite grand medieval castle that was designed as a fortification as well as a palace. It still is used today as a residence. Then on to lunch in the picturesque town. The Countess had stopped pressing Gabrielle about what was so troubling realizing it would only make things worse. She knew Gabrielle would tell her what happened in due time. Of that, she was certain. Her sixth sense about people and her life experiences gave her patience. After lunch, which Gabrielle hardly touched, they continued on to Surrey where the Countess had such fond memories of her childhood. Her home was still there and the surroundings looked the same. As the Countess stood there reminiscing about those sweet and idyllic days, tears welled up, filling her eyes, and flowing over in a steady path down her cheeks that had to be wiped away with a tissue.

With that, Gabrielle came back from the dead, waking up from her imposed numb state to give her dear friend a supportive hug. She still did not want to tell her what happened but she began to speak, chatting away about nothing in particular. In truth, Gabrielle herself was tired of her imposed silence and relieved to give it up. Not her normal state of being. Coming back to life, and keeping thoughts of the encounter, as she called it, at bay, she became animated about their plans for the next day. It was to be a shopping and eating day at Harrods. Having the Rolls take them everywhere and wait for them continued to be an amazing perk of their hotel. And there it was the next day to cart them around in style once more.

Gabrielle was taken aback by the large, impressive building housing the store. Its facade featured Egyptian designs, terra cotta tiles, Art Nouveau windows and a baroque-style dome. Inside, the food halls were over the top in their abundance and design. It looked like Christmas with all the colors of the fruit and chocolate trays displayed in glass-enclosed shelves under the elaborately and colorfully painted yellow dome lighting. Gabrielle got her appetite back with her elevated mood and they ate a tasty lunch from an enormous salad bar that also had assorted cheeses, a variety of breads, and sweets. Afterwards, they browsed the high-priced couture clothing and shoes. Both of them enjoyed browsing the fancy soaps, bath oils, and lipsticks that needed no dressing rooms. They shopped unhurriedly for hours. Not wanting to go empty-handed they settled on several of the soaps as well as teas and jams made exclusively for Harrods. The Countess wanted to show Gabrielle the memorial for Princess Diana but they were told it no longer existed because Harrods had been sold. Oh well.

Continuing their eating extravaganza, they had Afternoon Tea at Claridge's, one of the best teas in London. It was served in the hotel's elegant 1930s' inspired art deco Thierry Despont's foyer. The delicious items of finger sandwiches, quintessential scones, clotted cream, and petit fours were beautifully displayed in a specially designed stand for the hotel and then placed on their signature blue-striped fine bone china. They listened to an exquisitely played piano concerto by a student at one of the numerous music schools around London and left a generous tip. The tea was perfect. Couldn't be more perfect. Gabrielle mused that perhaps they should serve afternoon tea at the inn on weekends. The Countess thought that was a grand idea and added, "Too bad Irina won't be there. She could make a fantastic tea when she was in the mood." The Countess surmised that Gabrielle had not gone to see Mark Davis because that was the day she was the most distraught. So, she never brought up tea at the Howard Hotel. No sense in getting Gabrielle all riled up when she had finally calmed down a bit. *All in due time*.

The next day was reserved for a final drive around London and all the popular tourist sites. One last look at Parliament, Big Ben, Westminster Abbey, Buckingham Palace, and the West End theater district. Afterwards, they had the Rolls drop them off at Trafalgar Square where they decided to walk to Covent Garden. They strolled around the shops in the glass-enclosed market, grabbed a pork pie at a vendor, and then visited Petersham Nurseries the Shop at Covent Garden where they found knick-knacks and doodads and tins of loose teas for the inn.

A very pleasant end to a trip with mixed reviews from Gabrielle. She still hadn't mentioned a word about her upset and it still made her overwhelmingly uncomfortable to think about. A sense of humiliation would creep up on her when she least expected it and jolt through her body. Throbbing, throbbing pulse, blood pounding in her head, quickened heart rate. She would stop and take deep breaths to calm herself. She did it covertly so the Countess wouldn't see her distress. *Everything will be alright once I get home and start running the inn. Thank goodness he lives here!*

When they got back to the hotel, the Concierge called them over and handed a note to Gabrielle. Her stomach clenched but then she saw it was from Captain Davis. He was waiting for her in the lounge. Would she please join him for a drink? She relayed that information to the Countess, who gave a smile and a wink. And then told her pointedly that she was glad that after Gabrielle abruptly canceled their date "for unknown reasons to me," he was not completely put off. The Countess would supervise the packing and for Gabrielle to take her time. She reminded her that the flight was at 10:00 am and they would have to leave the hotel by 7:00 am. Gabrielle nodded, "Just having a drink," she said slightly annoyed at the implication and then realized that the Countess was innocent to Gabrielle's feeling like a perverted harlot. "I'll be up soon," she said sweetly recovering from her mistake.

She saw him immediately because he stood up from the bar where he was waiting with a clear view of the entrance. As soon as he spotted her, he quickly finished his drink and walked over. He looked great. Being casually dressed suited him as much as his uniform. A light-blue crew neck cotton tee over blue jeans showed off his fit chest and small waist. He looked sophisticated and elegant as he padded over in soft expensive loafers. A bit sorry she didn't meet him the other day, she air-kissed him "hello" in the European fashion but his landed on both cheeks. He took her arm and led her over to a secluded booth, called the waiter over, and ordered a split of Champagne.

"I'm so glad to see you. So glad you decided to meet me this time," he said.

"I'm sorry I stood you up, but I had an unexpected meeting, as I said in my note.

"I don't mean to make you uncomfortable. Naturally, I was disappointed. But it turned out that I bumped into some old friends and we wound up partaking of the Howard's wonderful tea together. I hope you've had one here at the hotel. Quite good if I remember."

"Yes, it's wonderful. And we also had the one at Claridge's."

"Oh good. Glad you didn't miss out on a quintessentially British experience."

They continued to make silly small talk. She recounted her sight-seeing adventures. He spoke of dealing with the necessities of life after being away for several months. Both felt the excitement of being together. A validation of their attraction. On a superficial level, she thought him quite appealing, and he thought her beautiful. But there was something more, something unexplained. She admonished herself for being so easy during the "encounter," not being used to so much attention from men and not knowing how to handle it. He felt sexually charged around her and was turned on by her innocent feminine wiles. The way she pursed her lips when taking a sip of water, her cute self-conscious laugh. Her manicured fingers when she tossed her hair out of her eyes.

The Champagne arrived and was poured. He toasted to their meeting again. He asked her to tell him which was her favorite tourist experience. She started going through the list, naming the ride on the Eye as at the top. He got up, came around, and sat next to her. He moved closer and discreetly snuggled her neck. Rubbed her shoulder.

"It's sad for me that you're leaving tomorrow," he said. "Would it be okay if when I came to New York, we could meet?"

"Yes, of course," she said. "Or if you had enough time in port, maybe you could come to Vermont?"

A meeting in a strange bar late in the day that would probably be their last but they pretended they would meet again. They planned and schemed to see each other again. She gave him her phone number. They would keep a connection, through FaceTime. He paid for their drinks and then they got up to head for the elevator but, instead, he surprised her and led her to a quiet salon off the ballroom corridor. There he grabbed her and kissed her passionately for several minutes. They became very heated but had to stop when they heard someone enter at the far side of the room.

"I must go," said Gabrielle.

"Yes, I'll walk you to the elevator."

When she got in the elevator, she finally asked him, "How did you find me?"

"It was easy," he said. I just asked the staff that handles the luggage for the ship. It was labeled with the name of your hotel for disembarkation." They both laughed. "Have a safe trip home," he said. And then the door closed. Once in their room she saw the bags were packed at the door with an outfit for the trip home the only item hanging in the closet. The Countess was eating a light snack and watching the news.

"He seems like such a nice man," she said. "Did all go well?" she asked cautiously.

"Of course. I'm sorry now I canceled the date. He says he'd like to keep in touch when he comes to New York. We'll see." With that they both put on their nightclothes and went to bed.

As Gabrielle lay there, her mind wandered to the unspeakable. She was in this situation because she didn't have the tools. Never having been a girl who was in demand by men, she had no skills. Wasn't prepared to handle the attention. She was like a naive child. Flattered and turned on by the attention. Couldn't resist the attention. But also, these men were quite handsome. She had never attracted such handsome men. Had she known the name of the man who had taken her upstairs at Sofia's she would have never gone with him. Never, never, never. But she didn't ask him his name. Had sex with a man *without even knowing his name! How could she?* And Mark, acting like a hussy with him in a public place. This wanton behavior must stop. It *would* stop. She was determined to become the *Gabby*, she used to be. Well, maybe she'd keep her new hairstyle, her clothes, her name. But she would get smarter. Not be such an easy target. Vermont would be a safe haven. A place of business. Not monkey business. Eventually, she fell asleep.

Chapter Eleven

The Group Is Now Complete

Journal Entry:
Home! Finally, home!
Safe and sound...perhaps not.

"More tea, Countess?" asked Gabrielle as they had a light breakfast of tea, coffee, fresh fruit in season, and assorted rolls.

"Yes, thank you, darling. I've been thinking. Why not call me Tasa, like my close family does since you are like family to me."

They toasted with their drink mugs and that was that. The Countess and Gabby had started on this adventure but Tasa and Gabrielle would be who returned. All as it should be except for all the others in their group. No one else would give up the formality of calling her the Countess. So, it became very special for Gabrielle and a symbol their closeness to call her Tasa. After breakfast they took their last trip in the Rolls to get to the airport. The loss of this splendor made them fantasize about getting one for the inn to transport guests around town. It would be quite the perk for a rural Vermont inn, they laughed. But where would they get it serviced? And so, the idea was dropped before it even took hold. Fun while it lasted. Once seated on the plane they decided to have Bloody Marys and became quite sleepy. They woke up at JFK, grabbed a beat-up taxi that made them miss the Rolls even more, and went to Tasa's New York apartment to stay the night.

At first, Tasa thought a burglar was in the apartment because there was noise coming from within when she opened the door. "Who's there," said Tasa in a stern voice hoping to frighten the intruder. But then a delightful surprise.

"Irina!" she and Gabrielle shouted at once.

Well, just as the Countess had predicted after the first blush of excitement wore off and reality set in, Irina found herself living in an intolerable situation. None of his people spoke English. Living with his mother was most unpleasant and afforded them no privacy. She also noticed quirks about his personal hygiene and personality that began to bother her immensely. Realizing, she no longer found him attractive and didn't enjoy sleeping with him, she packed a bag, hopped on a plane, and came here. She had been there for two days and was quite perturbed. Why do you have suitcases? Why wasn't the Countess living in this apartment? She had looked around and all her clothes were gone, no food in the refrigerator or pantry. She began to be frightened. What to do next? Go back to London? Stay? So, needless to say, she was very happy and relieved when they had shown up.

"Oh, Countess, seeing you is such a relief, such a relief," she kept repeating.

"Well having you here is such a wonderful and thrilling surprise as well! Let's have a nice pot of tea and I'll tell you all that's happened," said the Countess.

Then Gabrielle and Tasa suddenly shouted together while laughing, "Afternoon tea at the inn."

They explained everything about the B&B to Irina. The bottom line was of course she would come. She would oversee the kitchen and the licensed chef they would hire. And yes, Irina enthusiastically agreed that offering a typical British afternoon tea on weekends was a great idea! They chatted all day and caught up on all the news while scheming and planning and ordered a pizza to be delivered and a car to drive them up the next day. Irina pulled Gabrielle aside and said the change in her appearance was quite dramatic and very positive. She now looked like a sophisticated New York model. Irina would also refer to her as Gabrielle as the Countess had done. She suggested that the name change might have been the Countess's idea and Gabrielle nodded in agreement.

"Your new name for your new look matches perfectly. It quite suits you," she said cheerfully.

As the car made its way to Vermont, Gabrielle's excitement began to grow and also the comfort of being miles away and a life away from London. They had called the Captain and he told them the rehabilitation was nearly finished. Everyone had come through quickly. Ordered fabrics had come early and so the sofas were done. Wallpaper was nearly all installed and the rooms had all been repainted. Gabrielle was on pins and needles to see the results. And finally, they pulled up in the driveway. She gasped. She'd forgotten how big and imposing the place was. This is mine! Irina was impressed as well and said so. And they all walked up the steps to the front porch in a state of reverence. Their new home. Their new life.

And then the ground beneath them shuddered and the house heaved and swayed as a seismic shift passed through the earth and knocked them all down. As soon as the shaking stopped, Gabrielle helped the older ladies up and they staggered toward the front door. When they opened the door, the Captain ran over to them asking if they were all right. After they assured him everyone was fine, they hugged "hello" and assessed the damage. They were shocked and relieved. There was no damage. Nothing of any consequence. A few chairs had slid from their place, sofa pillows were tossed onto the floor, knickknacks from the fireplace mantel had smashed onto the hearth, and some of the wall art was askew. That was all.

The kitchen also had minimal damage since there weren't many items just lying about or hung on walls. The dishes in the cabinets had not moved and were in perfect shape. Same for the glassware except one glass had knocked open the cabinet door and crashed onto the floor. Probably there would have been more problems if the quake had lasted longer. They were lucky. Lucky indeed.

As we step away from this important moment in time to assess the situation, we can wonder. Are there earthquakes in Vermont? Well, yes but rarely and usually mild. But there wasn't an earthquake at all that day. When they tried to find out about it later, they discovered that the quaking shuddering event had not happened anywhere else. It had been local, very local. The shaking was just at that property, just at that house. Unbeknownst to all of them, they had put themselves in the middle of a fierce battle for the soul of humanity and the ecosystem of the planet. An epic situation to be sure and to be revealed to them in snatches as time went on. It was the beginning of everything changing...for all of them. But right at this moment, this little group was too fragile and naive to be of any significant help.

In time their purpose would be understood. In time, they would come to know that they were handpicked to be there. Although hidden negative forces had tried to shrug them off, they would not be stopped. They had picked themselves up and gone inside. Their first show of strength. Both Gabrielle and Tasa sensed the import of walking into the house after being knocked down by the quaking house. And once inside, they stood straight and wore an expression of fierce ownership. As Gabrielle looked around, she thought to herself, *Whoever you are, you can't stop us*, but as yet did not know why she had had that thought.

After they set their suitcases down in the owner's quarters, they noticed a small study that could easily be made into Irina's bedroom. It was perfect. There was a powder room right next to it that could be expanded to fit a shower. They would hire workmen at once to get started and furnish it tomorrow. Tonight, Irina would share the Countess's bed. Then they showed Irina around. She was amazed at the majesty of the place. The ambiance was so relaxed and friendly like being in the middle of "a tangle of tree trunks," she kept saying over and over as they looked around the upstairs and kitchen. The paint choices in the bedrooms were perfect. The rooms had a monotone feel so they could be referred to by color, rather than a number, in the future. Much more friendly to refer to the green room, or the blue room, rather than to Room 208, and so on.

All agreed that the rooms were cozy, well-appointed, and quite welcoming. Irina offered to make some tea and coffee so they could all catch up with their latest news. They sat in the breakfast room off the kitchen.

"As you can see, the living room sofas are done and the chairs will be finished next week," said the Captain. "You saw that all bedrooms have been painted and the new linens look great, so we are right on target to announce our opening for Labor Day weekend. Mrs. Jones has identified a chef. You can set up an interview once you're settled in."

"Thank you, Captain, for doing such a good job, "said Gabrielle. Irina is now an official member of this company. She will oversee the kitchen and provide some specialties like British afternoon tea on the weekends. Also, Russian specialties, recipes that have been passed down for generations if we decide to open for dinner or she'll cook just for us. She used to be Tasa's cook and housekeeper and companion and now that she's back, it's perfect that she handles that for us. We're very excited to have her. By the way, we can all refer to the Countess as Tasa, her childhood nickname for Anastasia, if you like. More familial."

The Captain nodded his approval of bringing Irina on but wasn't sure about calling the Countess Tasa. "To me," he said, "she will ways hold that regal title of Countess." He added that he loved living up there and keeping the grounds. He thought he might stay on and continue doing that and he would continue to stay at Mrs. Jones's and keep her grounds as well. Gabrielle thought that was a wonderful idea.

"You should get rid of your New York City apartment and move up here permanently. What fun that we are all here together!" said Gabrielle. Then they got to the strangeness of the quake greeting them as soon as they tried to enter the house. Gabrielle checked the internet for information on earthquakes in Vermont. They were perplexed to learn that it was very rare. Then she checked for reports of the magnitude and discovered there were none. It was as if the earthquake happened only right here at *this* house. When the Countess finished her tea, she took her cup and studied the tea leaves.

"Well, this explains it," she said after studying her cup for a few minutes. "That was no earthquake. That was a warning. To us. It seems this house is enchanted."

"Mrs. Jones told me that magical things used to happen here years ago," said Gabrielle, "but they suddenly stopped. It drew people to stay here and when it stopped the clientele dropped off. It only started to pick up lately when people forgot about the stories of magic and came just for the usual reasons. Beautiful scenery and skiing."

"What sorts of things?" asked the Countess. And so, Gabrielle recounted the tales Mrs. Jones had told her of writers getting rid of writer's block, students getting better school grades, and marriages saved.

"That makes sense from what I see here in the tea leaves. Now I know why I was so drawn to come here. I think I've been summoned. Gabrielle was the instrument to get us all here. We will help the flow of energy once again. Right now, there's a tug-of-war between dark forces and light. Between destruction and redemption. We are at the cusp of some monumental change in our planet as well. Some catastrophes that we might be able to stop or mitigate.

"This disturbs me and I must meditate on it to understand it fully. I will figure it out and our path forward. We are strong in our convictions and we will persevere. We are meant to be an army of sorts. Of that at least, I am sure. But let's not focus on that right now. Let's settle in and unpack. Our greater purpose can wait for now. One thing I know for sure is that we belong here and we are meant to help with some grand plan."

Gabrielle was thrown by this information. Summoned? This stayed on her mind all night. The Captain went into town and picked up Chinese food for dinner. They sat on the porch in the rocking chairs munching off paper plates and marveling at the view. How lovely it was up here they voiced individually as they ate. But all wondered if was there something ominous going on? Hidden from view? Then Gabrielle remembered the woman with the flaming red hair and she almost jumped out of her chair. The first time she had seen her was in the house! As she sat there, a creeping anxiety began to form a knot in her stomach. Did she really want to be involved in this strangeness? That didn't seem to be the plan, at first. It was a business. An inn. A livelihood. A safe haven. A refuge from her lonely life, a refuge from her dark unspeakable behavior.

This negativity was about to swamp her. Take over her spirit. She forced herself out of these thoughts and looked around. This place captured her heart. The not-too-distant mountains looming majestically framing the landscape. The meadow of dewy grass with wildflowers sprinkled here and there added a touch of color peeping out of the sea of green. The shimmering lake reflected the sunlight glistening off the light chop. Deer off in the distance chewed on the abundant vegetation.

She always trusted the forces of the cosmos. Gave thanks for all her good fortune every day. If she were needed, she would answer that need. She was comforted in this thought, "Tasa will know what to do." And just then in the far-off distance, the figure of the red-haired woman in white appeared among the deer and they gathered around her. Just like they gathered around Gabrielle that first day she had come to this house. She watched mesmerized and felt a kinship accepting the strangeness. *Whatever they need, I'll do.*

"More egg foo young or kung pao chicken, Gabrielle?" asked Irina.

"Maybe a little more chicken," said Gabrielle and after Irina put some on her plate, she turned to continue her observation of the woman in white. But she was gone.

They spent the next days and weeks preparing the inn for its grand re-opening. There was much to do. Putting ads in the paper and creating a web page with pictures showing the remodeling's success. They hired the chef Mrs. Jones had recommended. He was rather young but could prepare a wicked breakfast of brioche French toast and crisp bacon. His name was Peter Lambert and he had grown up in Vermont but went to the Culinary Institute in New York and was hoping to open his own restaurant someday. His elderly mother lived nearby and he was looking after her since his Dad passed last year.

Gabrielle was getting better at noticing when a man looked at her with sexual interest. She felt the spark given off from the young chef when he first arrived for his interview. She tried to send indifference toward him. When Tasa suggested Gabrielle show him the rest of the inn, she made an excuse having learned her lesson in London. So, Irina took him around. After he was hired Irina took him grocery shopping and between the two of them, they put up enough stores for a month with a full house of guests. It was fun to see the giant fridge, freezer, and pantry all stocked up. It felt safe. Cozy.

Filling the role of innkeeper was a learning curve for Gabrielle but Tasa took to it quite easily, probably because she was used to having household staff. Gabrielle followed her lead. They hired housekeepers and groundskeepers to help the Captain and a handyman who could fix electrical problems and plumbing issues and whatever else needed to be repaired. They also got a list of workmen from Mrs. Jones. Harmony prevailed and it seemed the opening would go off without a hitch. Mrs. Jones and the Captain had developed a close relationship and it was lovely to witness. Whenever they gazed at each other it was with such a look of pleasure that observers felt they were intruding. Gabrielle felt happy for them and wistful for herself. But periodically, she still had strong feelings of shame whenever she thought of the BIG MISTAKE. This frame of mind wouldn't disappear and she shunned Mark when he called, lumping him with her shame as she had done before when she canceled tea. No reminders of London were welcome in her new life.

They all fell into a routine and enjoyed the breakfast surprises offered by Peter. One day they decided to try a typical British afternoon tea. It was passable except for the clotted cream, and Peter offered to find a shop nearby that might have something similar. He asked Gabrielle if she would like to accompany him and she was torn between wanting to see the surrounding towns and spending the day with him unprotected. She decided that notion of not being able to take care of herself was silly. She was in charge and could handle anything and she needed...wanted a day out. So, she went.

All in all, it was a most pleasant afternoon. They stopped in Killington, a rather quaint small town. There were no shops that carried anything British, but they decided to stop for a coffee and get to know each other better. Peter grew up in Burlington and loved Vermont. Skiing in winter and sailing on Lake Champlain in summer or taking the ferry over to Essex, NY just for the fun of it. For two years, he went to the University of Vermont and lived at home. Watching cooking shows with his mother, who watched them incessantly, spurred his enthusiasm for becoming a chef. And he had a knack for it. A talent for picking spices to alter recipes for the better and a pleasurable experience. That led him to transfer to the Culinary Institute. After his graduation, he got a job as a sous chef in NYC for two years but missed the outdoor lifestyle that Vermont affords. He worked the past year at a resort in Killington but this B&B seemed perfect for his ambitions. Small and informal with a chance to expand to his own restaurant, a plan on the table for the inn that was conveyed during the interview.

As he spoke, Gabrielle, assessed him. He was adorable. A youthful excitement with wide blue eyes and thick bouncy black hair. Unsophisticated but sincere. A comfort after the assertive men she had met in London. And with that thought her face began to turn red with shame.

"Have I said something to disturb you, you seem to have gone red in the face," he said.

"Oh, no, sorry. I'm feeling a little warm just at the moment," Gabrielle said feeling foolish.

"Let's go then and I'll show you what's on Killington mountain. The ski trails and hiking trails are part of the beautiful Green Mountain range and maybe we can take a Gondola ride to the peak to cool off. I think there's a dairy farm on the way and I can check out some of their cream products."

Peter was a pleasant companion. Visiting the dairy was a great idea. So rustic and down to earth with the bellowing and lowing cows and milking equipment. The scent of cow manure was strong and earthy. A real connection to nature. Simple living. Peter decided he liked the quality of the cream and would find a recipe to prepare it like the clotted cream from Devonshire. Then they drove to the Gondolas and thoroughly enjoyed the ride to the top with vistas of the mountains all around them. The view at the top from a bench outside the ski lodge was spectacular. It was a marvelous day, relaxing and comfortable. Peter was friendly and not pushy about holding her hand or touching her in any way. She liked this young man quite a lot. As they sat there, he said something that startled her

"Do you see the shadow people?" he asked. "I call them that but they're not really shadowy."

"What did you just ask?" Gabrielle was shocked to hear this.

"Various women in long robe-type garments or something looking like that, like Greek goddesses. I see them from the corner of my eye but when I turn to get a better look, they're gone. I had been told that this B&B had a history of unexplained events." He noticed her frown listening to him. "Well, the stories were positive. People flocked here to bask in the good energy. But I also of late have felt a darker energy. A conflict between the two forces."

"It's interesting that you're sensitive to that. We, too, have had a run-in of sorts with the dark energy. It happened as soon as we arrived. We thought we were experiencing an earthquake but it was just the house shaking. It knocked us all down. Tasa, I call the Countess Tasa a family nickname as you've might have noticed, Tasa has seen a premonition of tension between these forces that also has to do with mass changes happening with our planet. We don't know the timeframe, so we are just going along getting the inn ready for occupancy. Perhaps something will show itself, perhaps not. Does this frighten you?"

"No actually, it intrigues me. Adds another dimension to this job as well as another way to understand reality."

I like how this guy thinks. Gabrielle deliberately put her hand in his and he squeezed it in acknowledgment of his pleasure. He looked into her eyes and smiled. They stayed at the peak for a little while enjoying the view and grabbing a coffee in the lodge at the top. They strolled the trails for a bit and then took the Gondola back down. He told her he would love to take her to Burlington for a day before the inn opened. They both agreed that after the opening a day off would be rare. On the drive back they both silently enjoyed the scenery and Gabrielle thought about the shadow people, as he referred to them. She hoped they wouldn't ruin all her plans. She must talk to Tasa about anything else she might have discovered in her meditations.

After they got back Peter and Irina handled dinner and they invited Mrs. Jones and the Captain. Dinner was a delicious combination of ground beef with tomato sauce and an abundance of spices, cut up fresh mushrooms, and served over pasta. Red wine was abundant and everyone got slightly tipsy.

"Peter's seen them," Gabrielle blurted out.

"Who?" asked Tasa.

"He calls them the shadow people. All of them women. They dress like Greek goddesses. Right, Peter?"

He nods.

"I haven't told you, Tasa, that one of them followed us to London. Or I should say, me. I saw her the very first day I came to look at this place with Mrs. Jones. She appeared in the reception room as soon as we got the door to open. The door was stuck and had given me trouble at first. Then it flew open like it was being pulled from the inside and there she was red flaming hair and all, but Mrs. Jones didn't seem to see her. And in a flash, she was gone. She also gave me quite a fright that first night we stayed here after the storm. She appeared in the bathroom mirror when I used the bathroom in the middle of the night."

"What do you mean she was in London?"

"She appeared at your cousin's dinner party and then the next day when I went alone to the Eye."

"How bizarre," exclaimed Tasa.

Everyone murmured in agreement.

"I've only seen one but Peter has seen quite a few. What do you make of it, Tasa?" asked Gabrielle.

"It's time to look at the tea leaves once again," she said.

And after they finished dinner, Irina steeped some tea and served a fabulous peach pie that she had made that afternoon. *Having meals like this every day is not too shabby but I must start exercising!* thought Gabrielle. They all enjoyed dessert before Tasa took her cup and tried to read the future. She studied the leaves for quite a while.

"What I see disturbs me." Everyone got very quiet and appeared concerned. "There are going to be climate changes of epic proportions sooner than later. This inn will play a role but I'm not exactly sure how. We will have the help of these 'shadow people' as Peter refers to them but we first must rid ourselves of the dark forces that are trying to take hold and prevent our mitigation of this catastrophe for the planet. Since we don't know the timeframe of all this, I see us opening the inn on schedule. Getting more adept at handling the running of this place, so when we are needed, we are a smooth-running operation. All we can do for now is move forward, be diligent, and expect more unusual weather episodes. We are safe here, perhaps even protected."

"Well, that doesn't add much more to what you read before, and it still alarms me," said Gabrielle.

"It's good if the tea leaves reveal the same story as before. That gives it validity," said Irina.

"Climate change has been buzzed about for years. I always felt safe here from rising sea levels," said Mrs. Jones.

"I think you've just hit on why this place is safe, higher altitude protects us from rising seas and rising temperatures," said the Countess.

They decided to clean up and call it a night. Peter went back to his apartment and the Captain and Mrs. Jones went back to their inn.

The next few weeks went smoothly. The reopening weekend was soon and the advertisements announcing it went out. The phone starting ringing with reservation requests. And they were full in a few days. Everyone was excited and nervous. Peter and Gabrielle spent time together going to movies and to the Paramount, the local community theater in Rutland, where they enjoyed a production of *Man of la Mancha*. Peter learned how to create a perfect clotted cream that equaled that of Devonshire and they enjoyed a typically British afternoon tea prepared by him and Irina replete with scones, assorted jams from Harrods and Petersham Nurseries, finger sandwiches, and petit fours bought at a Rutland bakery.

All agreed it could match the tea at the Savoy in London. They were enjoying one last quiet dinner before the first guest was to arrive the day after next. Mrs. Jones's inn was already open and had come over with the Captain for dessert. After the tea and coffee were poured there came a knock at the front door and then the bell rang. All were startled at that most unusual occurrence. Why it was Mr. Whitehead. How strange. Gabrielle jumped up saying that she was thinking about showing him what they'd done to the place and was sorry she hadn't invited him sooner.

"Please join us for some dessert," she said as she walked into the dining room with him.

"May I speak to Miss Gabby Bernstein," he said rather confused.

"Oh, Mr. Whitehead it's me, Gabrielle. I've changed my hair."

He paused with a stunned look and then realized his mistake. "So sorry not to have recognized you, Ms. Bernstein. You've had quite a transformation. But I will say, and I hope you take it the right way, a change for the better, my dear. And I see, you've freshened up this place quite nicely. Charming, lovely, and very friendly." *Just like this gorgeous young woman*, he thought.

"Well, please join us for coffee and dessert." And everyone murmured their approval.

"I have some important information. Perhaps, first, we should go somewhere more private."

"No, just please sit down," and she pulled out a chair. "Whatever you have to say is perfectly alright to say here. Peter, will you please pour Mr. Whitehead some coffee, and Irina please serve him a piece of this wonderful German chocolate cake."

Whitehead sat down and sipped his coffee slowly and ate slowly. What he had to tell her would not go over well now that he'd seen how much work went to rehabilitating this place. *She must have spent a good deal of that cash*, he thought. He delayed the news for as long as he could. Everyone had stopped speaking and was looking at him with anticipation. He must tell them all…and *now*!

With obvious dread, he said, "Well it seems there's been a slight mix-up. We never received the paperwork forfeiting Mr. Barnstable's interest in his inheritance from his attorneys. And it seems now he has changed his mind."

"What?" said Gabrielle aghast. "Well, if it's the money, I have some left we could give him."

"No, it's not the money. He wants to activate his partnership."

"But…he lives in England!" Gabrielle almost shouted quite disturbed. Nobody knew the half of it! Her stomach clenched. This is a nightmare. Her sick behavior will be exposed!

"Well, apparently, he suddenly decided to give up his professorship at Cambridge and move back to the states. He's already in New York and will be here tomorrow for a meeting."

Gabrielle started to shout, "No! This can't be! I hate him! I know he's my half-brother and my only living relative. But he is the embodiment of my father's unfaithfulness to my mother when he was still married to her and I was already born. He was carrying on with this Barnstable woman when he already had a family, *me*, and broke my mother's heart and destroyed her very essence. Because of this relationship, I never had a normal childhood. He destroyed any chance that I would have a caring, nurturing mother. And my father never came back, never came to see me. Despicable. Abandoning me to be with his other family. It hurts so much just to think of it. Beau Barnstable and his mother got all my father's love and care. I will hate him until my dying day. If he insists, I will just walk away and go back to New York. I refuse to be his partner."

"Wait, you don't..." said Whitehead when the bell rang again.

"Who's that now?" asked Gabrielle. "I'm not in the mood. Much too upset," she said nearly crying.

The Captain got up to answer the door. There were raised voices at the door and then they burst into the breakfast room.

"Oh. My. God!" shouted Gabrielle and ran from the room.

The Countess stood up recognizing Beau from her cousin's dinner in London.

"Mr. Whitehead, please ask this gentleman to leave. He frightened Gabrielle in London and ruined the last part of our trip. I believe he attacked her. If he doesn't leave, I will be forced to call the police. We might press charges anyway. Now everyone please excuse me, I must comfort Gabrielle." And she and Irina left the room.

The Captain and Peter walked over and menacingly stood in front of Beau and Mr. Whitehead then grabbed his arm, "C'mon, we best leave," he said and they both left together. The others cleared the table and left soon after.

Chapter Twelve

Beau

The story of Beau was simple. He was the devoted son of a single mom and lived out his childhood at this B&B. Independent and curious like most normal boys, he also had a flair for the romantic pretending to be the captain of a pirate ship, or a wilderness explorer when he was deep in the woods. He was a solitary child, a trait that most of this group shared making them perfect choices to form new strong bonds between each other without any extraneous loyalties. Charming, sweet, and brave with a love of the natural world, Beau made a perfect leader to this group. A glimpse of Beau's life reveals his character.

"Beau, Beau, come inside, Beau," his mother called out to him while he played in the yard. "I'd like you to meet someone."

And that's how life as he knew it ended and not for the better. He tossed the jar containing a butterfly onto the lawn and it immediately escaped flying high into the sky before landing on a far-away bush. Shrugging his small shoulders, he went inside grudgingly. Another one of her boyfriend's stood in the reception area of his mother's B&B and their home. Even though he was only 16 years old, he knew his mother had horrible taste in men. She always managed to pick losers, gold diggers, and men who had no desire to be monogamous, like his dad. Or maybe it was his mother who had no idea how to be in a relationship. Either way, the progression of relationships was always the same. After a few months, sometimes weeks, never years, his mother was left alone and crying or screaming in a rage and kicking the guy out throwing his clothes all over the lawn.

He never knew or even met his biological father who had left before he was born, never came around, and then was killed in a motorcycle crash. At first, the holidays were hard for his mother without a male companion, but then she got used to it. Beau thought it was better when it was just the two of them and no new boyfriend. He was the happiest then. It had been that way for about a year now, but he knew it wouldn't last. Not with his mother's tendency for bringing men into her...their lives. She was one of those women that couldn't be without a man and that trait bugged him. It was always peaceful when it was just the two of them and he didn't understand why she always had to introduce chaos.

He was sick of the routine, so he wasn't interested in meeting this new boyfriend and kept his head down and grunted when his mother made the introductions. His name was Philip Bernstein from New York City but originally French Canadian from Quebec. What was different about him was that he would work at the inn. Help out with various chores. Check-in people and carry luggage, that sort of thing. *LIVE THERE WITH THEM!* his mother said and she looked happy as she always did... at first.

"Nice to meet you," Beau mumbled before he ran back outside.

It was also very different at the inn when it was just the two of them and the guests. But most importantly, the special women in flowing white gowns who appeared in the shadows or peeked out from the corner of your eyes came more often. When things went bad with a boyfriend and his mother was depressed or when he was just alone with his mother, the women whispered to him and brought pretty insects, like that pretty butterfly today. They also sang beautiful melodies when he was down by the lake alone and out of earshot. The sounds brought the deer and he glowed in their nuzzling as they crowded around him feeding on the lush grass and wildflowers. Things changed when Philip Bernstein entered their lives.

The special women appeared less and less. A huntsman's presence started coming around bringing a negative force. The magical happenings at the inn changed as well and it was magical no longer. The good events it brought to guests staying there stopped happening. Pretty soon all the special women and even the Huntsman stopped appearing. It made Beau sad. Over time the clientele started to return not expecting magical events because the tales of these special events stopped being spread around, and people just forgot. It became another beautiful B&B in a beautiful Vermont setting for skiing and fall foliage. No real harm done.

Then Philip Bernstein and his mother decided to marry. Their wedding day was a terrible day of bad weather. An omen. The thunder and lightning were fierce, felling trees and knocking out electricity. Attended by very few people from town and those who worked at the inn, it was a somber affair with the storm's rumblings replacing any music since there was no power. The candlelit reception had atmosphere but it was creepy. The few guests quietly ate the finger food and cake and left in silence soon after.

Phil and his mother made the best of it gorging on the left-over cake and sandwiches put out for 25 guests when only eight showed up. The question that Beau kept wondering about was why Phil attracted such negativity. He was an ordinary enough person. The only thing he knew that was pretty awful was that he had left a wife and young daughter. Just up and left. Like his father. But other than that, he didn't yell and he was a big help around the inn. So why were the goddesses opposed to him? He knew that because they told him so. What was it? Maybe his lack of loyalty to his own family was enough.

Beau grew up as a normal kid save for his ability to see other realities like the beautiful goddesses and his detailed memory of his past life during the Reign of Terror in Paris. He remembered fighting in the revolution as a patriot but then being betrayed and arrested for treason. He escaped with his life and managed to cross the channel into England where he spent the rest of his short life as a French teacher and writer of love stories. No one knew of these visions and memories, Beau believing it quite normal to have them and not worth talking about. His mother only became concerned when he fell from a tree hitting his head and began speaking fluent French.

This strangeness lasted a few days when Beau recovered and spoke English again as if nothing had happened and his mother never talked about it not wanting to give it any credence. As he matured, he developed a total dislike for anything French, especially and including Phil Bernstein with his Quebec connection. For his undergraduate studies, he went to Boston and for graduate school, he went to Stanford. He chose to settle at Cambridge and joined the faculty returning to his past life country of refuge. More importantly, he hated being home and went as far away as he could. He didn't trust Phil. Felt the Huntsman's dark energy was taking over Phil's soul. He warned his mother, who just laughed. He knew he must leave Vermont and he seldom came back. Eventually, he stayed away for good even when his mother died under mysterious circumstances of being locked in their walk-in freezer. The cover story even to him was a heart attack. No use scaring off potential business.

The goddesses during that period had gone away having been summoned back to wherever they came from. At the goddesses' retreat to their sacred place, they learned how important Philip

Bernstein was to their future strategy and that his presence was ordained by powers greater than they. There was a silver lining with Phil for all of them including Beau. So that even though Phil would attract the Huntsman because of his amoral nature, selfishness, and desertion of a young child, it was a necessity. They all agreed and came back to join forces and fight the Huntsman's negative energy. But, alas, they could not save Abigail Barnstable from his evil plan. But unbeknownst to everyone, it was as it should be. Good always concurs evil...eventually.

While at Cambridge, Beau decided to take a trip to Paris to see for himself whether his memories were real and his hatred justified. As soon as he landed in Paris, he was overtaken as if in a spell that propelled him to places and buildings from his past life. He was able to understand what everyone was saying although he was not able at first to speak the language. Suddenly in a shop when asking to buy a croissant, he spoke fluent French. Just blurted it out. Quelle surprise! He walked streets he realized he had walked before; ate food he had eaten before and was overcome with sadness for the loss of Gabrielle. The woman he cherished, the love of his life. She had been by his side always until the very end when they were supposed to meet. His abiding love for Gabrielle was deep and pure but, alas, she was not there in the chaos of his escape from prison and rush to leave the country. He was never to see her again. Never to know what happened to her. Now he understood his hatred. Although he mourned his past life and the loss of Gabrielle and all the accompanying sorrows during those dangerous times, he fell in love with modern-day Paris. Walking the narrow streets of the Left Bank. Strolling the Champs-Élysées, he felt alive, even though there had been so much death in his awakening memories. The self-inflicted banishment to England brought sadness to his soul. Paris owned his heart. Paris defined him. But always back to the loss of Gabrielle. The heartbreak. He could almost imagine his precious love with her porcelain skin, chiseled features, and flowing dark hair. He could taste her sweet lips. Inhale the scent of her flowery perfume. Gabrielle. *My love*, he thought. And felt glad that at least he was capable of deep love even if it was in a past life because in this life, he seemed to be devoid of all those feelings.

Until he saw her in London when he went to dinner at Sofia's

Chapter Thirteen

A Different Worldview

Journal entry:
The shame, the hiding,
then the blossoming.
The goddesses make themselves known
and are indeed my friends.

Three soft raps. "Gabrielle, dearest, may I please come in?" It was Tasa at her bedroom door. Gabrielle was about to ask her to please come back in the morning when she opened the door and barged in.

"Your behavior is most extraordinary. You've got me so worried and upset. What is it? What did he do to you? Should we press charges?"

"It's not him. Not his fault. It's mine. It's unspeakable. Why am I being hounded? By him, now by you. I just don't want to talk about it!" Then shouting, "WHY MUST I?" A pause with sobbing and tears. "I'm so ashamed. Why couldn't he just stay in London? Why am I not allowed to just put this behind me?"

Irina came in and stood solemnly next to the Countess. "I know what it is," she said. "You had a sexual encounter with him."

"Oh my God! Why do I have to tell you? Is there no privacy? ALRIGHT! ALRIGHT! YES!!! YES!!! But I didn't know who he was. I was drawn to him. I had no idea he was my...*BROTHER!* Half-brother but still. It's too awful. Incest, a taboo, FORBIDDEN! I can't breathe every time I think of it! Every time, I can't breathe. It's too awful! I'm so ashamed."

"He knows who you are because he's here. Is that right?" asked Irina interjecting some logic.

"What? ... oh...yes...he must."

"Well, why isn't he ashamed? Why is he pursuing you? Why did he come? Maybe you should ask your lawyer if you *really* are related."

"Oh..." Gabrielle got quiet. She lay back on her pillow. "I'm confused. My father's Will referred to him as *my son. I* don't know. I need to go to sleep," she told them in a soft voice full of anxiety.

They left quietly and she fell asleep puzzled and hopeful she was not a twisted and perverse person. In the morning, she decided to call Whitehead to ask him that most important question but he was in a meeting and his secretary told her he would call her back. She soon pushed it down, shoved it away, would deal with it later, because there was much excitement today at the inn. Their first guests would be arriving tomorrow. Opening Day! Everything must be gone over thoroughly. Peter made them the breakfast he would be serving and later on he would prepare afternoon tea.

They ate the wonderful breakfast of steeped English tea, coffee, bacon, eggs, toast, and muffins with Irina contributing blinis in sour cherry sauce. At four o'clock he would serve clotted cream, scones, assorted petit fours including French macarons, and finger sandwiches. They had a fabulous selection of tins of loose teas from England and China and the jams that Tasa and Gabrielle had bought at Covent Garden and Harrods. All through these festive food tastings, her stomach kept doing cartwheels. Tied into knots. Nervous about opening day and nervous about...him. *Would he take this away from her? Could he?*

After Gabrielle inspected the eight bedrooms and reception area, she decided to sit for a bit on the porch and gaze at the lake and mountain range in the distance. Serenity. It gave her a chance to think, to contemplate everything that had happened to her in such a short time. Doo sat on her feet and it felt cozy for her to do so. She was grateful for the path of this new life, of new adventures. She had no remorse for choosing to accept this gift from her father. She was suddenly filled with positive energy and recalled what Irina had told her the night before. Of course, he wasn't her brother. Of course, he wouldn't have come if he knew he was. This calmed her immensely. Much better to grab hold of *that* idea. They were NOT related. He was NOT her father's son. So much better to think that on so many levels.

As she sat there convincing herself that her upset over what she thought was a travesty was just a big misunderstanding, she became filled with a sense of purpose. *This place will be a safe haven for mankind* fluttered through her mind. *Many such places are being created now. Floods from rising seas, epic fires, and contagious diseases will befall humanity. We will help you. All of us are here to help. We will awaken the Divine Feminine in all females to help us.* It was as if someone were talking to her nearby, so she turned around and boom there she was. The woman in white with the red flowing hair. She was smiling, lovingly. "Who are you?" asked Gabrielle and as the woman faded, she said, "I am called Venus or Aphrodite," and then she completely disappeared.

Gabrielle was shaken. This ethereal creature had been following her, ever since she first came to this house. Even to London. *Why?* She just now had imparted knowledge to Gabrielle about the planet's changing climate and its potential impacts. Yes, that first night with everyone at Mrs. Jones's. The horrific storm. Downed trees. Newscasters saying it was most unusual for Vermont. What kind of a safe haven has storms like that? But at least they were safe from rising seas. She said that they would all help. Who were *they*? It was troubling but at the same time, comforting. They must have magical powers. They must have been the ones that showered this B&B with their magic. She sat for a few more minutes hoping the Venus spirit would come back, so she could ask her questions about the future and what they were expected to do. After a short while, she got up and walked down to the lake after she noticed a few deer darting in and out of the trees.

She tried to quiet her mind as she sat on a bench with little Doo on her lap. The bench had been placed there for just that purpose to enjoy the calming scene of the lake and the friendly deer. How lovely was this beautiful spot with its manicured green lawns and lush trees that framed the still, mirror-like water?

"How lovely it is here. I came down here quite often to fish or swim in the icy water on hot summer days."

Gabrielle jumped up and started to walk away.

"Wait," he said. "Don't go. Let me explain. Explain everything. Please...please sit back down."

So, with trepidation and overwhelming curiosity, she sat at the far end of the long bench and he at the other. And he began.

"Whitehead informed me of your confusion. Thinking we were related, half-brother and half-sister. In short, we are not. My biological father left right after I was born when my mother inherited this place from a maiden aunt. He had no desire to turn it into an inn and run it. It was too conventional a life for him, he being a free spirit. He was killed in a motorcycle accident soon after he left. I was 16 when my mother met your father. He had driven down from Quebec and stayed as a guest. She was between boyfriends and they started seeing each other. He took a job here to help out and after a while, they decided to marry. I never liked him. Bad energy seemed to follow him. I left as soon as I could. I probably should have stayed to watch over my mother because she died under mysterious circumstances.

"She got locked in the walk-in freezer but the official cause was a heart attack. No use in causing bad publicity for the inn. But she knew how to get out of there if it locked, there was an escape latch. There was some evil energy surrounding the inn that started around the appearance of your father. I don't know if he was the cause or just the vehicle for it. Anyway, it disturbs me to think about all that. She was taken before her time at just 52 years old. It's kept me away all these years until I saw you.

"I'm assuming you have seen the goddesses or at least Venus. She told me about you when she came to me in London and coaxed me to go to Sofia's for dinner. I couldn't believe it when I saw you. I was so stunned by it. When we found ourselves alone, I couldn't resist you. Do you remember...us? Before? Together in Paris? It was terrible times. During the Reign of Terror. We had decided to meet in London, but you never came. I mourned for you. I thought you remembered me in London, but you ran away, like you didn't remember us. How can that be when I remember so clearly?"

As he spoke, Gabrielle studied him. His eyes were captivating revealing so much tenderness and love. They bore into her and she, too, felt strong emotions, reawakened emotions about him. A familiarity in those eyes. Flashes of scenes of violence and war. Shouts of soldiers and people dragged to guillotines. "Je t'aime, Je t'aime," he shouted as he was dragged away by the gendarmes. The soldiers were rough as they knocked him about. Now she remembered his uncle had been in the clergy. All clergymen were suspect. She brushed away the thoughts and concentrated on the man in front of her.

Now it all made sense. How she was so drawn to him immediately. Her fascination, as a child, with this time period in France. Her dreams were not made-up scenes but memories of living there in a past life. This was validation from the cosmos. She was dumbstruck. Shocked. Speechless. This was their destiny. So much life had happened to her in a just few months. All the highs and lows. For so many years she had been an outsider watching others feel the love of family, while she was bereft of closeness to relatives, mother, father, aunts, and so on. Now there was an abundance of what she had longed for. Now she had a family and now on top of that, she seemed to have the love of the perfect man, someone to cherish and with which to share her life.

They lost each other once but now they had a chance to make it right. She was overwhelmed with her good fortune and tears welled up and she blinked them away. *Yes, I loved him in a long-ago life. I knew him so well, but I know nothing about him now, except those...eyes.* She let him continue his life story, his dislike for her father and estrangement from his mother because they were married. The bad energy that took over the inn with her father's arrival. There was a riddle there. She remained quiet until he finished his story and she remained quiet for many moments after. They sat. They pondered feeling like strangers when there had been passionate love in the distant past and passionate lovemaking in the recent past. These kinds of thoughts were new to Gabrielle. Reincarnation, past lives. She had read about these strange occurrences but it never before pertained to herself. But now it felt so real. So honest.

"I do remember some things. When you were talking just now. Scenes flashed through my mind. But I also remember dreams that I've had throughout my life where I'm wearing period clothing. So real that I can feel the soft blue silk fabric of an elaborate dress. A man, it must have been you, would speak to me in French and I understood what was said, even though I cannot understand French today. It's a bit much to take all this in, especially right now. Just before I walked down here, the goddess Venus who has appeared to me quite often came to me while I was sitting on the porch and told me what she and all the goddesses want and need from me."

He interrupted, "Oh, my. Look over there by the side of the lake still on this property. There, see the deer crowding around. There. There are the women. The goddesses. Frolicking with the deer. Over there can you see them?" he points. "They are in their see-through mode, transparent so it's hard to make them out."

"No, I don't see anything. Oh, wait, yes, now I see a few. How many are there?"

"I see five or six."

"Is that all of them? I've only seen Venus."

"Oh no. There are many more. I never counted but they kept me amused and not lonely when I was a kid growing up here. I loved them all. Ruined me for any woman who lives in our world...except for you." He looks at her meaningfully and they both turned away and sat silently watching the deer and the goddesses fading in and out.

"I finally went to Paris last year," he said suddenly out of the blue. "It changed everything for me. I have hated all things French because my dreams and visions made me sad and lonely. But as I walked the streets where we, you and I, lived on the Left Bank, lovely thoughts were awakened in me. You and I together, we shared a life, we shared a great love. The memories flooded back. And the food, what fabulous food. I came back to London renewed. Acknowledging our love was a good thing. At least I had that kind of love once, although several lifetimes ago. In this life, I've been quite lonely. But then I saw you at the dinner. I couldn't believe it was you. My love for which my heart has ached for so long. Will you give us a chance in this life, Gabrielle? The universe works in mysterious ways. All the events that had to happen to lead us to sitting on this bench on this day in this life. Quite remarkable."

"I, too, have always embraced the wisdom of the cosmos to direct me on the right path."

He moved closer and reached out and took her hand. Comforting electricity pulsed through her. "Now tell me what Venus asked of you earlier." And she did.

They watched the goddesses play at the edge of the lake and float over the water. Boats rode by and people walked near but none seemed to see them. Excitement was in the air for the changing season and coming holiday weekend. A mild and cool breeze with the hint of fall caressed them. Here and there among the leaves of the deciduous trees was a bright spot of yellow or deep reddish maroon sprinkled with nature's orange paint as their leaves were starting to get ready to disappear for the onset of the winter months. A clear azure blue sky made the scene an artist's or photographer's vision in its glory and specter. They sat together holding hands as Beau told of the influence of the goddesses on the collective consciousness of Vermonters. It's no wonder the climate crisis that is at a tipping brought them here to help. This has been their mission since he was a young boy, he told her

"So many laws have been passed to preserve the environment in this state," he continued, "and it's owed to the persistent messages from the goddess realm. Gentle and calming, these wonderful spirits gave Vermont its lingering goodwill to all. People feel happy in Vermont. Unfortunately, there are always negative forces that try to bring down the goodness." And then Gabrielle told him about the house shaking when they arrived.

"Yup, the Huntsman likes to shake things up. I'm sure he attached himself to Phil and stayed here after he passed. Somehow, he must have been responsible for my mother's death and Phil's. We have to rid this place of his evil meanness."

They sat for a while until the goddesses disappeared. In the intervening time, Gabrielle had completely changed her mind about him. She was glad he was here and very glad they weren't related. An understatement. Beau knew that he was where he belonged finally and sensed he had won over Gabrielle. This house had been a place that he loved until Phil came. It hurt him to leave but he was not sorry. He was glad that he had seen some of the world, especially Paris where he was able to rekindle his strong emotions for, and connection to, Gabrielle, and now here she was in the flesh. How amazing. And he was grateful beyond words.

They never spoke about what they would do about their relationship going forward. Never spoke about making it known to everyone. They just walked arm-in-arm back up to the house. Stopping once under a tree, Beau leaned down and gently kissed her and they hugged for a few minutes before continuing on. As they walked onto the porch, Venus appeared smiling and bouncing around them as a bubble of laughter. As soon as they walked in everyone stopped their preparations for the big opening weekend and stared at them.

The body language of everyone said it all. Beau and Gabrielle were now a couple, everyone except Peter was pleased and accepted this relationship as something they expected. Then all started speaking in a rush about how the last room was finally reserved so there would be a full house. The first guests were expected to check-in early at 1:00 pm and stay in the Greenroom. As a celebration for the opening, Peter decided to offer a dinner menu on Saturday night by reservation only and for additional cost to the guests to see how it went over. Everyone was excited and exhausted and felt the inn looked perfect.

The Captain and Mrs. Jones joined them for a celebration and they decided to order Indian food from a local restaurant in a small nearby shopping center. Beau offered to treat everyone and said he had an announcement to make later. As they feasted on samosas, chicken vindaloo, chicken tikka masala, naan bread, and basmati rice they chatted about the coming opening the next day. It was a party atmosphere. All their hard work paying off. The Countess stood up to make a toast. She looked very elegant with her hair pinned up, bejeweled fingers, and a grey knit dress that matched her hair.

All raised their wine glasses as she said, "I want to send my love to all of you but especially to my darling Gabrielle who has brought me a new lease on life. Because of her, I have embarked on a path that never would have been afforded me, especially at this age. I love this spectacular scenery in Vermont, the loveliness of the architecture of this B&B, and the prospect of making new friends with the guests who stay here. I have met my bliss late in life, but it's really never too late to find it."

They clinked their glasses and said to "To Gabrielle," and then "To the Countess." And all came around the table and hugged each other and laughed and laughed. Then Beau clinked on his glass with a spoon and asked everyone to have a seat.

"I have a very unusual tale to tell you," he said. "Please open your minds. There are some of us that can tap into other realms of consciousness. A random gift. I am one of those individuals. I didn't realize that it was unusual as a child. I thought everyone could do that. It began with seeing the shadow people at the inn. Women in white flowing gowns. I didn't realize they were goddesses until I was older and studied about them in Ancient Mythology. As a young boy, the women kept me from being lonely and sometimes played a part in keeping me from harm. I loved to climb and there was plenty of opportunities to do so around here. Trees with wide sturdy trunks and big heavy branches and an array of cliffs hidden in the thick woods. Once I tripped on a ridge and nearly fell several hundred feet but I was grabbed by one of the women and carried to safety."

As he spoke, Gabrielle watched his every move. The more he spoke, the more she realized a feeling of love was stirring inside her. A love she felt for him that perhaps had lasted centuries. She studied him most carefully wanting to imprint him in her mind. His hand motions, his stance, the confidence he exuded, and of course his obvious intellect. She was captured and enraptured by his large piercing eyes. He was such a handsome man and she was lost and under his spell. This was it. He was the one. The cosmos had brought him to her by creating all the unusual circumstances that led them to meet. And as we know, she always trusted the cosmos.

Unbeknownst to the group at dinner, peeking out from the corners of the ceiling were the faces of the goddesses who had shared this B&B as their residence on and off from its beginning. Their wide smiles indicated how happy they were at this turn of events. Events they had engineered but were never really sure of the outcome, humans being so unpredictable. The safe haven for the human race was beginning to form with the assemblage of this group. Venus and the goddesses not held hostage under the Huntsman's power had immediately gone to work to put right the wrongs befallen Gabrielle ever since her childhood. Gabrielle's dedication to the positive energy of the cosmos and being the daughter of Phil Bernstein, who was an intermittent conduit for the Huntsman, was necessary for this mission and so they created the inheritance that brought her to this inn. She had the necessary combination of positive and negative forces within her to be a formidable asset against the darkness wherever it might lay in waiting. Creating a connection to Beau was key.

The goddesses had finally put to rest the Huntsman and his negative energy after the quaking incident trying to stop Gabrielle and the Countess when they arrived. How foolish he was in thinking these strong women would be frightened off. Destroying the Huntsman's power had been a long time coming because for many years a good number of them had been trapped by him, literally trapped in the trees surrounding the inn. The Huntsman's power had also declined with the changeover of Phil Bernstein from being selfish to being remorseful at the end of his life. The Huntsman could no longer feed off his selfishness and his strength declined. All of the goddesses' energies were needed now for this most important endeavor, so the timing of their gaining strength was important. They were blessedly freed from their entrapment with the arrival of the positive energy engulfing and surrounding the very essence of Gabrielle.

With that increase of positive energy, they were able to banish the Huntsman and his followers from ever setting foot anywhere on Earth, at least they thought they did. Unfortunately, there always remained a remnant of evil that could survive and grow. Humans, also, had perpetrated their own evil onto the planet's delicate symbiotic balance. The destruction could not be stopped as the goddesses had tried to do but failed. Perhaps the impending tipping point could be mitigated. For their new mission, these people at this B&B would be their army. They were jubilant in their mission being cemented with these declarations about to be revealed by Beau. Outside the songbirds gave forth their melodies, happy chickadees roosted in the trees, and the waterfowl danced in circles of joy.

Beau took a sip of water and continued, "I also had the knowledge that I had lived before because vague memories would flash through my mind. I knew things about the French revolution in Paris before I ever studied the history surrounding that time period. My incomplete understanding had me detest all things French because a great sadness overtook me whenever snatches of my past life came through in my dreams or musings. I finally went to Paris where my memories became more complete, clear, and real. I loved walking the narrow winding streets of the Rive Gauche also known as the Left Bank, and the fabulous epicurean delights. I understood all that was being said as if I spoke the language fluently.

"I saw vividly in my mind's eye the woman to whom I gave my heart. Her hair, her eyes, her lips. I relived the deep passionate love we had for each other and I came to understand that I lost this great love after I was held prisoner in error. I was rounded up with a group of men I happened to be standing next to on the Champs-Élysées during the Reign of Terror. My uncle, a priest was one of the men and clergy were despised. So many people were taken in a frenzy of arrests and beheaded by the numerous guillotines all over the city. I managed to escape from prison with the aid of the gendarmes who I had fought with side-by-side against the monarchy. I managed to get to a boat and cross the English Channel to safety, where I thought Gabrielle, my love, would meet me. But, alas, she never came."

As soon as he said the name Gabrielle everyone was audibly shocked and sucked in their breaths and then murmurs went around the small group. Beau stared at Gabrielle with love in his eyes and walked closer to her. "A true miracle has happened after centuries of separation. I have finally reunited with my Gabrielle."

Beau then told everyone what they had already probably guessed that he decided to stay, accept his inheritance, and help them run the B&B. "I hope you will all agree with this change in ownership."

"Of course, we do, don't we Gabrielle?" asked Tasa. Gabrielle just nodded still not trusting her emotions and trying not to cry. She never realized what an easy crier she was having it never been tested, and now she seemed to cry all the time. "Another pair of strong arms will be most welcome. But I'm sorry to tell you, we have no place for you to stay, 'there's no room at the inn' as they say."

"Well, that's no problem because after my mother married Phil, I didn't want to stay in the owner's quarters, so they built me my own suite in the attic space. It has its own key which I never gave anyone so that's what is behind the locked door up there."

"What a relief," said Irina. "We thought a diabolical monster was living as a caged animal devising ways to get out."

And they all laughed.

Chapter Fourteen

Finally Open

Journal entry:
Magic, glory, and happiness blending with me
and the cosmos.
We are all in sync.

The opening weekend was a sold-out rousing success. Four families, two of which rented two rooms, and two couples were the first guests to initiate the reopening of the B&B, now under new management as it was advertised. They came away all abuzz. Being the very first paying customers they were treated to some very special amenities. Breakfast had several selections including brioche French toast, varieties of pancakes and any kind of eggs, grits, breakfast patties, and toast. Going forward breakfast would have fewer selections. On Saturday starting at 3:00 there was a complimentary afternoon tea, henceforth to incur a charge. There was a wine tasting at 6:00 pm and dinner served from a fixed-price set menu. Serving dinner was a test to see if there was much interest and all guests reserved a spot. A success. Some guests at Mrs. Jones's inn also partook. Everyone thought Chef Peter's offerings were expertly presented and as tasty as those of the finest restaurants anywhere.

Mr. and Mrs. Abernathy, a neat and compact couple who stayed in the Greenroom suite and connected room with their very tall teen-aged son, were convinced the inn was enchanted with happy spirits that manifested positive energy into their lives. Charles, their tall, lanky, shy, and awkward teenager with greasy hair and red-pimpled face, was unfortunately afflicted with a stutter. For many years, overcoming this handicap had eluded the professional coaching of speech therapists, psychologists, and the like. It tragically impacted every aspect of his young life and brought him much misery.

As soon as they stepped into their quarters young Charles felt a tremendous sense of calm. He slept so peacefully through the night that he was extremely well-rested and quite surprised to experience an unusual emotion (for him), glee and optimism when he first awoke. Sitting down to breakfast while making casual conversation they suddenly realized that Charles no longer stuttered. It was a miracle they celebrated the entire day enjoying listening to Charles speak stutter-free while walking about and shopping in town. A miracle as certain as any miracles in the Bible.

Jolene and Joey, known as J&J to their friends, were one of the two couples staying there who decided that this B&B must have a life-changing positive energy flow. Having unsuccessfully tried to conceive for many years, now Jolene was at a precarious age where fertility issues start to appear. For some mysterious reason, Jolene's fertility temperature registered perfectly on the basal thermometer for the entire weekend. She thought she felt herself conceive on the first night there. After they got home, she took an early pregnancy test (EPT) not wanting to ruin the weekend by bringing one. Lo and behold she was pregnant and better still with twins, a boy and a girl. After she found out at the appropriate doctor's visit, she called the hotel soon after to convey the news. They felt the peace of having a family that was going to be complete. Jolene could stop worrying about her age factor and just enjoy her life and her babies.

Beau was ecstatic when he heard these stories. It brought him back to his happy childhood when it was just him and his mother enjoying their lives alone together and the magic. All guests had a story. The second couple was older and after being married for 40 years were thinking about divorcing. They had stopped getting along years ago. After one weekend at the inn, they fell madly in love again. One of the remaining families had been awaiting the results from a recent cancer screening to determine whether or not their child's cancer had returned. They received the good news that the child was cancer-free while they were there.

The largest suite housed a blended family whose children argued the entire time they were checking in. Two boys and two girls each became overnight stepsiblings and seemed to fight constantly making a scene at the front desk that the parents were quite embarrassed and upset about. As soon as they stepped into their suite the fighting quieted down and the staff noticed pleasantries at breakfast, tea, and dinner. In short, the war of the families seemed to have reached a peaceful conclusion to the happiness and benefit of all, which included the other guests and staff. The remaining quests all declared that hadn't felt so free of allergies in years or slept as well.

During this very successful opening weekend, there were also several stories happening behind the scenes. First, there was Beau and Gabrielle and second, there was Peter and Gabrielle, and third back to Beau and Gabrielle. When Beau got his things and went up to his attic hideaway after dinner, Gabrielle was sitting by his locked door. She stood up when she saw him and he grabbed her and kissed her assuming that was what she came for, but she broke away.

"What's wrong?" he asked.

"Apart from needing to have a real conversation with you about us, I've come here because I'm in possession of a diary that belonged to your mother."

"A diary? How odd. She didn't strike me as the type that kept a diary. Are you sure it's hers?"

She handed him the book and he opened the door with his key and she followed him into his quarters

"I didn't try to open it. I would have if you hadn't come here, but now, it would have been wrong of me to snoop," said Gabrielle.

She looked around the charming two-room suite tucked into one of the turrets so there was a curved windowed alcove perfect for reading a book. A nice-sized living room was separate from the bedroom and bath. She saw that the TV was an older model and quite small but the furniture was in good shape and comfy looking. The kitchen was one step up from the living room and had a selection of cabinets upper and lower and was completed by a four-top wooden table and chairs, microwave, sink, and mini-fridge. A haven for a young Beau. Gabrielle sat down in the grey suede-like microfiber armchair that matched the full-size sofa.

"Would you like a drink?" asked Beau as he pulled a bottle of Irish whiskey and a bottle of red wine from his backpack. Gabrielle immediately chose a much-needed whiskey to soothe her ragged nerves. Beau poured two drinks with glasses he got out of the mini-kitchen cabinet that he rinsed off first. They clinked glasses and toasted. "To the cosmos," they said in unison and laughed. She took a big sip and felt the strong drink burn down her throat and immediately relaxed. Beau sat on the sofa and tried to jiggle open the lock on the diary to no avail.

"This was some setup you had up here," she said.

"As a young impressionable lad who was not fond of my mother's boyfriends, it was perfect. She had her privacy and so did I.

It was quite simple at first but was fully furnished after she and your dad married. It was also a secluded getaway from the guests. My own private hideaway. In between her boyfriends, I would move downstairs. Once she married Phil, I stayed up here until I went to Boston for my undergraduate degree at Harvard then soon after left the East coast for my graduate courses at Stanford. I hardly came home during that time. I loved this place but it has had its ups and downs. It's like it's located in a vortex of opposing forces. Positive and negative energy fight for dominance.

"Most of my early childhood was kind of blissful. The inn seemed to be bathed in positive energy and we were prosperous. It became known as an enchanted and magical place and people came from far and wide. When I think of that time, I see morning rainbows that seemed to attach to all the trees and hover over the lake. I see afternoons full of sunshine and robust flowers that filled the branches and made thick the bushes. And of course, the women in white happily dancing in the moonlight. Then things began to change after Phil, your father, came to live here. I suffered through those times when the negative energy forces took hold. I often wondered what Phil might have done. And now I know that he deserted his wife and young daughter.

"I couldn't wait to leave and it became easier and easier to stay away. The few times, I came back were filled with awfully sad events. A child drowning in the lake, arguing guests, and the like. Eventually, I stopped coming back. Even when my mother died. We spoke on the phone some, but she was always distracted. I made a life for myself. Loved living in London. I never thought I would come back here. Never. But the universe had other plans, I guess. I had forgotten how happy I felt here most of the time and I've missed that sense of belonging."

As Gabrielle listened to him, she felt moved by his loss of innocence. At least his childhood was not completely bereft of joy like hers. She realized he was never the monster she had imagined who had stolen her father's love from her. He too wanted to have a father but sadly for him, he didn't want her father. How ironic that he loathed the father she craved for, the very one. She began to see him as more than just a man who stirred her, but as her destiny, and she always resigned herself to destiny. Even though she didn't quite understand the past life connection intellectually, she felt it organically, believed it wholeheartedly. She remembered her fascination with that period in history. She did not remember being alive as vividly as he did. Did not remember him as detailed as he remembered her. Perhaps there was some greater power at work to have them find each other in this life. Perhaps their continued relationship would reveal some clues and their past life would become more real for her. Gabrielle walked over to him and kissed him tenderly and then passionately. He got up from the sofa and led her into the bedroom and the diary was forgotten.

Chapter Fifteen

A Wedding and Sorrow Came to Visit

Journal entry:
The carousel spins. It starts all happy and playful.
But suddenly it stops and there is pain.
What happened to the brass ring?
A grim future portends.

The next few months were marvelous bliss. The B&B was swamped with reservations and not only for weekends. The fall foliage colors outdid themselves that season. The orange and yellow colors looked like firebombs dotting the landscape, the reds were rubies, and the deep purples were royal in their splendor. Together the color palette was rich, luscious, and awesome. Every morning, Gabrielle awoke in Beau's arms with Doo snuggled at her feet. She would sit on the balcony of Beau's suite with Doo in her lap while sipping a cup of coffee and absorb this season full of wonder and glory. She was so grateful each and every day for her new life and this glorious setting. Never take anything for granted was her constant inner voice. *Always be mindful and presen*t. And these days, it was easy to stay true to her motto.

They all decided to make the restaurant permanent with only Mondays closed and people came from all around for Peter's fabulous menus and Irina's Russian influence. Afternoon tea on weekends also was a hit and breakfast was to die for. Peter became key to their success but he hadn't been in a good mood lately and approached Gabrielle for a private conversation that was still waiting to happen. She was prepared to give him a raise even though he had really just started, he was that good.

In the midst of all this, Mrs. Jones came around with an announcement. She and the Captain would be getting married and they wanted the wedding to take place at the inn because of all the good vibes. It would be a small affair and Peter would cater the reception dinner. Mrs. Jones asked us all if we could please refer to her by her given name Emma since she would be taking on the Captain's last name and henceforth be Mrs. Ostrowski. However, for the guests at her inn, she would remain Mrs. Jones. We all hugged and set aside a date for the nuptials, the first Monday when the restaurant was usually closed and there were no reservations at the inn. We blacked out the date in November, excited and thrilled. Then we all wrote notes to ourselves to remember what to call her depending on where she was at the moment.

It was a cherished day. The wedding took place in a small and austere white clapboard village church that was built in 1850 when it was originally a gathering place for those of the Dutch Reformed faith. Today it was a welcoming Non-Denominational house of worship. It made sense since the Captain was Catholic and Mrs. Jones a Lutheran. She walked down the aisle unaccompanied in the elegant walking style of the runway model she used to be. Her gown was an heirloom from one of the townspeople who donated it to her for the occasion. It was white paisley floral lace tulle with a sweetheart neckline and long lace sleeves. The dress was narrow at the waistline and then billowed softly to the floor with a short train behind. The veil flowed just to her shoulders. Her thick curly hair was in its splendor, framing her face while falling loosely down her back.

The Captain stood at the alter all red-faced and awkward and beaming. He wore an ill-fitting tuxedo and he kept shooting his cuffs and adjusting his front jacket button. When it was time for their vows, he did something a little different and took a step forward to face the small gathering.

"Hello everyone. Emma and I are so happy you came to witness the best day in our lives. Down in New York City at a small neighborhood public library, I'm sort of famous for my storytelling. So as part of my vows today, I want to tell you all the story of Emma and Jimmy, better known here as Mrs. Jones and the Captain. I met the love of my life late in the game spending most of my adult life in the Merchant Marines. And, boy, it was an exciting experience. I saw the world but I missed out on the simple pleasures of life, a family, and growing old with one special person. I never thought, at this age, it would happen to me. The choices we make in life can seem random but these choices lead us down a unique path that gives our lives purpose and becomes our destiny.

"I moved to NYC when I retired. Because I missed the sea life, I would sometimes recreate that atmosphere by going to the zoo and watching the sea lions play and hear their barking, smell the sea air in their scent. These visits were good for my soul. On one such day, an elegant older woman came by who I had seen there often. As she made her way toward a bench, some young boys attacked her grabbing for her purse. I jumped up and was knocked down but managed to wring the purse from their hands before I fell. I had a small wound on my head and the Countess took me back to her place to clean it up and bandage it. We became dear friends from that day on never realizing that this was the start of the path that would lead me to my destiny and the love of my life."

He continued on recounting the first day he drove us up to the B&B and the first moment he set eyes on Emma. He knew he wanted to marry her but thought she was already married because everyone called her Mrs. Jones. By the time he found out she was single, she had fallen in love with him as well. Every day, he blesses the day he met the Countess at the Central Park Zoo. Now he has replaced the scent of wind filled with the salty and fishy aroma of the sea with the organic and seductive scent of newly mown grass. From riding the ocean's waves, he now rides a lawnmower as a groundskeeper and has started a very lucrative business. There was only one last thing left to do. To embark on their journey through what's left of the rest of their lives together. And then he stepped back and turned toward her.

"Dearest Emma, I vow to protect and keep you safe in sickness and health for the rest of my life and help you with the dishes and laundry every day going forward. I will always love you and respect you, oh and I vow to always take out the trash. From this day going forward, you can always count on me."

Everyone laughed and applauded. Mrs. Jones just hugged him in lieu of her own vows, being so shy and private. They exchanged rings. And that was it. They were married. The goddesses watched from the rafters and nodded in glee but also knew how serious his vow was to keep her safe and how it would be tested in the near future. All was going to plan for right now. And just then the goddesses were put on alert sooner than expected. While this wedding was taking place, the massive ice shelf in Greenland had started to crack, a small spark from a campfire had ignited the water-starved underbrush from a year's drought in Yosemite National Park, and the volcano under Yellowstone had started to slowly come alive. Birds began migrating haphazardly, an unexpected early blizzard fell in the Rockies, and the Alps spawned raging rivers.

The wedding guests who were old friends of Mrs. Jones from her fashion days and townspeople she dealt with for the B&B had no clue this was happening as they ate, drank, and partied back at the inn. Walter had come all the way from NYC with his family and would be staying the night. It was so good to see him after all these months. He never retired as head librarian because his wife's family found another relative to run the dry cleaners. He was very happy about that turn of events but missed everyone. The joyful atmosphere was contagious and the guests made speeches and gave toasts to the happy couple and laughed until their sides hurt. Champagne poured freely and Peter was complimented over and over again for his fabulous Coq au Vin, Beef Stroganoff using the Countess's recipe, and the beautifully decorated five-tiered white buttercream wedding cake filled with mousse au chocolat.

Peter pulled Gabrielle aside to speak to her privately but she was whisked away for a dance with Beau. The Countess was in deep in conversation with an older gentleman who was a renowned sculptor and lived on a remote farm that also was a warehouse for his giant hand-carved marble figures of Greek goddesses with a modern turn. He lived up this way for many years because it was convenient to be near the quarries that supplied his raw material. His work was showcased in museums and in front of office buildings in New York City and Chicago. Irina was showing Walter and his family the porch views and beautiful lake and Emma and the Captain were dancing cheek to cheek to Pandora's love song channel. Peter felt the odd man out and sadly no one noticed.

When Gabrielle finished dancing with Beau, she went looking for Peter but couldn't find him. She assumed he went to his own apartment because he never showed up again. The next morning Irina served a light breakfast of croissants, jam, with creamy Irish butter, and lots of brewed tea and coffee. Everyone was hungover and subdued but the congenial atmosphere prevailed. The newlyweds would come by before lunch to say goodbye to Walter and his family and revel in the atmosphere of their special occasion. When Irina finally decided to start cleaning up, Emma and the Captain arrived, and so she delayed that task to have another cup of tea with the newly minted Ostrowskis. It was a glorious bright blue cloudless sky day. Fall was subsiding with only a bright yellow or bright orange leaf here and there, winter's dominance and accompanying brisk temperatures had begun.

"Let's take a walk down by the lake," said Beau to Gabrielle as he handed her a sweater. They stood for a moment on the porch taking in the view and Beau put his arm around her waist.

"I didn't realize how much I missed this place. My feelings were so wrapped up in the dynamic between my mother and her relationships, especially after she married your father. Something was definitely off. The bubble of joy around this place was replaced by darkness. But being here with you now, I don't think about that. I can fully enjoy the setting and the loveliness of the natural beauty. I have longed for that without realizing it."

They slowly sauntered down to the edge of the lake where the family of deer emerged from the tall grass and nibbled on the sparsely remaining wildflowers. They watched in silence enjoying the connection.

"It's so odd how often they come around when I come down here. They came on the very first day I checked out this place and surrounded me as they nuzzled my bare skin exposed by my short-sleeve shirt. They were not all skittish that day," Gabrielle said softly so as not to startle these innocent creatures.

"They're part of the magic. They're singling you out. To let you know you're accepted and needed for the harmony here, just like me." Gabrielle turned to look at him and Beau continued, "What I mean to say to you is this wedding made me realize that you've become my sole focus. I need you in my life now and forever. Somehow, I have a feeling that our being together is important. Bigger than both of us. I know it sounds silly but it has seemed almost like a driving force and I can't rest until you agree to share your life with me."

Gabrielle was taken aback. She knew deep down that this felt right but it was very fast. It also felt urgent that they needed to make this pact. Something was bigger than them. Something that had brought her up here, brought her to London, and now back here with him. Something to do with the goddesses, the climate changing, and building some sort of refuge. But it wasn't very clear. She was about to speak when they heard shouting. Irina was running from the house and shouting. When they could finally make out what she was saying they heard, "Something awful has happened. Come quick back to the house. Awful just awful."

Racing back to the house they heard sirens and an ambulance. Once inside they saw everyone gathered in the kitchen. The walk-in freezer was open and then the EMT workers rushed by and went in. Beau had a sense of dread. This felt like something evil was being played out again. And it was. There inside the freezer was the body of Peter, stone-cold dead. A most horrific end to a joyous few days. Gabrielle began to cry overcome with guilt for not giving him a few minutes of her time when he wanted to speak to her. The police came in next and started to ask questions. Did anyone have a reason to lock him in the freezer? Was there a safety latch inside to prevent such a terrible accident? Beau answered, yes, there is one that was specifically installed so an accident like this couldn't happen. *But it had happened before! Covered up as a heart attack!* Beau walked over to the liquor cabinet and grabbed a whiskey neat and drank it in one gulp. And then another and one more all tossed back quickly.

"What? What is it?" asked Gabrielle noticing Beau's distress.

"I have to face this now. My mother's death. I couldn't bring myself to come back here and investigate. Too cowardly, but now I must. Something fishy is going on. Is it human or just an evil force? Will it bring negative energy to this place as it did before? I shoved all that away because being with you felt so right. Maybe we should sell this place and leave."

"But you were just telling me how happy being here made you feel. I'm concerned too. There are definitely opposing forces centered on this place. Otherworldly energies. I wish we could get some guidance on what we should do to keep things from turning dark. If not for this negative energy, life is wonderful here. I've never been so happy."

Poor Peter was carried out to the ambulance to be delivered to the Rutland Regional Medical Center morgue for an autopsy. The detectives stayed a little longer taking notes and testing the inside latch which seemed to work. While they were there a sense of anxiety permeated the group. The newlyweds had decided to leave earlier to perhaps recapture some of the joy that was overshadowed by this tragedy. The Countess asked those who remained to convene in the breakfast/restaurant room to discuss what to do next. Walter and his family decided they should go back to NYC and they said their goodbyes.

Sometimes there are historic moments that call upon some of us to step forward. Sometimes a leader emerges, a volunteer who feels compelled by internal voices of encouragement and necessity. If not me who? If not now when? Such forces descended on Countess Anastasia Ivanova and she knew it was time to reveal her true self. Her role. She was chosen for just this moment and for this group of ordinary people with extraordinary abilities.

She had chosen well by instinct and with care. It was a long time coming. A lifetime but she was ready. History would remember the need to capture the power of the Feminine Divine. She was ready, finally ready after her preparations and travel abroad to take her rightful place. She loved her sisters in spirit, the goddesses, and their love for humanity. The heartbreak of messages being ignored by the very ones who were destroying the environment, the continued disrespect for this Earth, and all who dwell here by those who take it for granted and don't understand this is their only home. And the reveal began in a simple way.

"Irina please make some tea and let's catch our breath while we say a little silent prayer for Peter Lambert. He was such a lovely and talented boy," said the Countess.

After the tea was poured and the prayer was said, the Countess suggested they call the Captain and Emma on FaceTime so they could join in this important discussion.

"I hope we're not disturbing you, but we have a rather important decision to make that concerns you as well," said the Countess.

"No, no certainly not," Emma said. "Jimmy and were just starting to prepare a hardy vegetable soup for later. It can wait. Jimmy," she called out, "come over to the computer in the office for a minute. Something important."

And so, with everyone assembled the Countess began to speak softly, determinedly, and emphatically.

Chapter Sixteen

We Are Beginning to Understand

Journal entry:
Wow

The group sat mesmerized in high anxiety wondering what the Countess was about to say. Even Irina who had known the Countess her entire life sensed she would learn something new today. It was interesting, but unfortunately, alarming information that would bring purpose to all their lives. And so, the Countess began. From a young child, she had had a deep respect for all creatures whether they be large or tiny insects. She would never knowingly smash even a small bug but shooed it away or if found in the house put it carefully outside. "Tasa," her mother would yell, "there's really no need to do that, dear."

Oh yes, but to her, there was a need. It was necessary, quite necessary. Because Tasa understood that all life on this planet is connected and dependent on one other. She cherished the beauty of the fauna and flora at her country estate but also found joy in the natural world even in the heart of London. She fed pigeons in the parks and kept a collection of ladybugs in a glass enclosure in her bedroom. Not having any idea where this commentary would lead, everyone sat silent and still. A curious flickering on and off of an otherworldly glow surrounded the Countess as she spoke. This apparition calmed the growing anxiety of the group.

The Countess continued her life story not paying any attention to the light that illuminated her. Her soft melodic voice told of her inquisitiveness and appreciation of all living things arose from her gentle nature but also stemmed from a deep wisdom that was implanted in her from another realm. A realm of ethereal creatures that joyfully directed her to explore her ability to visit that realm through deep meditation. As she matured, she slowly began to understand the miracle of being alive and having a consciousness. She was grateful every day for this gift of life never taking it for granted. Too many of us sleepwalk through our lives and never take the time to bless this awesome gift, the gift of life, and our human experience on this planet.

Through the wisdom she received from the ethereal realm where goddesses transcended time, she learned how there is a connectedness to all things. She would meditate and see realms not available to other humans. Scientists now know what the ancient wisdom teachings have known for millennia: that at the quantum level, where the world is reduced to the smallest particles, all is connected. At this level, tiny particles of everything swirl and whizz around in a vastness of space so that one cannot discern a cat from a human or humans from each other, or a table from a person. The Countess could become as small as a particle in her meditations. She could validate the particle world firsthand. But also, she was amazed that we can see this connection manifest itself at the macro level as well. As in the murmuration of migrating birds where they appear as a cloud that turns and weaves as one unit or schools of fish that swim as one giant sea creature when they quickly dodge a predator. Bees and ants create colonies and social hierarchies. Herds of antelope that run as one.

Now is the time for the human race to come together as one giant brain to conquer our life-threatening climate change, threatening all life as we know it. This B&B has been designated as ground zero to create a refuge from the rising seas, a bubble of safety from the drought that brings fires, and a source of fresh water and food. We must start to prepare. The time is now. We have been left a book that will explain how to proceed. And the goddesses one by one will reveal themselves. There are many more who will travel here from all the corners of the planet. Many more places of refuge will be created on higher elevations in the mountains around the world as the fertile plains become dry and baren and islands become engulfed with rising sea levels. We have much work to do. She also told them that this truth was revealed to her in small doses over her entire life so she didn't understand the complete picture until now. Until she took up residence here. This book is the key to understanding everything.

"A book?" asked Gabrielle.

"Yes, I hope we can find it," said the Countess. "Does anyone know of such a book?"

"No, not really."

Everyone responded.

"Why don't these goddesses just tell you where it is?" asked the Captain.

"We must keep proving we are worthy, that we too feel the urgency."

"Is there no way to stop the rise of the seas before mankind is doomed?" asked Irina.

"Unfortunately, no, but perhaps if we can't turn things around, we can prevent them from getting worse with the help of loving spirits. Humans have been blind to the consequences of their actions and never have stopped polluting. I am sure the love and power of the Feminine Divine can save us if we can access it. So, we must find the book. I was told we were given such a book, but I'm not sure I've seen anything like that. We must look for it at once."

The session ended with everyone numbed by the new reality facing them while they straightened up the inn and looked for the book. There would be guests over the weekend so they needed to clean and hurriedly find a new chef. Everyone sobbed thinking about the loss of Peter and wondered if there was a dark energy that locked him in the freezer and hid the book? Had the Huntsman come back with a vengeance? While the vacuum was running someone shouted, they found the book and everyone ran over but it was just a book that had fallen from a library shelf. Finding this book was top of mind. But its whereabouts were a mystery.

A detective came by and had information about poor Peter's death. As soon as he walked in a chill of fear shot through everyone. What actually happened was easier to digest than evil energy. At least that was somewhat calming. The autopsy revealed that Peter was quite inebriated and most likely passed out in the freezer while looking for something and was overcome by hypothermia. Plain and simple, he froze to death accidentally. A tragic accident. Everyone was relieved it wasn't foul play and planned to attend the funeral. Gabrielle could not shake blaming herself for not having the time to speak to a distraught Peter who obviously drank too much over her rejection of him. She had immediately moved out of Beau's room after he was found.

Accompanying the sorrow from Peter's death with the dire situation told by the Countess, the usual lightness of being at the inn was overshadowed by a cloud of darkness and dread. The words of the Countess rang in everyone's ears as if a mantra. Climate destruction.

Need for a refuge. The entire planet and all species were at risk. It was a harsh reality. A reality that had been just under the radar. Flaring up occasionally and then forgotten. No one wanted to give up driving gas-fueled cars. The majority of humans were meat-eaters and could not imagine that methane produced from thousands of heads of cattle could affect the atmosphere.

Isn't beef a staple in South America as well? Americans had been outraged by this notion of giving up hamburgers and juicy steaks. They pounded their fists in defiance. The public had learned well under the thumb of a cultist leader who had lied constantly throughout his presidential term. Just believe what feels good and throw away the uncomfortable truths invigorated by science. Scientists and their warnings of pandemic disease, of ancient viruses released when the Siberian permafrost melts, and worldwide famine were just fairytales. Extinction was just a word. Global warming was a joke, a hoax even, why, just look at this snowball!

This denial had gone on for decades. But the day of reckoning was nigh. A collective understanding was at hand. The remedy was beyond the scope of what humans were prepared to do. Beyond the tipping point for repair. Powerful forces must be marshaled. Forces from ancient times had been watching covertly but now waiting to help. Also, modern technologies of communication were in place to get the word out. The world must come together and quickly. But how?

And where was that damn book?

Chapter Seventeen

A Surprise Visitor

Journal entry:
Taking stock for a bit.

"Gabrielle. Please...talk to me." Beau came into the kitchen as Gabrielle was making toast for breakfast. The funeral was that morning and the Captain was driving everyone in his large SUV. "Let me drive you to the funeral. We haven't spoken in several days," said Beau with a tremor in his voice.

"Don't you understand? I am overcome with grief and guilt. If not for my feelings for you or had you not come here, Peter would still be alive. I need to digest this. All signs are now pointing to the opposite of what I had thought. I keep thinking it's wrong for us to be together. Your mother supporting my father's abandonment of his family. Did she ever wonder if he had a wife and child? Did she not wonder why he just showed up in his late 40s alone? Did she ever ask about his life before he came to this inn? Did you know about me? Because I never knew about you!"

"These questions are very understandable. I wondered about your dad but my mother didn't seem to care about his past. And I didn't want to engage him in my life. I hated him. He took over my mother's every decision. He seemed angry and sad. Not a pleasant person. He and my mother began to drift apart. Was he responsible for her death? The Huntsman seemed to inhabit him and he became worse. I couldn't take it but had I thought he was capable of hurting my mother I never would have left. I was told she had a heart attack. The stories of her being locked in the freezer were sent to me by anonymous missives when I was already teaching at Cambridge, many years after the event. That's why I was angry about the Will and his ploy to make me feel that he cared. "Please Gabrielle, can't we just start over? Now that we know we are being called upon for a higher purpose, to build a refuge, let's do this together as a couple. Let's face this uncertain future as a team. I love you beyond any expectation I've ever had about how much I could love someone...could love someone as much as I love you. Please forgive me for any insensitivity I may have had concerning Peter. My thoughts have been only for you and about you, so I never noticed anyone else."

Gabrielle walked over to him and held his hand, "Okay, but let's take it a little slower. Really get to know each other. My attraction for you is beyond logic as if preordained. So, I want to understand why our being together is so important. I'll stay in the owner's quarters with the Countess and Irina for right now, and then we'll take it from there." With that, they held each other and kissed and it felt right again for Gabrielle.

On the drive to the funeral, they noticed the remnants of how special Fall was that year. A great showing of delights for which Vermont and New England were famous. Being in love, having this connection with each other and these glorious gifts of nature gave them a sense of purpose to try to save humanity and all life. Such a daunting task but one that was imperative, necessary, and one they would do all they could. They both knew the goddesses existed because they had seen them. But they did not know how to summon them. How to harness their energy and work with them.

The funeral was a conservation burial. Peter was laid to rest in a biodegradable container. The area of hallowed land would return to its natural state and be protected from development in this conservation cemetery. The trees and grasses would remain peacefully intact as a park for future generations to enjoy. Many such cemeteries were opening up in Vermont where the populace respected and promoted a green abundant earth. The funeral was a perfect reminder of how humanity must respect nature and how we are comforted by it. We should rejoice in the cycle of life and not fear it. They all became more committed to halting the ravages of climate change. It was a calling, a mission that must be heeded. This planet was so special giving and supporting life in the vastness of space where so far other life forms had not been found. This is our home. Humanity must wake up to its responsibility.

Afterwards, they ordered take-out Thai food for dinner at the inn and strategized the next steps.

"Should we remain open?" asked Irina. "I can handle breakfast but the restaurant would need a real chef."

"What do you think Gabrielle, Beau?" asked Tasa. "Well, making money would help for whatever we need to do here to turn this place into a refuge. So, I vote for leaving it open. We don't need to have the restaurant open for dinner and Irina says she can handle breakfast. So that will save some money. Afternoon tea can stay on the weekends because Irina has provided most of it before but we will charge a little more for it now if you all agree. Until we find that important book, we are sort of in a holding pattern," said Gabrielle and Beau agreed.

It had been a very profitable Fall season. Mrs. Jones suggested a chef to prepare a Thanksgiving feast in the restaurant and have it stay open for that weekend. All the guests signed up and the staff had a private ceremony where they all gave thanks for all their good fortune on the eve of the feast. They stood in a circle, clasped hands, and bowed their heads as Gabrielle led a prayer of gratitude. This ceremony had started spontaneously but quickly became a tradition after everyone checked out on Sundays. Tonight's prayer was not only to honor the Thanksgiving holiday but also to honor Peter.

After the feast was over and all went to bed came a grim reminder of their purpose and mission. A violent storm descended that was as brutal as the one when they first came up and were staying at Mrs. Jones's B&B. The weather had been quiet for months with just some light rain or drizzle. There had been numerous seasonal hurricanes but the storms petered out when they came near New York, making a right turn to the sea or traveled along the coast up to Maine. Vermonters were spared strong winds but not the heavy rain, making the grass and leaves shine a bright luscious dewy green.

This time they were not able to escape the winds that came with the torrential rain. A tornado ripped through the Rutland business district, blowing out store windows and flipping over cars. Then it traveled to the outskirts. The rafters of the inn shook and shimmied as the fierce wind whooshed against the windows. The windows held together as did the roof and the front door beat a rhythm against the frame of the house as if a wild animal was trying to get in.

Suddenly when the storm reached a crescendo of noise, everything got quiet. The guests and owners ran out of their rooms to the downstairs lobby waiting for something terrible. The quiet made them more nervous than the noise because they could see the fierce blowing wind and the rain coming down in sheets. The inn seemed buffered by a bubble of calm floating above the fray. They huddled together expecting the worst. But nothing happened. For hours. And hours. Out of fatigue and boredom, they all went back to bed. At breakfast, everyone revisited their experiences from the night before and all agreed that when the shaking stopped it was even more frightening instead of calming. Each had gotten under their covers waiting for something catastrophic to happen but nothing other than the downpour of rain happened and then sleep prevailed.

While they ate their breakfasts, the news was on the TV showing the devastation in Rutland. A loud gasp went through the group because the inn and the grounds had not been touched. Every tree was standing tall with all their remaining leaves intact. There was not even a chair misplaced on the porch. They knew this because the first thing they all did when they awoke was to walk outside. Have a look. Remarkable but most welcome. After breakfast, the owners went to their rooms and hugged each other relieved that the inn remained unscathed.

This bubble of calm must have been just like what happened during that first storm when Mrs. Jones's door blew in and windows broke but this inn had remained in perfect condition. They explained that to Irina who was taken aback. How? Why were we spared? The Countess just nodded and repeated over and over "Our protectors, the goddesses. Who else?" The arc of the bubble must also have extended to Mrs. Jones's place this time because she called to tell them her inn was spared as well. She was part of their group now.

They decided to close the inn for a few days after the Thanksgiving weekend to get it ready for Christmas. Beau suggested he get the tree and asked Gabrielle to join him. They hadn't spent too much time together recently because he had been asked to help with a paper for a colleague at Cambridge and he was busy writing and researching on his computer in his room. He was finished now and ready to party. Gabrielle was ready too. She loved Christmas but had never really celebrated at home because her mother wasn't capable and well...she was Jewish.

However, New York City was a marvelous place during the holidays and she would go with friends to skate at Rockefeller Center and see the giant tree. She had loved the hot roasted chestnuts sold by vendors on various street corners and the warm doughy pretzels. And of course, Macy's windows with the animated figures and winter scenes telling tales of Christmas. She also made sure to never miss Saks Fifth Avenue's light display projected onto its facade. But she never had her own tree. Never celebrated at home. Moreover, she never celebrated Chanukah either or received presents for her birthdays.

This was her lost childhood being relived right now. She would throw herself into celebrating it all. She looked up Chanukah on the internet to find out what was traditional. She would light the menorah candles, make the potato latkes, the challah bread, and brisket. She was lucky Chanukah and Christmas were at the same time this year. And this might be everyone's last chance for festivities before the looming climate crisis changed everything. Gabrielle would enjoy herself to the fullest. She had her new family, her new love, and she was the proprietor of her own business. It would be perfect if not for the looming danger. *Things could be worse.* The collapse of our ecosystem could be happening *right now.*

She and Beau would buy all the decorations and be in charge of making the inn look like Christmas. Gabrielle felt utter joy. Her very first Christmas tree! Irina would make fudge, assorted cookies, cakes, and pies. The inn would be overflowing with goodies. On the ride to the Christmas tree lot, they drove through back roads where she had gone with Peter on their first date together and thought of him while blinking back tears. A tragedy that would forever bring sorrow when she was reminded of him. However, by the time they arrived at the makeshift lot with its abundance of trees, she had recovered somewhat and was looking forward to this unique experience for her.

The strong scent of pine permeated the air as they strolled around the tree varieties. This scent would forever signify Christmas for her as it did for everyone else who put up real trees. She had no idea what would be considered a good tree or how to choose between them but Beau knew exactly what he wanted. Happy with his choice, it would be delivered to the inn later that day because this very large tree could not begin to fit on the roof of her SUV. He called the Countess and told her where to have them put the tree by the staircase. A perfect spot for all the Christmases at the inn. "Don't be put off by the size, it will fit." he said, "I grew up doing this."

After the tree was chosen, they went to a Christmas store pop-up in Rutland to get decorations. As soon as Gabrielle walked into the shop, she felt the warmth and glow of Christmas envelop her and she took a moment and basked in her feeling of joyfulness. Just then she heard a female voice, "We must all do what we can to preserve this planet. To share joy and love for all life for our time now and especially for the future." She turned around quickly but there was no one there. "Yes, I remember. You can count on me," Gabrielle said softly so as not to alert any nearby shoppers. Then she focused on her pleasant task.

As she walked around this charming place, she saw trees fully decorated and loved how they looked. She chose one she especially liked that had red and green ribbons, large glass ornaments, colorful dangling Santas, and globes. She took a picture of it and bought all the ornament types that were on it, planning to replicate it for their own tree. The next few days were a blur of cooking, cleaning, taking reservations, and decorating the inn. The tree took the most time and it was grand to listen to all the standard Christmas music while everyone made the place ready. It looked like a Christmas wonderland when they finished putting the lights on the building and porch.

The B&B had turned into a veritable charming postcard of the season and they decided to pipe music outside so that when anyone drove up wonderful standards like "I'm Dreaming of a White Christmas," greeted the weary traveler and cheered them up immediately. A marvelous time of year everyone agreed but the gnawing worry was waiting to take hold, *how many more would they be able to celebrate?* When these thoughts popped up, just like the consciousness of humanity, they shoved them aside and forgot about it. Being mindful and in the present became a huge help. So far so good, no chaotic weather event for a while now. The goddesses watched the creeping disregard take hold. They knew reality would come soon enough to not be ignored.

A new chef, Arthur Page, had been hired and everyone was satisfied with his skills and talent. He was a master at hearty breakfasts and delicious pastries for tea. He had complete autonomy to come up with a menu for evening dining. The group decided on a few dishes that he prepared quite well and told him not to try any more until after the holidays. He could just rotate the menu for now since people stayed at most four days. It was working out well in the lead-up to Christmas.

Gabrielle got a surprise that threw a monkey wrench into her relationship with Beau. She had moved back in with Tasa when they decided to slow it down and get to know each other by going on normal dates to restaurants, movies, bowling, and skiing. Getting to know him this way was sweet. Telling him about herself gave her the sense of closeness to another person that she had never experienced during her lonely childhood. One morning in early December, Gabrielle decided to glance at the reservation calendar to see how booked they would be for the next few weeks leading to Christmas and New Year's. They had hired a young townie to answer the phone and take reservations who informed her that, happily, the inn was quite full through the holidays. In fact, they had just that morning gotten a last-minute booking from a fellow with a charming British accent.

Coincidentally, just as she was reading his name, she heard someone call, "Gabrielle!" An unexpected shock threw her off-kilter. Captain Mark Davis was standing there in the flesh, wearing street clothes, so for a split second, she didn't recognize him. But then when she did, she quickly ran to embrace him and exchange kisses.

"Oh my! What a surprise!" she exclaimed. "How did..."

He quickly interrupted, "I'm an amateur sleuth," he laughed. "We put into dry dock unexpectedly, you see, because there were mechanical difficulties during the crossing. We've delayed the return for a week, much to the dismay and disappointment of our passengers. Messes up the entire calendar. But I thought, why not enjoy myself seeing you at your inn during the delay. So, I researched and it was quite easy really. I googled bed and breakfasts, your last name, and Vermont. Voila, your inn's detail page came right up." he paused for a moment and looked around. "I must say this is quite impressive."

Just then the Countess came out of the back offices. "I couldn't believe my ears. My word. What a wonderful surprise." She called out to the young man who carried the suitcases up "Allen, please put Captain Davis's suitcase in the green room." Irina came out and the Countess introduced her asked her to make some tea. "Come let's catch up and plan your stay. There's so much natural beauty to see here. What fun."

Unbeknownst to Gabrielle, Beau had walked in from the back entrance just as Mark arrived and he witnessed the entire reunion. Needless to say, he was quite perplexed. This Mark person was someone who seemed to know Gabrielle quite well and he wasn't pleased about it. He decided to join them for tea but would wait a bit. Linger nearby and listen in. One thing's for sure, Gabrielle kept surprising him, he laughed to himself. No other woman had ever affected him like her. Once tea was poured and the sweets served Mark said, "This B&B is quite spectacular with all the wood and charming reception area and this cozy breakfast room."

"Thank you. I'm so happy I decided to move up here with Gabrielle, as I told you on the ship. Every day that I'm here, I love it even more. The beauty of this structure and the surrounding natural beauty." said the Countess. "On the weekend evenings, we serve dinner here from a set menu. It's quite lovely and since this is Saturday, oh wait, by a strange coincidence we planned just a private dinner before the rush of Christmas guests. And it's as if we knew we'd have a British guest because for dinner tonight we'll be serving beef Wellington. How perfect! So, of course, you'll join us, Mark. But tell me, isn't it unusual for your ship to need major work between crossings after arriving in New York City? Please don't get me wrong it's such a treat to have you stay with us for a few days," she said.

"Most unusual, I'm afraid. The crossing was extremely rough for this time of year, and it lasted for nearly the entire voyage. People were quite ill. No one got their money's worth. The dinners were deserted. Quite awful. In all my years doing this, I've never seen weather as bad as this. Frankly, if this becomes the norm no one will want to travel by sea. I wouldn't blame them. It was quite frightening. The swells were so high there was real concern it would swamp the ship. I should say, I was concerned. Much worse than on your trip, I'm afraid."

A gasp went through the small group bringing them back to the mission presented by the Countess right here in this room. They all realized they had pushed down the concerns of climate change in preparation for the holidays, just like the rest of humanity had done for years. It was too alarming to deal with, much more comfortable to go about one's business and not worry about it. But unfortunately, reality would not be ignored. Just then Beau entered the room and Mark stood up to shake hands and was about to introduce himself when Gabrielle jumped in and took over.

"Beau, I'd like you to meet Captain Mark Davis. He was the Captain of the Queen Mary 2 when we crossed from New York City to Southampton this summer. He invited us to sit at his table one night for dinner and we became friends. It was an amazing ship and our suite was beyond anything I could have ever imagined. Unfortunately, we encountered a storm as well, otherwise, the voyage would have been beyond perfect."

"I've never crossed the Atlantic by ship," said Beau. I can imagine rough seas would take the fun out of it." And he sits down and Irina pours him some tea.

"Beau is the co-owner of this place having inherited it as well from my father who was married to Beau's mother, the original owner before she passed," said Gabrielle continuing the formalities.

"Well," said Mark, "it looks like you have a piece of paradise here. I'm looking forward to my stay in these lovely mountains far away from the sea." He sips his last bit of tea and gets up. "Time to freshen up. Do you serve cocktails?" "At 3:45 pm in the reception area. We love to sit on the porch as the sun goes down over the mountains and nurse a whiskey neat. The sunsets early these days," said the Countess.

"Sounds lovely," said Mark. Gabrielle offered to show him to his room and Beau remained seated as they left. He looked at the Countess to explain what was going on. She made light of it saying Mark was quite helpful and charming as was the rest of the staff during the rough spot on the crossing. She mentioned that Gabrielle had met him for drinks right before they flew home. "That was it. Nothing really," she said trying to sound nonchalant.

Meanwhile, Gabrielle felt slightly apprehensive as she led Mark to his room. Once she opened the door, he moved toward her for a kiss but she backed away. "Something wrong? You're not happy to see me? Our last meeting made me feel like there was, I don't know, a spark, an attraction between us. At least for me, there was."

"Yes, you are right but something unexpected happened in my life. Beau..."

"Oh," he interrupts and backs away. "No need to go on any further. It's fine. No problem. I understand perfectly." He immediately recovers, "We can still enjoy each other's company as friends and you can show me the sights. I've never been to Vermont. Do you ski?"

"Not really, but Beau is excellent. He grew up here. Knows all the really good trails."

"Sounds quite fun. I'll change for dinner and be right down for drinks."

"We're very casual here. Corduroy and wool."

"Sounds like just what I need. I'm ready to relax and I didn't bring any formal wear as it happens."

When Mark came down, he looked like a local in a red-flannel plaid shirt with a tan lambswool cardigan thrown around his shoulders, tan corduroy slacks, and hiking boots. He certainly knew what to wear in chilly Vermont. It didn't go unnoticed by Gabrielle that he looked smashing and it awakened her former attraction...but only slightly. She was giddy with feeling the center of attention of these two fabulous males. Pouring him an Irish whiskey, they clinked glasses before they went out to the porch. As they enjoyed their drinks, the desk clerk came over with disappointing news. Arthur, their chef just called to say he had come down with a mild cold. He decided to take the night off not wanting to get any worse for the busy holiday season.

"We will have to make do with leftovers, I'm afraid," said the Countess.

"Nonsense! Whenever I'm on leave I love to cook. Beef Wellington is my specialty by the way. Show me the kitchen after we finish our whiskeys."

Beau joined them on the porch and as the sun dipped behind the mountain peaks, it spread a warm glow over the valley and became reflected in the mirror-like stillness of the lake. For Gabrielle, each sunset was a moment of gratitude and solace as a gift of the precious natural world bestowed upon observers and the wise. When the show was over and the stars began to twinkle in the night sky, they toasted in homage and respect for witnessing this miracle. As they continued to sip their whiskies, Gabrielle mentioned Mark's interest in skiing and Beau was happy to oblige having wanted to go since the first snow the week before. He also suggested snowboarding and Mark was most enthused having always wanted to try it.

As they sat there growing their friendship, Mark went into more detail about the nail-biting crossing. The giant swells caused water to get on the bridge and short out some navigation systems as well as the thrusters and other propulsion equipment in the power plant. It was quite worrisome getting to port and took careful maneuvering. The crossings seem to be getting more dangerous of late, he told them, and he was even thinking about another line of work.

"Well perhaps after tonight, we might offer you a position as chef," said Gabrielle and laughed. "Climate change is real and we might be positioned here at this B&B to respond." Then she told him of the magical events that had happened there, the interaction with goddesses, and the mysterious book that will serve as some sort of guide. Of course, he was startled and in disbelief but he knew the crossings were becoming more hazardous.

"I'm glad that attention is finally being paid to this problem, albeit from some magical energy force. Humanity has ignored it for too long," said Mark.

"Well, so far we've not done anything because we haven't found the book. But it's preying on our minds and spirits."

"Just ask those magical goddesses where it is."

"If only," said Gabrielle. "Finding the book is like saying 'Open Sesame.' A test perhaps of our commitment. It's the key to unlocking everything. We'll find it, of that, I'm sure."

Mark then clapped his hands together, "Now, let's get things going to eat my world-renowned beef Wellington or perhaps I should say, its future name, beef Davis. Show me the way to the kitchen."

After he donned an apron, he set to work while remarking how he loved the kitchen ambiance with its giant fireplace, brick walls, walk-in pantry, and freezer. He made the puff pastry and sauce after Irina got all the ingredients. She had seared the meat earlier and it was being refrigerated while waiting for the next steps. Mark finished it off with the seasonings Irina had provided and added some from his own recipe that were in their well-stocked pantry. When he was satisfied with his rub, he wrapped it in the pastry and popped it in the hot oven while Irina made the salad. Beau went to the wine cellar and picked out two bottles of Cabernet. It was a lively and delicious dinner. Everyone agreed if Mark wanted to change careers, there was a job waiting for him. Fresh fruit and cheese rounded out the meal with a very nice and expensive Port wine.

After dinner, Beau and Mark headed for their rooms since their skiing and snowboarding day would start early the next morning. Gabrielle decided not to join them, she was a snow bunny and would prefer to enjoy a relaxing day reading by the fire since there was a short respite before it got busy. Everyone was relaxed and at peace. No one had any idea what the next day would bring.

Chapter Eighteen

The Unexpected

Journal entry:
OH. MY. GOD!

The morning weather could not have been more spectacular. A cloudless azure sky, calm air, temperature just below freezing to keep the fresh overnight snowfall like powder instead of icy. Irina provided a substantial breakfast of meats, eggs, and pancakes with plenty of robust hot coffee. The men would stop at an outfitter in Rutland to buy gear and clothing. The shop had everything from goggles, snowboards, boots, bindings, gloves with matching wool scarves, and hats. Both men bought overalls to put over their jeans. After a major outlay of cash, they looked like pros and the shopkeeper was very happy. Off they went on their adventure with high expectations and smiles. They chose Killington for its expanse over the smaller Pico. Beau would teach Mark how to snowboard and if he didn't like it, then he would rent skis. "I'm sure you'll love it, snowboarding is very cool and freeing," said Beau.

Mark enjoyed sightseeing the beautiful scenery as Beau drove along the backroads leading up to the ski resort. They avoided the subject of Gabrielle and arrived at the Killington ski area unfortunately at the late-morning rush but easily parked at a premium-priced area that Beau, anticipating crowds, had reserved.

"Quite a shock to see so many people," said Mark.

"People come from all over southern Vermont and the neighboring states to ski here. At least there are enough trails to keep the experience from feeling too crowded. That's why it's so popular."

Mark, an accomplished skier, picked up snowboarding easily. He loved the freedom of just sailing down the slope twisting and turning without holding cumbersome poles as he zipped past traditional skiers. They stayed on the close-in trails until Mark became very comfortable and then they ventured out to the more intricate and challenging slopes. Snowboarding for hours while increasing the trail's difficulty, they felt invincible as they went all the way to the top of the mountain where they ventured to an off-trail pristine area marked with a warning sign. There was no one else around. It was exhilarating. Until...

Explosion. Roaring sound. Thrown into the onslaught. Tumbling. Trapped. Suffocating. Total ...darkness.

Word of the avalanche spread with the same sickening speed as the avalanche itself. The Captain and Emma had been out for a drive near the ski mountain when they heard a loud rumbling in the distance. As the cascading river of snow picked up steam it dislodged waist-deep piles that joined the flowing explosion. The Captain jumped out of the car and in pulsating fear put his arms up when he saw the approaching mass. Just like that everything froze in place and the snow never reached their car. He was able to turn around quickly and drive back from whence they came before the snow started to move forward again.

"What in the world just happened?" asked Emma.

"We got lucky," said the Captain purposely ignoring the meaning of her question and called Gabrielle as well as other neighbors. The roads leading everywhere would be blocked from the massive snow dumps when the avalanche ended its powerful journey downhill.

Gabrielle went white and sunk down on a chair after she listened to what the Captain had to say. "On my god, oh my god," she said over and over crying hysterically. "Are there survivors, Captain, any survivors?" The Countess and Irina ran into the room after they heard Gabrielle wailing. She could barely speak. "Avalanche," she whimpered and then between sobs, "...oh my god Tasa...at the mountain. Beau...Mark." And she collapsed in utter despair. Irina and Tasa started crying and turned on the radio to hear the local news. It was all out-of-whack, so they shut it off.

The Captain had no answer for Gabrielle about survivors because he hadn't reached the ski area. He saw helicopters flying overhead as he was racing back to their own B&B but now after speaking with Gabrielle, they changed their destination because they learned that Mark and Beau had been snowboarding. Everyone sat stunned in front of the big screen TV in the owner's quarters. The sharp detail of the picture display made the broadcast more real and more gruesome. There was footage of the avalanche taken from the vantage point of the ski lodge rooftop bar by a guest with an iPhone.

It was horrifying. Then video clips from the helicopters came on. They saw skiers trying to outrun the oncoming massive flow who didn't make it. Watching in real-time as the skiers disappeared from sight under the sheer mass, strength, and speed of the snow. They gasped in horror. Sobbing and wailing. It was an awful sight to witness. In their heart of hearts, they were convinced that Mark and Beau were casualties of this rare but deadly tragedy.

In shock, they poured whiskey and ordered pizza that no one ate. Gabrielle called all the hospitals near Killington and Rutland hoping Mark and Beau were listed as patients. She called the police rescue team. No one had any information. They sat together talking about how horrible this catastrophe was for everyone on the mountain that day. They told stories about Beau and praised Mark in his capacity as captain of an important cruise line and wondered if they should notify Cunard of the terrible news. They decided to force themselves to be positive and wait at least until tomorrow. Hope against hope that the both of them would show up, or one of the hospitals would call them, or the police would come by with good news. The Captain and Emma left and Gabrielle went to bed in Beau's room exhausted from crying and quite drunk from not eating and drinking shot after shot. She brought a full bottle of Irish whisky with her.

After spending several minutes throwing up she lay down on his bed and sobbed into the pillow. His fancy cologne scent was everywhere. It covered the pillows and the duvet. It was unbearable. Even though she was dizzy and nauseous, she got up and took another swig from the bottle to make the mental anguish go away. It worked and she passed out on the bed but woke up in the middle of the night and remembered why she was there. She was wracked with sorrow. She pictured Beau, the first night she saw him London, how she was drawn to him and he to her. How handsome with his thick curly hair and piercing dark eyes. He had enveloped her when they had kissed, his height towering over her. His strong masculine hands. Details of which she took notice.

How stupid she was to slow things down between them. Oh, how she wished she could get the time back. Time lost forever and she wailed loudly again thinking of her loss. Then she thought of Mark and blamed herself for Mark coming here and started wailing again out of guilt. She had never felt this kind of loss before and it was the most terrible feeling of pain and agony. Her mother's death and her father's abandonment did not come close to this feeling. This was pure devastating sorrow. She lay down again to try and sleep and must have dozed off because she was roused abruptly by hearing a commotion downstairs, then someone was calling out her name loudly and urgently as he hobbled into the room.

"On my God, you're alive, you're alive," she sobbed and she jumped out of bed and grabbed him throwing him off balance. He tripped and fell on the floor with her on top of him.

"I twisted and badly sprained my ankle, I'm not too steady," he said and they laughed in relief as they kissed passionately and deeply.

"Is Mark downstairs?" she asked.

"He broke several bones and had a concussion, so he had to be airlifted. The rescue team put me on some sort of sled and skied me down. It was kind of fun after thinking I would die of suffocation. The air, the setting sun, the speed of downhill. It felt great to be alive knowing I would soon see you again."

"Oh, my darling. I thought I'd lost you and my life would be devoid of any joy for the rest of my days." And with that Gabrielle got up and reached out to help him stand up but he waved her away.

Beau rolled over on his side and grabbed the edge of the bed to get support to hoist himself up on one foot. The bed shifted and he fell back on the floor with a heavy thud. He lay there for a minute trying to figure out how to get up while Gabrielle moved a heavy chair from the living room and placed it close to him. His foot had been put in a heavy support shoe at the hospital when he was admitted, making it clumsy to try and get up. He was able to rise up to a sitting position using the chair as leverage but then fell back on the floor.

"What's that under the bed?" he asked as he sat on the floor.

Chapter Nineteen

The Diary and Its Secrets

Journal entry:
We found it! Hallelujah!

Gabrielle finally helped a limping Beau stand up and come downstairs into the dining room. Irina and Tasa were making coffee and breakfast. The aroma made everyone's juices flow and euphoria stoked the prevailing vibe. Beau could not keep his hands off Gabrielle and she could not keep her hands off him. They hugged as they stood there and hugged as they sat down.

"We've got something important to tell you. Call the Captain and Emma to join us for breakfast and also let them know Mark and I are safe, well I'm safe and Mark is at least alive and being taken care of at the hospital," and he put his mother's diary on the table and everyone gasped and shouted at once.

"Wait! Isn't that Beau's mother's diary that I found?" asked the Countess. "Could that be the book the goddesses told me to find?"

"A diary is a book and it's the only book that Mrs. Barnstable kept hidden," said Gabrielle. "We need to open this and find out what's inside but my instincts tell me we will be given what we need in this diary. I'm sure this diary is the book we were told to find. Let's wait for the Captain and Emma and do this together. This concerns all of us. I think we can cut it open if we can't find the key. Maybe Tasa can look in the drawer where she found it?"

Irina made more coffee and toast while they waited. As they enjoyed the robust coffee and its savory aroma, they asked Beau to fill them in further on his near-death encounter on the mountain. *If it doesn't upset you too much*, they all chimed in. While he spoke, Gabrielle picked up the book and kept rubbing its leather cover as if she could magically discern the information inside through her fingers. Beau took a large drink of his coffee and sat back on the chair and seemed to be lost in thought for a moment. Then he sat up and started his recollections of that most eventful and frightening experience.

It had been a most enjoyable morning with no indication of the peril that awaited them. Mark easily learned how to snowboard as he was an excellent skier. There were crowds by the time they arrived but there were enough trails to snowboard without feeling encumbered by the large turnout. After a few hours, the crowds started to build becoming denser. Waiting in line for the lifts became annoying and they decided to call it a day. Then they spotted a pristine trail off the beaten track and Mark felt comfortable enough to try it. It felt daring and exhilarating and most importantly...empty.

The weather was ideal and the challenging trail with its twists and turns meandered through some glorious forest and wide-open downhills. It had been snowing lightly all morning but after it stopped the snow glistened in the sunlight. Everything in view was sharp and clear. Glorious. A cloudless sky, a light breeze, warm enough to ski without their jackets which they left in their lockers after they had stopped for a shot of whiskey at the lodge bar. It gave them more agility to snowboard just in their sweaters. So, they were doubly excited to go off on their own.

The rarely used trail was hard to make out so Beau yelled back at Mark to follow him. About 20 minutes down the trail Beau heard a loud *whumph!* just up ahead. It sounded like a heavy sack of potatoes hitting the soft fresh layer. Mark was several feet behind when the river of snow started to cascade toward them. Beau shouted for Mark to watch out as the snow quickly overcame them and they were wallowed by another heavy blast. Beau was smothered, not able to move. He couldn't tell how far under the snow he was but it was pitch dark with just a sliver of light coming through way above him bringing with it a small amount of oxygen. He started to lose consciousness from the heavy impact that had hit him hard on his head and the lack of oxygen when he felt movement near him.

Someone or something was causing the snow around him to move as if digging him out. He forced himself to remain conscious worried it might be a bobcat or bear. After several minutes of furious work, the snow fell away from him and he took large gulps of air while shocked to see the goddess with the red hair floating above him. Her white gown touched the pile of snow she had created in her desperate frenzy to free him from being buried under several feet of it. Venus, who had first appeared to him when he was a young boy. Who had protected him from harm and always came when needed. Who followed him to London. *Oh my*, thought Gabrielle, *she also followed me.*

Beau took another sip of coffee and continued in a shaky voice revealing how much the retelling of this horrible act of nature had frightened him. When he stood up from his snow prison, he shook his head to shake the remaining snow off his face while gathering his wits and watched in wonder as Venus floated over to another spot much farther down the slope where he realized Mark must be buried. He was afraid to move because he realized he had a lot of pain in his right ankle and could fall into a snowdrift, become buried again and be of no help.

Venus used her powers again to blow the snow away so Mark could breathe. Incongruously, when Beau paused for a moment to watch her, he took in the scenery and acknowledged how serene and beautiful it was up there now that the snowpack was quiet and still. It was almost hard to imagine the dangerous aggressive onslaught of a speeding snow tidal wave just moments earlier. Now it was blue sky, the gray stone and pine-tree green mountain vistas, and of course the pure white glistening snow. As he watched her, he realized at once that getting down with Mark would be a problem since there had been no acknowledgment from Mark that he was OK. Venus gave Beau the nod that Mark was alive but couldn't move. Something was probably broken. *Now, what to do?* He was frightened but he should have trusted his goddess protector to find a way. A rescue.

He heard the whirring sound of helicopter blades and up it popped over the ridge and Beau waved. The crew saw him and shouted their acknowledgement. As it happened, Beau and Mark were right at the apex of the avalanche and the snow passed beyond them down the mountain. So, the ridge behind them wasn't too deep for the helicopter to land. The rescue team came with two sleds. One for carrying Mark to the helicopter to fly him to the hospital because Beau had screamed at them that Mark was badly hurt. Then they used the other one to ski Beau down on the sled where he was laid flat and tied in.

Beau began coughing into his hand to camouflage his sobs. This natural disaster had taken a real toll on him and he hadn't realized how much he was shaken. Gabrielle noticed his distress and got up and put her arms around him. Then Tasa and Irina did the same. Just then the Captain and Emma came in and rushed over to Beau with hugs and warm expressions of love and relief. After everyone moved away from comforting Beau, the Countess told Emma of their find.

"That's the book?" asked Emma. "It looks like an ordinary diary but a little worn."

"Yes," said the Countess." I found it in an empty dresser drawer tucked away in the back corner. I have to admit I was curious what Mrs. Barnstable had to say about her life but I gave it to Gabrielle because she is the owner of this place. And then Beau showed up and she gave it to him."

"We put it aside," said Gabrielle, "because we couldn't open it without cutting it and then forgot about it. How it wound up under the bed must have happened when the cleaning people came. It must have dropped on the floor and then was kicked under the bed when they were vacuuming. What a strange coincidence that with Beau's twisted ankle he lost his balance and fell on the floor right in the line of sight of the book under these high beds."

"Not a coincidence, I should think," said the Countess. "Well, let me see if perhaps there's a key in the same dresser drawer where I originally found it."

Irina served more coffee to the Captain and Emma, who asked numerous questions of Beau and wanted news of Mark. Emma told them that of her many years living there avalanches were quite rare. One happened at Smugglers' Notch near Stowe resort two years ago and one had recently occurred in the Catskills. Before that, it was about 12 years past when an occurrence happened near Stowe at Mt. Mansfield, the highest mountain in Vermont.

"How unfortunate that you both got caught in such a freak accident of nature. We should all go and see Mark before it gets too late," she said.

Gabrielle went in to see how Tasa was doing in her search for the key. She had all the drawers emptied but was still furiously searching.

"We would like to visit Mark before it gets too late. Will you join us?"

"I've still not found it, and I have to clean up this mess. Please send him my best wishes. Let him know we'll take good care of him when he is discharged. That is if you agree."

"Certainly, he'll be treated like royalty as our guest."

"Okay, then I'll see you later. Irina and I will have dinner waiting when you get back."

Mark was not good, but alive. He was still unconscious and had a broken arm, a broken tibia on his right leg, and had shattered his spine in two places. The doctor informed them that he had barely escaped being paralyzed but that luckily, he would make a full recovery after his surgery. The recovery will be quite extensive—six to 12 weeks after surgery on his spine. The doctor volunteered, "He won't being going back to work anytime soon."

At least Mark's medical expenses would be fully covered by Cunard, so that was a relief. Working for a cruise line and stopping in ports all over the world put an employee at financial and health risk by just being covered under the UK's National Health Service. For places like the United States, Cunard provided the necessary additional coverage. Gabrielle gave the doctor her contact information for when Mark was out of surgery and the group stayed for a few moments longer after the doctor left. Mark would go to rehabilitation nursing care after he was discharged and then come to the inn. They discussed how they would all take care of him after he came.

"It's hard for me to take in how severe his injuries are," said Beau. "Apparently, he was right in the track of the cascading snow while I was just to the left of it. He got thrown into a tree and then was pushed down several feet and hit a boulder." He took several deep breaths to calm himself.

Gabrielle sobbed quietly visualizing what Beau was saying and horrified at the mental image. Emma remarked that at least the doctors seemed to know what they were doing. Mark would come out of this alive and would heal, for that all of them were grateful. When they got back to the inn a tasty and hearty chicken soup was heating up on the stove and the key was placed in the center of the table.

Chapter Twenty

We Are Stunned

Journal entry:
The key is the key,
the path is revealed, much joy
and much work awaits.

Beau was still an emotional wreck after seeing the state Mark was in and somehow feeling responsible. As if he could have...should have...been able to stop an avalanche. As they ate the soup, he blamed himself for suggesting going on that trail. He kept repeating, "The thought of an avalanche never crossed my mind when we were out there." It was an unexpected accident everyone told him with hugs. He had never taken a class in understanding avalanches. In those classes, skiers are taught that avalanches are triggered by snowpack conditions and by skiers crisscrossing on a slope with a snowpack that has a weak foundation. There had been no public warning of potential conditions until they had already started snowboarding and out of reach of getting any reports. Besides they were at risk anywhere on that mountain, not just that trail.

Weak layers in the snowpack can be created by weather conditions such as temperature, humidity, and wind. Also, early snowstorms followed by long dry spells are ripe conditions for avalanche-creating snowpack. Avalanche warnings by the local weather stations are not always heeded by skiers because they are only warnings and people who want to ski will take the risk. Anyway, Beau hadn't seen a warning, and there were many skiers on the mountain. It had snowed in the morning dropping a light fresh snow layer over an older layer. But that could describe most days.

Everyone comforted him by telling him that even if they had been on the normally used trails further down the mountain, it might have been worse with the buildup of so much more snow cascading on top of them. It was reported that several people further down the mountain had been killed after slamming into trees and being thrown off a cliff. A horrific loss of life.

Then they solemnly got to the business at hand. The diary would be read out loud. After some discussion, it was decided that Gabrielle would be the one to read it. They all had felt that Beau reading the words of his dead mother while in such emotional distress might catapult him over the edge. And so, they all got comfortable sitting on the plump sofas in the main reception room near the fireplace.

Beau prepared himself to be strong and also not to fall asleep, being totally exhausted and very stressed from his traumatic experience. But listening to his mother's words was surprisingly calming and soothing. It was good to feel her presence again and he forced himself to remain alert while silently aching inside as he pictured being embraced in her nurturing hug. As Gabrielle started to read a feeling of love permeated her as she touched the book. It was most pleasant. And so, with reverence, she shared Abigail Barnstable's diary:

Each night, in vivid dreams, dreams of startling clarity, I see my other self, the chosen one. This other Abigail, also known as Abby, is my enlightened and superior spirit on a quest, a journey for salvation and empowerment. The other goddesses, my mothers, have given me special gifts for this important task, a task not just for me and for them but for all women, and, in turn, for all mankind. A seeking, a commitment to the life force and profound knowledge that we all know but have forgotten in the three-dimensional gravity-bounded world. A world of greed, selfishness, and tyranny toward nature.

Sing the music of strength.
Sing the dream of joy fulfilled.
Sing the music of all living things.
Sing the flourishing of mother earth.
Sing the return to a healthy land.
Sing.

When dawn arrives, I am snugly back in my normal world bathed by the morning light. I am aware and awake and in my own bed contemplating my recent visit to my alternate existence. The heightened pulsating rhythm comes to life in my memory as I relive my escape to the nethermost point in the enchanted wood at the edge of reality. Immediately, and unwelcome, is the heaviness that comes over me when my daylight world encompasses me. I feel shackled, burdened by the limited dimensions of this plane and the limited abilities to perceive my surroundings. Here, in the everyday world, I am Abigail Barnstable, wife of Philippe Bernstein, mother of Beau, and proprietor of this cozy bed and breakfast inn on a lovely lake rimmed by stately homes, thick woods, and flowering fields. Magical to behold and magical to experience. I have much gratitude to experience such a life here and such a life in my enchanted wood.

As a young girl, I was filled with a rich imagination that was a slave to wanting more, wanting something special along with the weird contradiction of wanting something ordinary. And yet, I never can be ordinary in the true sense, because I have seen a world where all is possible. I have seen the ethereal and untold beauty in the world of my goddess mothers. Unbounded potential made real and whole. Perfection. Unconditional love.

As I reflect and cogitate on the truth of my visits to this alternative world or parallel dimension where wisdom resides for all eternity, I embrace my special gifts and acknowledge my calling, my destiny. And so, I have accepted the strangeness while leading my so-called normal life. I can fit in among the average persons, the unenlightened, as I float on the periphery. In my attempt to merge this dual aspect of my existence, I have woven a truth about my life. I am but an apprentice leaning in to understand this wisdom, a vessel to open up the world constrained by the five senses, to the spirit world, the eternal world. This is not an easy task and so I have attempted to write it all down and dissect it, examine it, and piece it all together.

There are those who will believe and those who will refute my unusual journey through life. My challenge is to convert the non-believers and to replenish the faith of those who do. This challenge is especially poignant for women, for we are the embodiment of the feminine divine. Have an open heart dear readers and an open mind. My journey might be a reflection of your own emotional journey. My acknowledgment of the Earth's need for the gentle but firm command of this power of the feminine divine is a ringing of the gong. We have the help of the goddesses who will show us the way. The goddesses who will come when summoned. They gave me the tools to summon them as I will give to you, my dear readers. I will impart some of their wisdom that has served me well.

Years are but moments in time.
All is relative.
Seek knowledge.

Always be in a state of becoming.

It is time to begin your own personal journey which is now a necessary journey for all mankind. Before you learn how we can save our Earth, our home, it is important for you to understand how my own awakening and enlightenment brought me the necessary skills for the change that's needed. My goddess mothers have been with me my entire life. They followed me to this inn where they wove their magic to create an atmosphere of happiness, not only for me and Beau but also for my guests. At some point, the dark forces, led by the one we've come to know as the Huntsman, whose role is to cause disruption and destroy any joy, came to this inn. He caused my death, thus hastening my passing over to permanently reside in the goddess world.

This saddened my family but it freed me to explore with utmost care and leisure the goddess realm that is now my forever home having been taken there as soon as I passed over. The Huntsman hadn't realized I was one of their chosen because the goddesses shielded his knowing the truth about me, his awareness of my role. Duped into strengthening their cause by not realizing I would join their army against him to save all life, including you dear readers of this diary, from extinction. He tried to remove me but to no avail. After I joined their forces against him and after much aggression, we drove him out. He is gone from the spirit realm at the moment but will most assuredly return. We must stay vigilant because he appears in many forms and takes on many roles in the gravity-bound, five-senses world, your world. He can be a member of our government or even a malevolent president aspiring to become a dictator.

The world is in grave danger when that occurs. This evil and cruel energy can exacerbate the ills this planet suffers. This country has had such a leader recently, it is the reason climate change is now happening at an accelerated rate, that pandemic diseases are having devastating consequences for humanity, and that there is an increased threat of nuclear war that would annihilate world populations. Any events varying from the norm can be disastrous when the energy of the Huntsman is in power. Religious people in the Judeo-Christian tradition call him the Devil. This demagogue was forced out by overwhelming goodness. Overwhelming goodness trumps evil. Always. But it is temporary. We must remain on high alert. We must work to keep the forces for good in power. To reverse the trends set in motion by evil and ignorance.

And so, I am sending out a call to fill our troops with goodness. All women have the ability to become goddesses imbued with their loving spirit and grace. But they must be awakened. This is my calling. This diary is the beginning of the awakening. It is written by me from the goddess realm enabled by the magical ability bestowed on me to communicate with your world. I am able to tell my story in detail in order to guide and inspire. I encourage you to watch for signs that are similar to what was presented to me, the hints and miracles that might be in your own lives right now to show you the way. Follow where it leads, as I did. Most importantly, to all who are reading this now, you are not here by accident. You were chosen. You are special. You are needed.

At this point, Gabrielle pauses for a moment wondering what everyone thought about what she had just read. Irina offered to make more tea or coffee. The consensus was they took the call for help very seriously. They were grateful to the goddesses for their work in awakening humanity to the dire situation of climate change, intrusion of evil in politics, and the need to come together as one people of one world, our only home. They wondered if Beau had any idea that his mother had been chosen by the goddesses and had visited their realm her entire life.

Beau cleared his throat before he spoke revealing his emotional upset. "These revelations both shock me and feel normal," he said. "The goddesses were always around me as a child but my mother and I never shared those encounters. I thought they just materialized for me. Never realized, it was my mother who was the real reason they surrounded me. It is so profound and comforting to know her spirit lives on. And that I might see her again as one of the goddesses. It's quite wonderful and at the same time...implausible."

After they stoked the fire, replenished their drinks, they resumed their positions on the comfortable furniture. Before Gabrielle returned to her spot, she felt the urge to rub Beau's shoulders in a calming and loving gesture and then went back to her chair and continued reading while tucking up her legs and leaning on its arm. She continued in her hushed and respectful tone:

For me, the experience of being in the goddess world always started the same way. As I lay in bed, in anticipation of a new adventure, I patiently waited until finally losing all sense of place, closed my eyes, and then started to dose. A flurry of activity seemed to tickle my closed eyes and popped them open. I welcomed the intrusion. Circles of white light, like ping pong balls, bounced back and forth, up, and down, here and there in the darkness of my bedroom. These lights illuminated tiny dust particles that floated lazily about my room. In a sudden movement, these dust particles collapsed to form shapes that turned into the words "Come." And then, "Hurry."

The anticipated visit of these dancing orbs and accompanying messages beguiled me. Their visits brought a fluttering of excitement, an expectation of impending joy, and a recognition of duty. As a young child, when the orbs first began appearing, I had no fear only a tingle of pleasure rising upward from my toes, along with unabashed wonder at this spectacle.

Then, the small orbs would begin to merge forming one large circle and rest at the foot of my bed, hypnotizing my thoughts. Signifying the next stage when the journey to the other realm began. The circle would grow larger and then surround me while reaching into the sacred part of me, the spirit of me, the everywhen of me—my eternal self. The total thrill of visiting my other mothers would morph into ecstasy, especially since my biological mother was distant and aloof.

Starlight and moonbeams would guide the way. A blinking of on...then off...then on again, a pulsating rhythm. A beacon, a beckoning call, a summons. The high-pitched sonar of whales from untold pods across all the seas of the world sang together in concert along with a thrumming primal accompaniment that became the soundtrack of my journey.

The Earth's song.
These calming sounds resonated within me, a harmonic response.
My heart soared in delight.
The submission, then the blending.
The light.
Me.
Now one.

There was a sense of elevation. A great height. A vista. My spirit was soaring above the trees and into the wispy clouds. Now, the wind kissed my lips. Like a majestic bird flying through space far from Earth, the journey was instinctive and laughter bubbled up from deep within my core. I was going home. Home, to the hidden place of nurturing love and hope. Home to the eternal beginning of all things. The gestation of the spark, the birth of intelligent purposeful energy.

Energy that manifests itself in all life and in the form of me, Abigail, the goddess/human. As I journeyed among the twinkling starlight to this other realm, my hair grew long and flowed gently behind me in the night sky. My skin became pale as alabaster glowing in the moonlight. I was becoming as lovely as the goddesses and as bright as the stars that marked my pathway.

When I'm in this other reality, my revered wonderland where my goddess mothers, mostly those worshipped in Ancient Egypt, dwell. I live in a simple small cottage at the edge of a deep wood, hidden, safe, and solitary. However, when I was but a child, a chosen mother goddess stayed and watched over me. This sacred place was my sanctuary, my respite. Here, I was at peace and where lessons about the human condition were taught by the counsel of stately leaders. They all cherished me and told me so, frequently.

"You are one of us in strength and a beauty to behold. Your power is in your wisdom and the divine feminine, such as is ours. You are a goddess in the truest sense, as all women can be," said Isis and all the others concurred.

"You have many gifts," Hathor and Isis told me, "and you will use them quite soon. It is an important task you have been given. The changeover must happen no matter how long it takes, even all of your lives."

Hathor, mother of Horus and the sun god Ra, and Isis, wife of Osiris of the Old Kingdom in Egypt, were first among the other avatars of the divine feminine, teachers of the cosmic truth of all things and ancient wisdom keepers. They nurtured and protected me and were not only the lead goddesses but my first mothers. Bathed in a warm glow that bent the energy around them, sometimes they merged together as one, sometimes they remained as two divinities. Even the powerful Nieth, goddess of war worshiped in the ancient Egyptian pantheon, recognized their position, and respected and loved them for it.

The mission was the ultimate progression for humanity, Hathor explained, as she floated on an unseen current of air. She wore a spun-cotton white gown that flowed like wings behind her and then as needed shaping to become her limbs. It was the enlightenment, the openness of thought and curiosity, the awareness that the energy of the feminine divine was needed to keep the planet from dying and in turn its inhabitants. Our role was to oppose the forces that pressed against the seeking of knowledge and the non-acceptance of the chaos to come with the impending climate crisis. For what had been slowly evolving but steadily moving forward as a mindset for emancipation from the dark and oppressive history of humanity, now seemed to be losing ground. Backward *in time to the beginning of the fight.*

The chant, the song, filled the air, filled the wood. Filled my mind. Seeking truth and fighting against climate change and foolish thinking must prevail.

Oh, the joy of the light of knowledge.
Oh, the pleasure of total awareness, total presence.
In the moment and in the now.
Singing freedom for all things.
The enlightened mind is life's gift for us all.

"The women of your world, in your country, in particular," Isis said, "have started to lose the power they had gained over many years of fighting and of struggle through either religious and political oppression, cultural decay, or poverty. A backward trend is starting after so much progress had been made. That is one of the reasons we have become active again. That distressing turn of events and the willful ignorance and avoidance of the changing climate on Earth. Humanity is in grave danger and it is always the women who suffer the most."

She told me I must help to clear the path for the changeover from earthly women to powerful goddesses. My mother goddesses had allowed the placement of powerful goddesses of all the ancient religions, among the mortals, the unenlightened, to help them create a sea change to create a society, like in Ancient Egypt when women had no shackles. The mission was to create enlightenment in the minds of women who had lost those thoughts of empowerment through subjugation and religious extremism. Some women had lost their divine spirit. Their femininity and nurturing instincts had been drowned by baseness and masculine tendencies. A merging of the sexes, but not in a good way for these women and, in turn, a threat to all women.

I knew that my life's journey would be heroic and challenging. I knew I would have to find these special enchanted women, to uncover their power without the help of my goddess mothers. That was the work, to discover their true selves was the test. The eye of Horus would lead the way. The symbol of the changeover. This cherished amulet adorned these women but hidden from view to the world and for some even hidden to themselves.

I would know when I was ready for this task and I remained alert, always alert, for the signs. But my work was cut short by the Huntsman's return. However, I kept copious notes. Writing down the wisdom of Hathor and Isis and the others in my journals so that the teachings would not be forgotten. I would chant my song. I knew instinctively that with Isis/Hathor as my mother, I was special, chosen. A child of power and a force for good. In the goddess realm, I even went into battle without any hesitation.

For even here, there were negative forces. My mentors told me that darkness made the light brighter. I learned that all creatures, all life from the smallest ant to the largest bear, both in this realm and the normal world, were filled with spirit and must be protected, not hunted. And so, I nursed sick animals of the forest and protected the weak ones.

All the spirits and creatures of the wood paid me homage, knew my mission was purposeful, and my intent pure. All sang my praises. And that is why in this gravity-bound world a herd of deer stayed close to the inn to this very day. To protect and find protection. Seeking my replacement at the inn, a young woman of strong moral character was selected. Known as Gabrielle, she was chosen many lifetimes ago and so all that has happened to her in her childhood was the ordained prologue for her destiny.

Gabrielle stopped reading visibly in shock and began to lose her breath and started to hiccup. She was physically and emotionally distraught. How did this woman know about me? A person I have never met. "Oh my," said the Countess. Beau sat up and said "Wow." "Irina said, "Of course," and the Captain and Emma said nothing but appeared stunned. Irina ran to get a glass of water that she handed to Gabrielle to help calm her hiccups. "Shall we stop her reading for the night and get our wits about us?" asked the Countess.

They all agreed to take a break until morning. There was still some time until guests arrived for the holidays and they would visit Mark in the afternoon. The Captain and Emma accepted their invitation to come to breakfast and everyone said goodnight. Gabrielle went upstairs with Beau. A somber and troubling mood hung over everyone. This knowledge made everything real. Very real. Not a silly game like playing with a Ouija board. The warnings, the important work, the gathering of these selected souls, this posse. It was overwhelming and quite worrisome. Danger was on the way. Real danger. Biblical like the flood and Noah.

"I feel so manipulated," said Gabrielle. "I know it seems childish, but it gave me some comfort that my father finally thought about me, even if it was at the end of his life. He gave me this inheritance after all the years of ignoring my existence, this inheritance that changed my life in so many ways. So, were all his actions controlled by the goddesses? Him marrying your mother? My meeting you? Bringing Tasa and the Captain here? Mark's accident that might mean he can no longer work on a cruise ship and possibly stay here? All planned like we are puppets? Come to think of it, Venus appeared a few times before and after I met you. Do you think the dinner was provoked by her, somehow? That our meeting there was planned?"

"Perhaps," said Beau. "But what does it matter? I'm happy about the way things turned out. Couldn't be happier, ecstatic actually. So, what if we're some Punch and Judy puppets with much less physical drama between us, of course," he laughs sheepishly. "If manipulating me means that we wound up together, that's just fine by me. More than fine. I could do without the end-of-the-world scenario that comes with it, though," he deadpans.

Gabrielle punches him in the arm. "Yes, our lives would be perfect except for one giant problem, will we survive, or will anyone survive the coming planet climate crisis?"

"I say, let's stick our heads in the sand and pretend it's all a hoax and that we will survive anything as long as we have each other."

"And the goddesses will fix it all," she said.

"Of course, the goddesses will save us," he said.

They went to bed and snuggled in each other's arms for the entire night waking up to a light dusting of snow. A hearty breakfast of hot porridge waited with the alluring aroma of fresh coffee. The Captain and Emma arrived as the snow started to get heavier and accumulating quickly. Irina called the greengrocer, the butcher, and the supermarket to get their order delivered ASAP before the snow piled on even more. They needed to stock up on fresh vegetables, meat, and canned goods to be stored for the guests that were due to arrive the following day through Christmas and New Year's. After the delivery and second and third cups of coffee in front of the roaring fire, they all settled down to hear the rest of the diary read again by Gabrielle.

This time she seemed a little anxious as to what waited for them, in particular herself, in her reading. She began reading quietly but then cleared her throat and read in her full voice

Of course, without a doubt, my visits to my other mothers on the tail-end of a moonbeam became for me the good part of a fairy tale, where there was always a happy ending. I was shown by my other mothers, the lovely goddesses, that there was a very different way of thinking about life and living life. Wonderful, beautiful, strong women populated my other world. The world I write about in this diary. A world that seemed so real in my dreams or deep meditation. These graceful and gentlewomen showered me with love, nurtured my intelligence, and gave me the tools for my personal strength.

Read on to learn how to summon these goddesses. Practice doing that. Ancient Egyptians believed speaking names out loud was heard in the spirit realm, so you must call them by name. Form a circle and hold hands. Have pure thoughts and a pure heart. When they appear, they will greet you one at a time to get to know you. I will be among them. You must also understand how I earned the right to be called one of their own and by doing so gave all mortal women this same ability. My quest, my mission was to prove my worthiness. Because I fulfilled my mission, I paved the way for you, dear readers.

When I was quite young, my mothers, who had been with me for my entire life, told me that as soon as I approached my blossoming, becoming a woman in the biological sense, I must begin the steps toward fulfillment. Start the process of the great changeover. Peel the layers to achieve my prize. "What is the prize," I asked? The quest will reveal itself as you progress, they told me. It began in the deep woods, hidden but not so hidden. I ventured into the thicket surrounding my cabin because it was the place where I alighted from my mystical energy field in the cosmos. I crawled among the bramble bushes and furrowed in the ancient forest like a tiny mouse, squirrel, or snake even. Bent low, I moved slowly scraping my knees and shins. Then it came to me, crystallized in my mind. I was searching for the mysterious mushroom, the fungus that gives you second sight. The idea was imparted to me as I began my descent into the thicket.

The hidden mushroom dwells among the pines and palm trees of the swamp, among the roots protruding from the ground. This sacred

plant would give me the knowledge of how to begin. I breathed deeply. The pungent lush odor of the swamp filled my nostrils and dissolved in my mouth. The taste of the deep woods coated my tongue, the thick foliage and fecund dirt became entwined with my biology, became enmeshed with my DNA. This is life. The source, the reason for the quest, the end at the beginning. Somehow, I knew that. Knew that I would come full circle.

For several days I returned there, or maybe it wasn't days but just moments, moments of thoughtfulness in the mortal world, the world of limited senses and linear time. Maybe not to this very spot but near, very near. I groveled and sweated but went home empty-handed. To my home in this wood, my second home, or perhaps it was my first, the home of my heart. The elusive mushroom did not frustrate me or bring a notion of defeat because the quest was the game. The quest was the reason for the quickening of my pulse. I knew that when I found the treasured mushroom, it would lead to another prize, like a treasure hunt.

In an effort to communicate with that which I sought, to bring forth the field of connection, I decided to quiet my mind and to concentrate. So, I sat upon the soft spongy ground and expanded my spiritual knowledge to communicate with the wisdom surrounding me held within the ancient trees. The tall trees can reveal their secrets of which there were many. My mothers, who went by many names, Hathor, Isis, Athena, Venus, Ishtar, and Neith had told me that. The canopy of the live-oak trees kept the searing sun at bay. And so, I sat and sang the ancient wisdom chant handed down from mother to daughter. The chant was soothing like the humming sound of a vibrating body—the calming sound of OM. The body wisdom. The heart beating, the breath coming in sequence, the rhythm of life. The harmonic throbbing of all things. The music of life.

I could hear colors. The color yellow of the tiny wildflowers was a sound bright and tingling. I could smell the sounds of small birds chirping, the aroma like a dozen sweet roses. All of my senses were altered and enhanced. My consciousness expanded and brightened and I was aware of my connection to all things and I sat this way for many moments. An hour even and then stood. I raised my arms and blessed this spot. Nature was the key. Love of nature meant love of all things. I was humbled by this love and renewed. The trees whispered their knowledge with the rustle of their leaves. The birds sang the lessons of seeing all with more than eyes.

The communication although unspoken was nevertheless relayed. Especially so for someone like myself who always has had special gifts of knowing another way, another reality. I preferred to leave behind the crusty and dust-covered reality filled with the darkness and evil shadows of meanness. In that other reality, the boxed-in reality, the confined reality of a world defined by touch and smell and sight, hearing, and taste, I realized my time spent there was full of yearning for something better. There, where the humdrum habits of understanding only what one can glean through five senses that trapped the soul longing to rid itself of cages and bindings. But here in this other reality was a world where mind and spirit were made real, were tangible.

Thus, I sat contemplating these opposing realities.

And finally spied what I sought.

With the magical mushroom within reach, I knew that the knowledge given to me would move me forward in my task. I was ready now for whatever challenges lay ahead. Delighted to be alive and in this skin, the crescendo of the pulsating energy field of particles propelled me on my way. Like a symphony, the vocal beauty of everything, the rhythm of the universe. And I carefully loosed the mushroom from its bindings and started to take my first bite, then thought, maybe it's better to wait until I get home. Since my reaction could be monitored there for safety.

"Mother, Mother, I found it, the mushroom!" I called happily to Nieth as I ran inside the cottage. "Look! Look!"

"Well, darling, that was very quick. Let me see it." Nieth took the mushroom and as soon as she realized what it was, threw it on the ground.

"Why are you doing that, Mother? I needed that to start the quest! You told me so!"

I bent down to pick it up. "No! You mustn't! Stop at once! It's poison!"

Then I stopped abruptly and looked confused. "You described it. I know I chose what you described. Why did you describe poison? And also, the trees told me. I listened to their whispers. And the birds. I might have tried some before I ran home, I don't understand. Do you all want me dead then?"

"Abby, darling, this is a trickster. A fake. It looks like one thing but is another. To all who see it, it appears as the sight-giving mushroom for which you had been sent. But there are always evil forces that surprise me. We cannot be that trusting of anything. It is good that this lesson came so early in the quest. Do not trust a thing to be what it seems. Do not take anything for granted. Be alert to falsehood. I had no premonition about this and thought I had sent you on a safe mission. It is a testament to the positive forces that you had not thought to try it before you brought it here. I am so grateful for that, my darling one."

With that Nieth came to her and hugged her tightly. "We must be on our guard. We must cover you in the pure light of protection. This travesty, must...cannot happen again!" And so Nieth prayed for protection. She called on all the positive forces to become stronger than the evil forces that had for so long remained dormant but now had been revived to thwart the quest, to harm or even murder the neophyte, Abigail. And we sat still and meditated together so that Nieth's strength and wisdom would infuse with my essence.

We sat, thus, for many hours.

Finally, Neith rose up and said, "I will provide the mushroom myself, but first I will tell you that the quest will take you far from here, will challenge you to be brave, and will demand your keen intellect to assess the correct path."

"I am afraid, Mother," I said. I do not want to leave here. To leave you. Is there no other way?"

"No, my darling one. No other way. For what we seek is the eye of enlightenment, and it resides in a place of mist. You have been chosen by all your goddess mothers for this enormously important task. Only you can perform it and you will save all womenkind and all mankind as well from the ever-waiting abyss of climate collapse that is at the ready to destroy our Earth. Please sit now, Abigail," said Nieth in her most powerful voice.

Then Nieth stood with her back to me and raised her arms and chanted the mystical words to bring forth the flame. At once a warming fire sprang to life in front of us and then Nieth sat next to me. The sound of crackling and popping kindling was the backdrop to this most important ritual. Nieth extended her right arm with her palm open and facing up. She sat, thus, for many minutes, she closed her eyes and a low humming sound vibrated from deep within her. I became mesmerized by the flames and the humming vibration and began to see images of myself against new and foreign settings. People came and went and I was always propelled forward. Suddenly, Nieth cried out, "Now!" And in her palm was the magic mushroom.

"Here, my sweet Abby," she said, "This is the one. Notice there is a yellow dot right in the center? This is what separates the special mushroom from the lethal impostors. You may need the aid of this mushroom on your journey and it is imperative that you memorize the true one from the false. Here, take it now. You must swallow in one gulp and then close your eyes. The mushroom will lead you to what happens next."

I did as I was told and my life force flew out of my body and took wing. In this state, I traveled far and wide and realized I was being given a glimpse of the places I would visit on my quest. Colorful villages tucked into fertile valleys, imposing cities set atop high ridges and cliffs, sparkling waterways dotted with fanciful islands. I smelled the trees chanting, and the sweet pungent odor of the protective song of the meadowlark. I listened to the bright yellows and dark purples of the flowers, their harmonies both a relaxant and stimulant that brought a brightness to my thoughts. My senses expanded in ways I would not have thought possible.

In an instant, I saw herself with many divergent beings. There were gods as well as goddesses, elves, faeries, magicians, and wizards. A plethora of communities and experiences. Always, I was given the wisdom to continue, the correct path to take for the coveted prize, the magical trophy of the end, and the beginning of the changeover and enlightenment. The experience of this vision was powerful down to my very essence.

I began to chant:

Oh, to the light of the mighty spirit.
The giver of all knowledge, peace, and glory.
Oh, to the wishing and wanting of wisdom and sharing.
The purposeful life is blessed.
Oh, the purposeful life is blessed.

The vision dimmed and I reunited with my corporeal self. My eyes fluttered open. As I became more aware of my immediate surroundings, I had a profound realization. The journey, the quest was no longer frightening, and a pulsating, throbbing excitement replaced any tentativeness and worry.

"Now, you are ready," said Nieth.

"Yes, Mother, I am, truly."

"Then, you will leave at once, my dear child."

And yet, I stayed. I made a big fuss about getting ready. About what I should carry with me and what should stay. I worried about knowing where to go on my moonbeam rides. How will I find my way back from those heretofore unknown places? Basically, I was afraid I'd get lost. Lost in this world and thus lost in the other, to just disappear with no one to realize my trouble, my helplessness. Nieth, Hathor, Isis, and the other goddesses grew restless and disgruntled with my procrastination. Why was I fidgeting with everything? Packing and unpacking? Didn't I realize all would be provided? But I could not get my confidence. The mushroom-induced vision did not propel me forward as I had thought it would. As Nieth thought it would. I was stuck. Stuck and disappointing my mothers with my attitude. I was letting them down, feeling like a failure. It was not good to be this way. Eventually, Nieth said, "We must find another neophyte. Abigail is not as strong as we thought."

I was devastated, but powerless to do anything. I could not leave them. I was attached and it could not be broken. I was paralyzed and heartbroken that I was letting them down. But find another to take my place? It was unthinkable. I must do something. Somehow get the strength to do what was expected of me. Somehow. I closed my eyes and tried to become one with the energy fields around me. Internalize the magic. Push out my doubts and replace them with an open heart and calm demeanor. I sat thus for many hours. Days even and then I opened my eyes.

There stood the most charming creature with a wide smile. She was a young girl like me and yet not. She had the wisdom of thousands of years in her eyes. When she reached out and took my hand, I knew immediately she would accompany me on my journey. She called herself Hebe and was the attendant to my mother, Venus. We communicated without speaking. She was inside my mind and I hers and I was immediately comforted.

And so, the quest began.

My mothers smiled.

It was a winding road that took me away from all that was familiar. Out of the dark wood and into the light we traveled on foot. Stopping to rest only to eat the food in the satchel prepared by Nieth. We leaned against a large rock at the entrance to a stone bridge. The rushing waters of a brook gave off an alluring melody of happy sounds as we ate our fresh fruits and other tasty delicacies.

"We have a long way, passing many villages and cities," said Hebe. "We must seek out Berwyn, a wizard that will lead us on the right path. He resides just there," she says as she points in a direction to the right of us. "It is far and will take us many days."

"Mother showed me the way on the map. I know where to go, perhaps we can bypass this stop and forge ahead. Straight as the arrow to our destination."

"That would be a mistake. Berwyn knows our quest and will give us tools to help us if needs be. He is expecting us and is preparing for our visit. We must not disappoint him, for his wrath knows no bounds."

This information was disturbing. My goddess mother never mentioned Berwyn the wizard. Can Hebe really be trusted? I tried to remember the vision. Tried to bring forth the image of a wizard and was at a loss. Then suddenly a flash of a blue satin robe and silk scarf. Yes, maybe, maybe. Perhaps that was Berwyn and my fear subsided.

And thus, I learned from Berwyn when we visited his cottage, of the harm to the creatures who thrive on this planet, the fauna and flora. How they will come to know the collapse of their habitats brought forth by the callous misuse and abuse of the natural world by the greedy ones. The humans who take no delight or comfort in the beauty around them, the springs and lakes, the abundance of fish and wildlife, the arrival of seasons, the pleasant warmth of the sun. They will lead this planet to scarcity with their greed and blood-lust sports, to excessive heat that withers the grasses and farmland with never-ending droughts and then causes what's left to wash away in floods.

All life will be jeopardized. And so, our mission is to slow down the destruction, create safe havens to wait out the losses, to nurture what remains in order to recreate the majesty that once existed. To awaken all women to the goddesses within them. To bring them into the fold to help with the important work of saving what we can. To create an optimistic future world of joy and abundance. To harness the power of the spirits, the power that lay waiting to help in this other realm. To be pure of heart in this quest for salvation. And we set out on our quest to gather seeds and awaken the animal kingdom to be ready to populate the five-senses realm.

The salvation of this most precious Earth and all life starts here in this realm with the help of the goddess world at this location at this inn. It starts now. Instructions are attached. Heed this important call, heed the fulfillment of this mission. You were all brought here through the love and well wishes of our own Roman goddess Venus, also known as Aphrodite. Similar instructions to build safe zones at higher altitudes have been sent to saviors all over the world to mitigate soaring temperatures and floods. You are among many who have been selected and we send you strength and love.

Gabrielle flipped to the attached instructions and then closed the book and said nothing. In fact, no one spoke, so taken aback with the powerful message and important mission assigned to this little group of ordinary people. Gabrielle passed the book around so they all could flip through the detailed instructions of building a safe haven and sending out a call to bring help from the Feminine Divine, women of this world who were also part of the goddess world. She also told no one that as she read the names of the goddess mothers, they appeared one-by-one and took turns hiding behind the furniture. The goddesses were still there observing the group's reaction and seemed enthused with the positivity emanating from the group brought together with such an important mission but also aware of everyone's apprehension and fear of failure and what that would portend for the planet.

The instructions were like an architect's rendering for building a self-sustainable village with areas set aside to grow vegetables, raise chickens and dairy cows for eggs and for milk. No meat would be consumed. Renewable energy would supply power and detailed instructions for building that power and weather stations were provided. Nature and the natural world would be honored and worshiped. Hope and joy sprang off the pages. The plan was to maintain this haven for as long as necessary.

After they browsed through the building plans, they chatted about why this group in particular was chosen for this very important mission and thought perhaps because some of them had special gifts. The Countess could read the future in tea leaves, the Captain could stop time, Beau and Gabrielle could see the goddesses and believed in them. Emma was perplexed as to why she was chosen and finally said,

"Well, I can make a mean vegetarian chili," and Irina chimed in "And I make a fabulous Afternoon tea." Beau added, "And Mark will learn how to make a vegetarian beef Wellington with his fabulous crust.

Everyone laughed lightening the mood when they suddenly heard a giant bang by the front door and all ran over. The door was stuck shut. Then everyone realized that the windows were completely covered with snow and blocked the view outside. At that moment the lights began to flicker and then went out. There was still some daylight getting through and Beau ran down to the basement to turn on the generator and then headed back upstairs.

"I think I know what's happened," he said. "This happened only once before when I was about five years old as I can remember. We were completely snowed in as we are now. It was shocking. Just like then, the snow is piled up on the porch covering the front door because the wind is blowing in this direction. The same with the windows. That noise was probably a huge branch breaking off from the weight of the snow or an entire tree falling over. It will take quite a few days to dig us out after the snowfall finally stops. No one can get in or out right now. We need to cancel the guests that are coming for Christmas until we know more. Emma, you'd better do the same because you can't leave right now. Luckily the cable company buried the line underground several years back, so we should still be online."

An initial feeling of claustrophobia overwhelmed everyone but then they decided to flip the feeling into feeling cozy. With all the stores in the pantry, a feast was planned and a festive mood prevailed. Gabrielle was about to make phone calls but the phone was dead. Then she realized the guests had canceled through emails because the storm covered the entire Northeast. Everyone was safe and for that she was grateful.

"I think since we can get on the internet, maybe we should investigate just how much damage this climate crisis has caused so far and what the scientists predict are imminent dangers. Perhaps we all need to throw our energies into preventing further escalation...as of right now. Let's give ourselves a couple of hours and reconvene to talk about what we found. We have a few computers in the business office next to the owner's suite and we also had bought a few tablets to lend to guests," said the Countess.

After several hours people started to wander into the main reception area and found seats by the fireplace. One could hear the excited murmurings of the few people who arrived first and then the others began to gather, some with notepaper, some with their tablets. All began talking at once and it was hard to understand what was being said. The concern and upset were written on everyone's face. There was no doubt the situation was dire. Finally, the Countess called for order and had everyone take a seat. The bottom line was it was frightening.

The first info to take the stage was how many places were already suffering from the rise in sea level. For example, certain parts of Miami Florida flood at high tide. So not caused by storms just normal tides every day. Miami residents who live below three feet above sea level need to plan for streets and roads that will be underwater. Some areas of the Florida Keys are permanently underwater and homeowners can't drive to their residences but must use boats to reach them. In the South Pacific residents of one of the islands in Papua New Guinea had to be relocated. Greenland and Antarctica have melting glaciers swelling the seas the are already rising. In the Solomon Islands, some islands have already been lost forever. And well-known vacation spots like the Maldives and the Marshall Islands are most at risk.

Everyone knows that Venice, Italy is sinking and has been for many years. But it has gotten worse. Now the threat of losing all the masterpieces of art and architecture for future generations is real. But did you all realize that London and NYC are also threatened with flooding from rising seas? The melting glaciers are causing another horrifying catastrophe, the collapse of the Gulf Stream. This would affect the climate on the East Coast of the United States and England. The current also offers greater speeds to shipping routes while bringing warmer waters that impact the temperatures along the nearby coastlines.

The Gulf Stream is like a conveyor belt where dense, salty surface water sinks at the north end and travels south and the warmer water travels north. With glacier melt, the surface water is fresher, less dense, and less salty so it doesn't sink quickly causing the conveyor belt to weaken or to stall. There are dire predictions of what would happen with a total collapse of this current. The impact on plant and animal life that thrive at these now warmer latitudes, not normally conducive to these species, would be devastating. Without the Gulf Stream, London will have the same climate as Siberia.

Then Gabrielle chimed in about the devastation brought about by rising land temperatures everywhere. Everyone has a story about how cool Europe used to be in summer and how that has drastically changed. Refitting buildings for air conditioning unfortunately is well behind the demand for it and also inadequate where it's installed. European theaters are too hot, hotel rooms uncomfortable. Strolling down avenues is uncomfortable when just some years ago, the outside temperature was quite pleasant even in early August. Temperatures elsewhere in the world are becoming life-threatening. In the Middle East in summer, temperatures can reach 125 degrees Fahrenheit and aerosols left in cars can catch fire and blow up. Arizona has also reached temperatures of 115 degrees.

California has suffered drought conditions for years bringing raging fires that have nearly wiped out the wine country of Napa Valley and burned redwoods that have lived majestically for centuries. When the short rainy season comes it brings mudslides because all the vegetation has been wiped out by the fires. We have all seen the devastation of the wildfires in Australia and the stress put on the habitats of wildlife, especially koala bears. Less rainfall has also put pressure on African elephants who need to drink up to 92 gallons of water per day. The opposite problem is hurricanes that are stronger and more destructive laying waste to any tropical island in their path. And the rainy season in Australia has brought torrential downpours and flooding. So, the planet suffers from too much and too little. The equilibrium is off kilter. Floods and droughts, much colder or much warmer. And we are not even at the tipping point yet.

Gabrielle also mentioned another growing problem which is clean drinking water. This crisis is spurred by pollution and scarcity. Around the globe, deaths occur daily from lack of water and diseases from lack of sanitation. Rapid urban development and poverty bring chemical waste, improper sewage disposal, and harmful fertilizer runoff dumped into drinking water. The rise of plastic all over the world has not only polluted our oceans but plastic particles are now even found in Antarctica. No thought is given that these plastics are not only polluting our oceans but also causing the extinction of underwater plants and fish.

After Gabrielle finished everyone rushed to speak exclaiming their upset and disturbed feelings concerning these findings. All realized what trouble they and all humanity were facing and it was daunting, overwhelming, and frightening. Suddenly the mood changed and a tangible excitement shot through the room. The goddesses began to slowly reveal themselves one at a time to the group. Everyone stopped speaking and stood in shock and awe. One by one the goddesses came over and hugged them. Nieth, Hathor, Isis, and Venus joined the small group of earth-saviors while the other un-named goddesses, of which Beau's mother Abigail was one, watched. It was quite an amazing sight to see them dressed in their regalia, creating a glow around them with their startling beauty and emitting a powerful light force. Like stars.

The goddesses that were named in the diary that Gabrielle read out loud floated over to the entrance of the room where they began to introduce themselves. The first goddess to come forward was the most important and dressed regally in her full-length gown and headdress of a sun disc between the horns of a cow. She was Isis, the divine mother goddess of fertility, motherhood, magic, and medicine. She told the group that she was also known as Queen of Heaven. The masses worshipped her ability to bring people back from the dead as she did in her myth story for her husband, the divine king Osiris. Her son Horus, the younger whom she protected, lost his eye in a battle but it was restored by the loving goddess Hathor. The eye of Horus, a symbol of Ancient Egypt was worn as an amulet to protect ancient Egyptians from evil and also represented the all-seeing third eye.

Hathor came next. She told the group that she had been the most powerful goddess until Isis appeared later in the Egyptian pantheon and that's why they both wore the same headdress and had similar powers. She was the mother or consort to Horus, the elder and the sun god Ra. She helped deceased souls in their transition to the afterlife.

Nieth came forward and told the group that she was the creator of the universe and all it contained, and she governed how it functioned. She was the oldest deity and the mother of Ra, the Sun God. She was the goddess of wisdom, weaving, the cosmos, mothers, rivers, water, childbirth, hunting, war, and fate. She was a warlike goddess. Neith wore war-crossed arrows and a shield headdress and the ankh and scepter, both symbols of power. Venus at the last came forward with her ravishing flaming red, thick, curly locks and just stood there to be admired, which everyone did in silence. Then Isis spoke again.

"We understand your distress over the coming climate crisis. We are here to help not only to build a refuge but to devise ways to try to prevent a tipping point of no return. To keep catastrophe at bay. We will all work together throughout the world to save humanity from the worst effects. Already, there are places where a grand effort is being made to plant trees to pull carbon dioxide out of the air, companies have been formed to clean the oceans, and companies to improve worldwide sanitation for clean drinking water. Also, there is research happening to create energy using fusion instead of fission currently used in nuclear reactors. And batteries with a very long life. We applaud these endeavors and we are hopeful. We are continuously sending energy forces to impart these ideas for mitigation and to help them succeed. Let's be joyful that we have come together to implement our strategies to save our beautiful mother Earth."

Everyone breathed a sigh of relief to hear these words of hope. After the goddesses made their presentations, they milled about staying in their full flesh form and socializing, except for Abigail Barnstable and the lesser goddesses who had floated off to their world. It would probably break some kind of natural law to have Beau chat with his dead mother. For Beau and Gabrielle, just seeing the goddesses in the flesh and not just apparitions from the corners of their eyes brought a sense of solidarity of help for this daunting and now common mission. The others also felt a sense of duty and being protected by this army of spirits capable of who knows what. They mingled together for several minutes murmuring greetings and gathering knowledge of their otherworldly guests. Then came an announcement from Beau that surprised the group.

"We have just been given the knowledge of how much we are needed to provide refuge and to give succor to all life forms, humans included. We are blessed to be armed with this knowledge of hope for humanity at our behest. It is an honor to be chosen for this important work. But we are also normal in our emotions. I have a wonderful plan to bring more joy and hope into this house," said Beau coming forward and surprising everyone. And, in fact, he did indeed. Quickly calling Gabrielle to his side, he looked at her with love in his eyes and then surprised her and everyone.

Chapter Twenty-One

The Grand Finale

Journal entry:
Virtual bells rang.
Our love was cemented,
pure joy.

Beau cleared his throat a few times and seemed a little nervous. Gabrielle looked around the room also visibly nervous in anticipation and fixed her eyes on Tasa who winked at her assuredly. Something good was the signal and she relaxed somewhat. The goddesses floated up to the ceiling to look down at this turn of events and the small group gathered close to one another.

Beau got down on one knee, and everyone immediately knew what was going to happen and a soft laugh of approval went around the room. He said:

"Gabrielle, I didn't realize how empty my life was before I met you. I beg you, don't banish me to a life of misery and loneliness without you in it. Please honor me by becoming my wife. My darling, I hope you will stand by my side while we build this refuge to protect those we care about, and all the others who travel here from far off or nearby places, from the ravishes of climate chaos of which we are getting a preview right now. I will love you with all my heart and soul until the end of my days and into our afterlife through time and space if the cosmos allows."

With that, he took out a diamond ring, "Will you marry me, my dearest?" and Gabrielle through tears of joy and hiccupping from emotion managed to say, "Yes, yes, of course, my love," as he slipped it on her finger. They kissed to everyone's applause. The ring was his mother's that Gabrielle's father had bought her. Love had come full circle. How perfect. Abigail had kept it in a special safe hidden in the owner's quarters that Beau knew about. Everyone expressed their joy and hugged them including the goddesses who had again joined the group from their floating observation point. A tearful Abigail had floated back also to witness this important moment.

"Since we are snowed in with no guests why wait? Let's have the ceremony tomorrow," said Beau. "Are you up for that, Gabrielle?" Gabrielle looked puzzled, not sure how Beau could pull off all the legalities, then he assured her it would be no problem. "I can get the marriage license online and the Captain can become ordained online and marry us. Would you be willing to do that, Captain?" "Of course," he said, "I might just make it a side hustle by offering our guests really romantic weekends," and he laughed heartily. It was settled. While the snow continued to fall all around them with the wind barely keeping the inn from being completely buried, a wedding would take place on the next day at 2:00 pm. From the mirror over the fireplace, Gabrielle thought she saw a look of satisfaction on the face of Venus, recalling that was the first goddess appearing to her when she came through the stuck door with Emma. This goddess had been her touchstone for her rebirth.

Perhaps Venus had been tasked with pairing her with Beau to help save the planet from being destroyed. But no one was more surprised than Gabrielle that she would be married to him and forge this journey to survive the climate crisis together. For with or without him, this crisis will befall all of us. And she silently thanked Venus for bringing Beau and his love for her. *Imagine all that has happened for me because of this inheritance,* she thought. *From the unluckiest child, except for impending global warming chaos, I'd be the luckiest woman. Sadly, now it's bittersweet. And I thank you as well, my father, for making my remaining life more meaningful.* And she bowed her head when she had this thought.

The planning now began. Little Doo as the flower girl would wear silk flowers in her collar from a vase in one of the bedrooms and walk with her through the room to the Captain standing by the Christmas tree. It couldn't be more perfect. There would be huge feasts with the goddesses attending who became quite excited for some delicious food. Everyone had walked into the kitchen to check the pantries to plan the feasts. Tomorrow was Christmas Eve and then they'd need a Christmas dinner as well. The feasts for Christmas Eve and Christmas lunch were chosen. A ham and goose for Christmas lunch and a traditional Feast of the Seven Fishes for Christmas Eve which was now also the wedding reception dinner. How lovely! Everyone was thrilled. The inn becoming vegetarian would wait at least these stores were consumed. One added benefit, there was no way from now on that Beau could ever claim he forgot the date of their anniversary. The menu for the fish dinner would consist of thawed out frozen shrimp and fresh fish and mussels that, luckily, were just bought that day.

Irina said a fish feast was traditional for Catholics to do on Christmas Eve and that's why she had ordered some, just in case, some guests wanted fish. Unfortunately, she had counted wrong and there would only be six and not seven customary dishes, but it was at least an attempt especially during this epic winter storm. Then, she had an idea about changing the seasonings and pasta sauce to make a new dish, and voila! The traditional Feast of the Seven Fishes would be served! They all declared that now actually having seven dishes as well as the snow not completely burying the inn was a miracle and Irina kissed her cross.

The Captain got busy with becoming ordained and Beau worked on the marriage license. Every once in a while, there was a crash and everyone held their breaths looking at the ceiling. Another tree or branch down but at least not through the roof. Emma checked her cancellations and prayed her inn would be unscathed by falling trees. They played Christmas carols all day and got into the holiday spirit while they prepared the feasts and sugary delights as the snow kept falling. It would certainly be a white Christmas and perhaps even until Easter by the looks of it. The snow just kept coming down and was mind-boggling. The weather stations were having a field day reporting on the accumulations.

Beau also thought to call the hospital to check on Mark. The hospital was operating under a shortage of personnel but still functioning. Mark had started to rouse and was resting comfortably. If the snow stopped, he could probably go home the day after Christmas. That was good news and added to the joyful mood. As Gabrielle helped with the feast, she tried to think of something appropriate to wear for her wedding day. Nothing came to mind and Tasa noticed something was wrong.

"You should be dancing on a cloud. Why so gloomy?"

"It would have been nice to find something new and special to wear for this, hopefully, once-in-a-lifetime event."

"Ah, yes, I see. Well, let's see. Have a look in my closet. Irina is a whizz with a needle and maybe something could be workable with a little this and that from her expert hand."

"Ok, I'll have a look, if you don't mind." And they went to Tasa's room and rummaged through her gowns. She spied a beautifully beaded white gown with lace but it was much too small.

Tasa was shorter than Gabrielle and smaller in the bosom and waist. It seemed hopeless.

"How about this?" asked Beau walking into the room holding up a vintage wedding dress.

"Where on earth did you find that?" asked Gabrielle.

She walked over to him laughing and touching the beaded silk fabric. Small buttons covered the arms and the full shirt had white roses, embroidered probably by hand, and meticulously placed for maximum effect. The gown was breathtakingly beautiful. Before he answered, a vision flashed before her eyes of Abigail Barnstable wearing this very gown when she married Beau's father. She saw them standing in front of her but in the other room. Right there in this inn in front of the fireplace. Just like they would be tomorrow.

"When I was upstairs, I decided to check out the attic. I remembered seeing photos of my mother when she married my father wearing the most beautiful wedding dress. It had been given to her by *her* mother who had, in turn, been given it by *her* mother. So, my mother, grandmother, and great-grandmother wore this dress at their nuptials. A family heirloom. And there it was sealed in a protective bag hanging from a clothes rack. It looks like it will fit you perfectly."

She tried it on after he left, and it did fit. As if it were made exclusively for her. A gift through time. It brought tears to her eyes. Despite the deep snow and the tasks that awaited this little group, all was right with the world. Right now. Today. Living in the moment because that's all we have. The man she first hated was now the man she most loved in this world. Whatever awaited, they would forge a life together. Who would have thought her life would turn in this direction? And she thanked the forces of destiny and the goddesses for her good fortune and said a prayer for surviving the hard times to come and helping as many people as she could. From now on, the precarious situation of an unstable Earth would always be on her mind.

The next day was bustling with excitement and mouthwatering aromas floated out from the kitchen. After Gabrielle took a relaxing perfumed bath, Emma gave her a manicure and while the food was in the oven and simmering on the stove, Irina did her hair.

She felt like a queen and it made the day just as special as anything that might have been planned at a formal wedding venue. To keep in the relaxation mode, she decided to catch up on reading in her old bedroom until it was time to dress for the ceremony. Doo did her business on puppy mats not being able to go outside and stayed at Gabrielle's side sensing the excitement all around and needing her calm assurance. It was so sweet to have her cuddle as she read. As far as she knew, Beau had no trouble getting the license and the Captain became officially ordained, easy peasy, all online and all automatic with no human input. When the documents were all printed out, they looked very official.

It was time to get ready and all the women helped Gabrielle get into her gown. Butterflies fluttered in her stomach. *Am I really doing this?* she thought. Little Doo was jumping around all excited and Irina found a small vase of silk flowers and wrapped them around her fancy rhinestone pink collar. All the women exclaimed at how beautiful Gabrielle looked. "Just like a fairy tale princess," said Irina happily. "Oh, good that reminds me," said Tasa as she ran into her bedroom to rummage through some boxes and came out with a tiara and placed it perfectly on top of the veil. "*Now* she's a princess," she said. Gabrielle gave her a bewildered look as if to say, *how in the world did you have this or rather, why do you?* Tasa shook her head and laughed. "Don't ask, but I was always very fond of tiaras and fancied myself a member of the royal family when I was married to my first husband. He was a third cousin twice removed or some such distant relative. What nonsense. But now worth saving all these years."

They heard the music begin to drift in from the living room. Someone must have found the wedding march on the satellite radio. That was their cue. Tasa took Gabrielle's arm with little Doo spinning in circles near them and they began their procession. As soon as they entered the passageway to the room an overwhelming scent of pine from the Christmas tree lovingly welcomed them and filled them with the joy of the day. It was like the joy of this season in a comforting snow globe scene come to life. Beau stood grinning from ear to ear in front of the tree next to the Captain. Gabrielle almost laughed out loud at their getups. The Captain had found a beautiful bedspread that he draped over his jeans and sweater and placed a colorful native American printed scarf around his head like a Shaman. Beau must have found a tuxedo suit where he found my dress and wore the too-small jacket unbuttoned and a white bowtie around his white crew-neck sweater over jeans.

A hysterical but also flawless impromptu wedding that Gabrielle could have ever imagined. As if on cue, sunshine suddenly poured through the windows even though it was still snowing. The goddesses floated nearby, all of them, so Abigail Barnstable watched the marriage of her son to his bride in her's, her mother's, and her grandmother's gown. The tradition continued. Irina snapped away on her iPhone and Gabrielle realized that someone had set up their tablet and Mark was watching from his hospital bed. He was smiling, sort of. A wide toothy smile that did not reach his eyes. As if to say, "Okay, if this will be my new home for a while, I'd better accept this turn of events. But it's not what I would have wanted."

The Captain recited some gobbledygook that he found on the internet. They burned a piece of paper that symbolized removing all their negative thoughts about each other for a fresh start. They lit one candle together which symbolized their union, and then they said their vows.

"I promise to love you Gabrielle for all time, I will stand by your side to help mankind survive this climate crisis, I will do the dishes and vacuum the rugs and fix anything that breaks. I will always cherish being with you and calling you, wife."

"I never thought there would come a day when I would stand before the man I love reciting marriage vows. The cosmos has been kind to me in arranging the circumstances for my meeting the love of my life, and I hope it will also provide the tools for all of us to stem the tide of the effects of a changing climate. I pray for a future where we can grow old together and enjoy the beauty around us as we do now."

A sigh of agreement to this sentiment went through the group but was especially acknowledged by the goddesses. Then the Captain finished the ceremony with the customary do you take this man...etcetera... and finally pronounced them Husband and Wife. The satellite radio was cued to play one of Gabrielle's favorite pieces, the lush, somber, but romantic, Adagio in G minor. Beau held her in his arms and waltzed her slowly around the room and intermittently hugged and kissed her as they then danced their way to the breakfast room/restaurant for the beginning of the reception celebration.

Irina went into chef mode with Emma and they started bringing out the delectable Christmas Eve celebration fish dishes to the several tables that had been left set up for the restaurant so the goddesses would have room to join them. Again, the author of the diary was not present having left with some lesser goddesses right after the ceremony. Beau looked around for his mother but understood why she was not there. He decided that when the time was right, she would interact with him. Gabrielle chose a table and decided to sit and watch the merriment as her favorite classical music filled the room.

She watched the goddesses taking dainty bites of the various dishes talking amongst themselves while expressing extreme enjoyment. Tasa sat with Gabrielle while Beau and the Captain were engaged in a serious conversation.

"How lovely today has been. My spirit has been so elevated with joy watching the two of you. This is so right, so perfect, and sends positive vibes to the universe. We are moving in the right direction," said Tasa.

"I can't help but remind myself how all this has come about for me. Meeting you was the key, I am certain. If I hadn't gone to London with you...well..."

"Yes, destiny works in mysterious ways and we are just along for the glorious ride. I, too, reflect on my good fortune meeting you. If not for meeting you my life would have been quite lonely and frightening as the climate crisis took hold. Now I'm part of the solution surrounded by friends whom I consider my family. I have much to be thankful for. And who knows, with all of us working together maybe we can slow down the crisis or even keep it from happening. I can be optimistic about it now."

Unfortunately, the Countess knew from her tea leaves that a catastrophe would come, but she didn't tell Gabrielle so as not to ruin this day. As they sat there, the crack in the giant ice shelf in Greenland had started to progress and if it calved a giant glacier into the Arctic Sea, it would cause a rise in sea levels swamping all beaches and coastal cities of the Atlantic Ocean. Expected not to happen for many years, this rapid crack formation was not predicted.

Unaware of the coming danger the party partied on. Beau and Gabrielle danced the night away in the restaurant after several empty tables were pushed against the wall to make room for a dance floor. Irina surprised them with a wedding cake decorated with flowers and hearts. The Captain took photos of the cut-the-wedding-cake ceremony. Afterwards, the photos would make it seem as if it were a regular wedding affair minus a large attendance. The goddesses somehow magically managed to look like ordinary folk dressed in normal clothes in the photos so the crowd looked remarkably denser. It always would thrill Gabrielle to peruse the electronic album and she would do so often. Taking pleasure in the captured joy on everyone's faces to cherish when times became rough.

Christmas breakfast and Christmas lunch were enthusiastically attended as the group was still riding high from pulling off this fabulous wedding in a blizzard. Mimosas were poured without end and by the time the Christmas goose was eaten and all the sides enjoyed, everyone needed to rest. Naps for one and all was the mantra of the day. The afternoon nap became an overnight sleep and the next morning everyone woke up to sunshine and warming temperatures.

After coffee, the Captain and Emma were off to see if their inn escaped any damage and the crew remaining cleaned up the inn to await guests and the arrival of Mark coming by ambulance. The rising temperatures created the conditions of an early mud season making driving a gooey mess and a fire engine/ambulance was better equipped for the sloppy trip. Whatever the cost it was worth it. Beau had told them Vermonters hated mud season and now they all understood why and it had just started. This giant amount of snowmelt was daunting. They feared for the deer getting stuck in the muddy field several inches thick. Sadly, several did and had to be lassoed out, hopefully without breaking any bones in the process. An extremely unnerving affair that eventually kept the deer away. The inn guests would be extremely disappointed to find themselves in such an unpleasant time of year that usually came much later.

The warm temperatures persisted for several weeks. Guests came and checked out early not enjoying getting mud all over their clothes and shoes. Rubber boots were a must. So, the inn made extra money stocking them. Mark remained indoors because he needed a cane and was advised to not slip or fall in the mud outside and break something again. He was content to amuse himself by searching the internet. When he notified the company of his condition, they suggested if he continued to need a cane that perhaps being a ship's captain would be too dangerous for him. With the crossings still on hold because weather conditions were not favorable and the seas too rough, would he consider a desk job?

Then and there, Mark decided he would stay put and help build the refuge when he could walk better. He enjoyed the camaraderie, although he flirted incessantly with Gabrielle which annoyed Beau. After all, he was unattached and she was the only young woman nearby, and let's face it, he was still besotted. His living quarters in London could be assigned to the next Cunard captain and his belongings shipped. So, with trepidation, Beau offered him a job. All hands would be needed when the refuge was up and running.

The happy lot went about their business after the mud season ended, welcoming guests and after their delightful stays waving and hugging them goodbye. Irina perfected her scones and afternoon tea was always fully booked. The restaurant got busy on weekends and was bustling with guests and locals. In fact, it became such a popular spot they all decided to keep it open during the week. Irina, in charge of the kitchen, hired a second chef who delighted the guests with his outstanding desserts.

Beau, Gabrielle, and Tasa enjoyed visiting Emma and the Captain from time to time, whose inn, fortunately, had no winter storm damage. Life passed pleasantly enough until springtime's easy temperatures abruptly ended and summer temperatures began to rise uncomfortably. Temperatures rocketed into the high 90's and an idea was floated to make the pool larger and create more swimming access points for the lake. At least scorching temperatures like those in Arizona and NYC with endless days of over 105 had not gotten up to this elevation. News of drought conditions happening around the world became a worrisome risk for wildfires.

Florida was losing the precious everglades to wildfires. Wildfires had scorched the forests and burned poor Koala Bears and their habitat in Australia during their summer and everyone sympathized until those dreadful conditions showed up in California and the entire Pacific Coast. Hurricane season starting much earlier. Puerto Rico was nearly completely wiped out, the Virgin Islands were swamped with massive storms, and New Orleans might never recover from the storm surge of the Gulf of Mexico.

Despite these events, there were no government regulations to stop offshore drilling, or switch to renewable energy, or make electric cars more convenient by having more charging stations built.

Some politicians opposed passing bills that would alleviate the crisis. People went about their business and took these unusual temperature swings in their stride. Gabrielle awoke each day optimistic and joyful as she looked at Beau sleeping beside her. Throughout the day, she relished watching him deal with the contractors who were planning the expansion. As she did when she was alone in her apartment a lifetime ago, she gave thanks to the cosmos every day for how grateful she was for this new life full of love.

But Gabrielle was no fool. When she stepped out of her cocoon of bliss she was drenched with worry. Worried, perplexed, and distressed about the insinuating problems waiting to be mitigated, created by creeping global warming and its disruptions to normal climate patterns. She was afraid to dream of their future selves surrounded by children and the inn thriving with skiers and fall foliage photographers. Because would there be a future where people vacationed? Would the seasons still change? It was not pleasant to think of this refuge that would be safe from floodwaters but only offered a subsistence level of existence. These worries were always at the ready at the back of her mind to spring out and waylay her thoughts.

When these thoughts popped into her consciousness, she grew anxious and extremely disturbed. She needed to distract herself when that happened and she would grab little Doo and take long walks into the thick woods surrounding the inn. As soon as she entered the wood, she felt the trees' magical connection to all living things. Their calming eternity. Growing up in the city bereft of thick woods, the abundance of trees was especially unique and awesome for Gabrielle. She went there in order to absorb the wisdom from these old-growth forests dense with plant varieties and animal species and to feel renewed.

These forests that had existed for millennia gave her a sense of peace and tranquility. She hoped in light of the coming climate chaos they would remain as such bringing solace to future generations. She needed to believe they would remain. The eternal nature of the wood with its buzzing sounds of busy insects and its strong sour smell of mud and humidity that provided the habitat for slithering worms half-buried in the dirt or among tree roots, would always be here, wouldn't it? She felt protected and connected to all life among these abundant stately trees. She felt it in her soul. On these ventures into the wood, she would find a large rock to sit and try to pause her thoughts and breathe in the abundant fecundity around her. Meditating and praying to still her anxious mind. This strong scent of moss in her nostrils was synonymous with the word "forest" to her. The hushed sounds and curtain of shade were a welcoming respite. A rustle of dry leaves, perhaps from the random steps of deer or possum. The flutter of wings from butterflies or birds. Bird song created the music of the woods, the cogent melody of life.

Overwhelmed by the mission given to them by the goddesses and reading more reports of flood, droughts, and rising temperatures, Gabrielle had changed at her inner core. The phrase things could be worse no longer worked. Because things were much worse than could be imagined and she was afraid. Afraid and sad that now when her everyday life should be full of bliss, she was tormented and stressed. The coming crisis was a perilous reality for her and her intimates, but only a handful of activists cared enough to send this message while everyone else in the world seemed not to give it another thought. These were dangerous times. Trying to slow the emission of fossil fuels needed immediate attention and yet ignoring the problem and pretending it didn't exist was the mindset of many. Once the tipping point was reached, there might be no going back.

Forests that provided mitigation by reducing carbon dioxide in the atmosphere were still being clear cut or burned to provide farmland to grow palm oil, a ubiquitous ingredient in multiple and diverse products. Making money was chosen over abating a climate catastrophe that affected all humanity, even the greedy. Always, money over humanity...over logic. Giant tears fell from her eyes when she sat there among the stately old trees visualizing the future horror. In the depths of her despair, one of the goddesses materialized and gave her hope. She reminded her that humanity may yet wake up and respond to reverse the current emission levels, to develop ways to remove carbon dioxide from the atmosphere, to create effective renewable energy sources. Do not give up on hope. She also reminded Gabrielle that the goddesses were planting these thoughts into the collective unconscious, pasting this narrative into dreams, and into the muses that help writers. Awareness will become mainstream. Soon. Very soon.

Buoyed by this encounter Gabrielle went back to her day-to-day but would often seek the woods and the comfort of the goddesses.

In this fashion, time passed. Mark was given Irina's bedroom on the first floor until he could climb steps. He and Beau developed a friendship that was marred by the obvious longing look in Mark's eyes whenever Gabrielle was close. They started to buy some milk cows and fenced in a portion of the pastureland. They built a hen house and bought chickens for fresh eggs in the mornings. *Why not?* Even if the climate crisis didn't happen, it would be a treat for the guests to have fresh dairy and visit the livestock.

They began excavation to enlarge the pool and investigated alternative energy sources. They held off on building the additional housing because they didn't want to disturb the guests with the accompanying noise. Hoping against hope it wouldn't be needed. Several months went by. Close to a year. The seasons changed. The rainstorms were more frightful. But not all of them. The group became complacent and uninterested preferring to ignore the climate and a foreboding future. The goddesses felt this change and waited until they were needed. Unfortunately, they knew they would be needed desperately and too soon for comfort. In the summer everyone swam in the pool and the lake. It was lovely and refreshing when the temperatures rose. They bought a little rowboat to venture out and see the beautiful homes lining the lake, the stately oaks and pines, and the manicured lawns.

It was peaceful. It seemed eternal. Life would go on as before. Here and there an article or newscast had a story about a flood, a raging storm, abnormal temperatures. But not enough to worry about. So, what if Miami flooded at high tide? That's at the coast. So, what if Manatees are dying off? What are they anyway? So, what if abnormal freezing temperatures caused a blackout in Texas? Just fix the grid. Going along in this fashion was easier than worrying every day. Gabrielle stopped taking the lonely walks with Doo. She remembered that being happy is a state of mind. And she chose happiness. She had Beau, she had little Doo and Tasa. She was complete. She was fulfilled. Then she looked at the early pregnancy test and saw it was positive. What joy!

At that very moment, unbeknownst to her and everyone else at the inn, the remaining giant Greenland ice shelf completely broke off and calved into the Arctic Ocean.